To Rita,
thanks for the
help.

JOEY

HIGH-RIDING HEROES

Joey Light

A KISMET® Romance

METEOR PUBLISHING CORPORATION

Bensalem, Pennsylvania

This book is dedicated to a remarkable family: MINE.

Nanny and Pop, Emmy and George, Marie and John, Flora and Lester, Dan and Julie, Ray, Angie and Christina Anne, Dean and Lisa, Eric, Roxanne and Danny, Angie, Matt, Ray and Mella, Mike and Tammy, Steph and Andy, Kimberly, Josh (Joey), and you, JJ.

The gentle man who has shared my life for many, many years, Danny.

I love all of you and if I didn't know love, I surely couldn't write about it.

Special gratitude and love to part of my extended family, Donald and Iona Hoopert of Tulsa, Oklahoma, for providing the research material on your fair state. Thanks for the taste and feel of it all. And, JJ, thank you for always sharing one of your most valued possessions with me—your unending knowledge.

JOEY LIGHT

Joey Light is married to her high school sweetheart, has four sons and lives in the foothills of western Maryland on a small farm. Joey has a predilection for a magical 150-year-old log cabin, full moon nights, music from classical to Croce, and retrieving newborn foals from knee-deep muddy pastures.

COME ONE COME ALL

Return with us to the wonderful days of yesteryear and live a day in the life of an outlaw, pin on a badge and become a sheriff, or swing your skirts on stage and be a saloon girl. Ride the stagecoach, try our horses. Join in a gunfight. How fast can you draw? Be entertained by our actors as they reconstruct the days you've only dreamed about, watched on TV. Browse through our Western shops, eat in the hotel dining room just as they did one hundred years ago. Visit our jail. Try your luck on the gallows. See our cowboys and champion riders on wild, bucking broncs. Watch them test their skills in the arena. Kids! Chase a calf for prize ribbons.

Fun and entertainment for all ages. Educational, exciting, and restful.

Open Tuesday through Sunday 10 A.M. to 10 P.M.

Free parking

_____ ONE _____

Late. Late. Some things never change. Adjusting the bonnet on her head with one hand and running, the long, full skirt of her period costume fisted up in her other hand, Victoria rounded the corner of Main Street. And collided with a solid wave of cowboy.

His hands shot out to grab her arms and right her. Still clamping the bonnet tightly over her curly hair, she looked up. And up. She blamed her sudden shortness of breath on the run. Certainly, it wasn't due to the tall man who stood smiling indulgently as he cupped her elbows to keep her steady until she found her feet.

"Whoa there," he laughed.

"Excuse me," she said impatiently, not unaware of the muscled forearms her hands rested on. Or the humor that sparkled in his beautiful dark eyes.

"Someone chasing you?" he teased. He idly wondered if he had wandered into the middle of one of the skits being put on for the tourists. He'd never seen such curls. A thick, brown mass of them surrounded her face and cascaded down to her shoulders. Green eyes. Emeralds that refracted the sunlight. A freckle or two had popped out on her nose.

"Not exactly. I mean, not yet. They will be. I'm on next. I have to catch the stage and get robbed," she added breathlessly.

As quickly as she had tossed herself into his arms, she was sprinting out of them again. He was instantly sorry. He would have liked to hold on to her just a moment longer. He watched as she ran across the dusty road.

So she *was* one of the reenactors. *This job might be gravy yet*, he said to himself as he turned to watch her scramble to the front of the saloon. His last view of her before she disappeared into the stomach of the coach was dust flying from her boots and a nicely rounded bottom covered in yards of swaying skirts designed with tiny rosebuds. Whew!

He'd heard men mention the term *bowled over* from time to time. Knocked off his pins. Shot into orbit. Had his breath knocked from him. Knocked him dead. Stolen his heart. Changed his life. Foolishness. All of it foolishness. Until now. Now he understood the term. One look. One collision and he felt, well, he didn't know what the words would be. Affected? Extremely interested? Curiosity aroused? Attracted? Intrigued? Fascinated?

In one brief encounter he had met a lady with zest. With a love of being alive shining from her eyes. Gusto. He shook his head. Ridiculous.

Wes folded his arms over his chest and leaned back against the porch post. He had been on his way to a meeting with the owner of Glory Town, but now he decided to watch. He'd been to Glory Town plenty of times but he hadn't seen this woman before. He would have remembered.

The voice coming over the well-hidden loudspeaker asked that the street be cleared to set the mood for the stage holdup. It was explained as the creaking, rocking stage was driven out of town by the dusty driver that it would come around the back of town and pull in from the other end with the bandits close on its heels. The tourists were challenged to use their imaginations and picture the event happening miles from any help. "Please stay on the sidewalks, folks. We don't want anyone getting hurt here at Glory Town, except the bad guys."

Wes looked around. The smart pop of cap pistols darted the air as boys and girls adorned in blue and red cowboy hats chased each other up and down the boardwalk. People from all walks of life lined up on the sidewalk to enjoy this latest display of frontier living. Babies watched from strollers beneath sun shades, and old people rested on benches or merely sat on the edge of the sidewalk.

Old buildings sandpapered smooth by the wind, faded by the unrelenting sun, leaned lazily while others stood stoically against the colorful backdrop of Oklahoma sky. Light blues, dull grays, and red dust that came with the breeze and rolled constantly, coating every flat surface. Hitch-rail brown, wrought-iron black and green. Lots of green. Tall buffalo grass swayed on the hill beyond. The deep, dark dusky green of the tree line below punched toward the cloudless sky towering above the sprinkles of bright yellow, purple, and pink wildflowers skipping along the edge of the pond that glistened from the hollow.

At the first sound of commotion from the other end of town, Wes turned his gaze, along with the crowd, to watch. The air was filled with actual and fabricated tension.

The stage careened around the corner and sped down the street to pitch and roll to a stop in the middle of town. It was surrounded by five desperadoes, handkerchiefs pulled up over their noses, pistols firing in the air. The stage driver slumped over in the seat after a brave attempt to reach for his shotgun. Dead. Ordered to disembark, the frightened passengers climbed down. The cowboy riding shotgun watched, helplessly, as the two men and lone woman proceeded to slide rings and watches and empty wallets into a cloth sack.

The man on top of the stage was ordered to throw down

the strongbox. And as he did, he reached for the same shotgun that did in the driver. He was gunned down immediately.

The bandits' horses skittered and danced a circle. A passenger made a grab for one of the holdup men and was booted in the face to land in the dust. The tourists let out a groan in unison. Wes smiled. It was like watching some bad spaghetti Western. Suddenly he itched to get on with his job. And then he saw her.

The woman dressed in 1870s garb who had blindsided him only a few moments ago lifted her skirt knee-high and wrapped her fingers around a derringer held tight to that smooth skin by a gaudy lilac and lace garter. A sound of appreciation worked its way through the crowd. He smiled and thought she must have legs up to her shoulders.

To the cheers of the crowd and the support of the kids and their cap guns, she planted herself in front of the thieves and fired at them. The little gun popped, and two of the big men grabbed their chests and folded, flinging themselves off their horses and dramatically to the ground. The remaining banditos, including the one with the strongbox over his saddle, hightailed it out of town in a cloud of dust and a thunder of hooves.

Just then, from behind the jailhouse, came a mounted rider, hat pushed low on his head, droopy mustache and dark eyes revealing his determination to capture the outlaws. He fired the shotgun and reloaded on the run. The hero took up chase and the crowd roared and clapped their support. Dust whirled to settle down once again. Tourists stepped off the boardwalk and began their explorations once more, smiling and enthusiastic.

Wes pinched the bridge of his nose between his thumb and forefinger. Shaking his head, he chuckled low. Three bandits ran from a lone woman with an empty derringer before the lone rider began his chase? No way.

Looking back out on the street, Wes watched as the reenactors loaded some of the kids into the stage and set out for a ride. Glancing at his watch, he turned toward the hotel and his meeting.

Buck was waiting for him. Seated at a table, the aging cowboy ate a cheeseburger and french fries, washing them down with orange juice. Wes grimaced and smiled. Who else would have lunch for breakfast? There wasn't another man in all of Oklahoma like Buck, unless, of course, it was his father. Put the two of them together and you had one hundred percent disregard for rules, regulations, and good eating habits.

If one didn't know this was all pretend, he wouldn't take a second look at the scruffy cowboy wearing worn boots, work-faded jeans, and a ten-gallon hat with a crinkled crown. His shirt had a rip down the sleeve and his suspenders were stretched out to capacity from long use.

At other tables scattered around the room, the tourists enjoyed a buffet that Wes eyed speculatively. He was hungry and the aroma of food reminded him how much.

"Morning, Buck."

Buck set his burger down to rise and slap Wes on the back. "Get yourself a plate, boy, and fill it up. We've got some talking to do." But when Buck spoke, he would catch attention. His voice was low and raspy, as though it was worn out from issuing orders all day long. His eyes were kind eyes, worldly eyes. A twinkle of his love for life shone through, along with a spark of the mischief Wes knew he indulged in from time to time.

Tickled that the show went well, Victoria pushed through the door of the hotel. Buck spied her on her way up to her room and called to her.

"Yo! Vic. Come on over here, girl."

He watched her cheerfully turn and head back at the exact same time Wes turned from the food bar. He had to swing his plate up and out of her way to keep her from bumping it out of his hand.

"Excuse me. I'm sorry." She laughed, recognizing him and feeling the flush of embarrassment pink her cheeks.

"Seems I'm developing a habit of getting in your way."
A ripple of anticipation rolled through her. She felt like
steel being drawn, sliver by sliver, toward a magnet.

Wes grinned and tipped his hat. "Some habits are hard
to break. In your case, I hope you leave it alone."

When they found they were both headed for Buck's
table, Wes pulled a chair out for her to sit. Some earthy,
flowery scent reached him as she moved past him and sat
down, smiling up at him. A long-forgotten explosion of
sensations shot through his body.

Manners. Victoria instantly liked the handsome cowboy
whose body she already knew was as hard as a rock,
whose smile was spontaneous, and whose eyes were honest and beautiful.

She looked questioningly at Buck when Wes sat down
with them.

Buck beamed and grinned, ear to ear, from one of them
to the other. And then he announced, "Well, here he is.
Vic, meet Wes Cooper. Wes, my new partner, Miss Victoria Eugenia Clay, formerly of Leesburg, Virginia."

She extended her hand only to have it lost in Cooper's
huge work-roughened one. He clasped her fingers tightly
and smiled.

Wes's interest peaked. So this was Buck's new partner.
Amazing. Simply astounding that he had failed to mention
she was a female. On purpose, Wes would bet.

"J. Weston Cooper. Wes. Hello." Her long cool fingers
warmed his hand. What kind of games was the old man
playing with him now? All he had said was that his new
partner was stubborn, Eastern, and unwanted.

"Nice to meet you." *Boy*, she thought, *is it ever*. He
was the handsomest man she had ever seen. He was tall,
well over six feet. His hair was black with a sprinkling of
gray. A well-shaped pair of thick sideburns grew down to
his jaw, Clint Eastwood style. His face was tanned and in
sharp contrast to his nice white teeth. Slashing cheekbones
met near a slightly Roman nose. A strong jaw and chin

indicated a stubbornness. The nice slightly crooked smile hinted of gentleness. And his eyes. Black. Almost black, beautiful, keen, see-right-into-you eyes. One thing she had learned from life was that you could tell a lot about a man just by his eyes. He seemed to have seen much in his life. At the moment his eyes were glued to her own green ones and causing all kinds of reactions to run along her insides.

"This is the man you wanted. The trainer." When Victoria didn't respond right away, Buck added with conviction, "The cowboy to train the boys how to shoot and ride and rope better."

Bristling, she felt the hair at the back of her neck rise as resentment twisted around inside her. It was her idea! She had planned to start her search for the right man for the job today. She had planned to make him her pet project and now Buck had beat her to the draw. Damn.

"What's the matter, Vic?" Buck asked, using his chosen name for her. It was only the purely innocent look in his eyes that stopped her from pulling his hat down over his face and strolling away.

"Nothing. I'm just surprised." She stammered and could have kicked herself. Annoyed at her quick temper, she folded her hands in front of her and forced them to be still as she rested them on the table.

"I've known this fella since he was knee-high to a cactus." Buck beamed proudly. "Was raised on a quarter horse ranch ten miles up north. His father still puts out the best animals in the country. He's been in the military as a weapons expert, so he knows about all kinds of guns and rifles . . . and he just quit the Oklahoma State Troopers, so he's free."

Buck sat back, satisfied with himself, and waited for her jubilance. He was still waiting as Victoria merely turned a very forced smile toward Cooper and asked, "Do you need a family-sized trailer or a single?"

Feeling and not liking the ice in her voice, Cooper opened his mouth to answer but Buck beat him to it.

"He wants a room in the hotel here. Said he wants to be on the scene all the time so he can get the feel of just what I want. You want. We want."

"The hotel has only one working bathroom," she managed through clenched teeth, her fingers now drumming a rhythm on the dark, scarred table.

"I don't mind," Cooper said with all the innocence of a babe. And the slyness of a cougar, she judged.

The smile on Cooper's lips was one of quiet amusement. He looked from one to the other and just sat back in his chair. It was becoming quite clear to him that Buck hadn't been completely open with him when he offered him this job. Or was *offered* the correct word? Coerced? Cajoled? Hoodwinked? Buck's story had been one of desperation. He needed Wes's expertise immediately or this horrible partner of his would take over. He claimed he only allowed a partner to come in because Glory Town needed money. He hadn't thought that partner would actually make a physical appearance and be a hands-on associate. And then Buck had gone into more detail about just what it was he wanted Wes to do. Now Wes was truly confused, but it wasn't up to him to decipher Buck's motives. He'd accepted the job of tutor and partner-chaser-away and he'd see it through. Only, there was a niggling question in the back of his mind. Did he really want to see this pretty lady turn tail and run?

"Why did he quit the police force?" she asked Buck, defiance clear in her voice.

"Who knows? Who cares? He's just what we need. Rides, ropes, rodeos, shoots." Buck sipped his coffee.

She stole his orange juice and took a gulp. Anything to keep her anger at bay. "I thought I was going to hire the man we needed. You didn't even give me a chance to look around."

"I would'a if I thought you knew where to look. You're green to these parts and you made it sound like we needed someone right this minute. Like it was some dang emergency." He grinned at her, the light glancing off the gold filling in his tooth.

"I was going to interview, see what they had to offer. This is an important step. We have to make sure we have the right man or we'll just be wasting our money." Her shoulders sagged a little. But only for a minute. She straightened up.

"You think I ain't capable of knowin' if this is the right fella? I just told you. I've known him all his life. He's good at what he does. He *is* a cowboy, so I know he can do the job and, boy, can he make a horse do what he's told."

"I'll just bet he sings and dances, too." Victoria pushed her chair back to leave them but Cooper's voice stopped her. It was smooth and rich, like hot fudge syrup.

"As a matter of fact, I do." A slow grin spread across his face. He was almost sorry he was finding all this so amusing. Almost.

Victoria glared at him. She had forgotten he was sitting there. Disconcerted, she stood and offered her hand again. "I'm sorry. I've been rude. It was just that you . . . all this just happened so quickly. Welcome aboard, Mr. Cooper."

"Wes."

"Yes, Wes." Cool and aloof, Victoria regally made her way out of the dining room. *Just what I need. A superhero. A genuine cowboy who's good at everything. He probably whistles and swaggers when he walks, too.*

Outside, Victoria walked purposefully up the road. The town functioned as usual, oblivious to the turmoil and resentment in her heart.

Two of the men rode through the street, their paint horses at a walk, the men exchanging small talk. The blacksmith shop was in operation, shoeing one of the horses. Children rolled hoops down the road and one little boy had his Matchbox cars lined up under the wooden boardwalk. The owner of the general store washed win-

dows while his wife swept the walk free of the stubborn
red dust that would simply blow back across the boards
in a little while. The tourists milled here and there.

It was as it must have been over a hundred years before.
Nothing had changed since yesterday. The town, the reenactors, the visitors, yet she felt defeated.

Water troughs offered relief for the horses that were tied
here and there to the hitch rails. The saloon doors swung
closed after the barkeep sloshed water while emptying out
a pail and finished mopping the floor.

After only a few minutes in the presence of J. Weston
Cooper she realized he might just be the flashy showman
this town needed. He seemed to blend, to mix in so completely with the surroundings. She wondered how she
could doubt that Buck had made a sound decision. She
shrugged in irritation. He was undermining her, making
her presence here uncomfortable. She took a good long
walk around the town, making mental notes of changes
she wanted to make, improvements she saw that needed
attention, that she would see to even if no one else did.

Taking a deep breath, she wandered off the grounds of
Glory Town. Half a mile out, she climbed a small hill and
looked all about. The Wild West. Untamed. Oklahoma.
She couldn't prevent the smile from forming on her lips.
It was beautiful out here. The tall grass, the prairie, the
rolling high ground. The low, meandering countryside,
unobstructed, unblemished by the passing of time. As
she'd become accustomed to, she set her mind free,
allowing her imagination to explore.

The red man. Kiowa. Apache. Arapaho. Shoshoni.
Crow and Blackfeet. White man. Ranchers. Farmers.
Schoolteachers. Preachers. Shopkeepers, healers, pioneers,
and outlaws. All brave and dauntless. All together, mixed
and mingled, joined in the ageless expansion of time. And
the souls. Still hovering, wandering, and haunting. Tradi-
tions and legends handed down from generation to genera-

tion. Glory. Victory. Defeat. Death and destruction. Growth. Life. Learning.

From her vantage point she could make out the groan of a tractor from a farm a couple of miles away, hear the song of tires on the highway hidden by the tree line. A train announced its passage with a shrill whistle. The roofline of a small development appeared tiny and far, far away. Looking down on Glory Town, she could almost believe she was really in the year 1872. Over the years the sun had faded it. Rain and humidity had warped and darkened the boards. The blue northers churned in, the steam-rolling winds harvesting the dust and rain to reap mud, splattering the countryside, dropping temperatures fifty degrees in fifteen minutes, challenging Glory Town to remain unresponsive for the next fifty years.

Victoria could see it so clearly. Prairie schooners bumping across the terrain. Children running alongside. Horses under saddle being guided across the hill. Mustangs running wild and chasing that free will.

Pulling a piece of grass and twirling it between her fingers, Victoria began the walk back. Determination drew her taller. No one was going to spoil this for her. Glory Town was half hers. Five weeks ago she had gotten off the plane with one hand holding her suitcase and the other over her queasy stomach. A greenhorn. A tenderfoot. She'd come a long way and worked hard at it. She wanted desperately to fit in. To be one of the guys.

Later, more relaxed and resigned to the fact that Buck had won again, she squared her shoulders and turned back toward the hotel, certain they would be gone by now. She had some serious thinking to do.

Pushing her way through the hotel doors, Victoria snatched a freshly made English muffin smothered in butter and a carton of orange juice and a glass. She headed for her room upstairs, which served as both her office and sleeping quarters.

When she had first moved in, she had pulled the huge

wooden rocking chair over by the window so she could watch the goings-on as she worked. The room was large but quaint. It needed work. Lots of it. The faded wallpaper curled in places near the seams and the carpet showed more hardwood floor than not. After exchanging her period costume for jeans and a white cotton shirt, she made sure the dress was neatly hung in the closet.

Victoria sat near the window with her glass of orange juice and rocked hard, trying to direct her temper elsewhere and bury her resentment.

Buck was an old goat, she had to remember that. She had to keep in mind that Buck hadn't accepted her as a partner yet, not seriously anyway. And he had just snatched her first chance to prove that she could do the job. She felt sabotaged. Damn him.

It had seemed very strange, at first, that Victoria didn't even know she had an uncle living in Oklahoma until the day the letter came. It turned out he was sort of a black sheep in the family, and since her father had died twenty-six years before, no one seemed inclined to mention his older brother. Of course, Buck was going to resent her inheriting his crusty old partner's half of Glory Town. It was rightfully his.

Interviews for the new show at the saloon were scheduled for six tonight and she needed to decide what kind of a show she wanted to produce. Maybe Buck had gotten J. Weston Cooper in here to stage all the routines, but at least she could handle the saloon performances.

She would just search until she found some really good talent and hope that would help draw more people into the town. And keep them there longer.

A knock on the door jarred her from her thoughts.

Walking toward it, she half expected to see Buck with an apology on his lips. Then she grinned to herself as she swung the door wide, knowing full well she'd never see that day. It was Wes Cooper.

She felt it. The lazy fire that was inside him, banked.

The power that was there, leashed. The energy and zest for living, contained. She didn't have to like him to appreciate that.

He didn't remove his Stetson but he did tip it. That was polite. Polite was something this gang of ruffians had forgotten. Maybe he could teach them that along with all the technical things Buck was extolling earlier.

"I've heard Buck's ideas and now I want to hear yours. I don't like the feeling that I stepped on your toes by accepting Buck's offer." Not one to generally give a hoot, Wes recognized a slight twist to his personality already.

Begrudgingly, she shrugged. She had no firm reason to dislike him since she really didn't know anything about him. It wasn't his fault he had been dragged into the middle of this, but the why is what bothered her. If he was such a fine fellow, so sharp and talented, as Buck touted, why would he waste his time on an operation like this one? And why did she have to waste her time talking to him now? She didn't.

"You don't have to apologize," she offered and moved to close the door.

He stopped it with his foot and the glare he gave her. "I wasn't apologizing. No one could have missed the look of animosity that took over your pretty face. I thought we could have dinner together tonight. I think we need to talk. You are Buck's partner." Just a little bit, he resented her resentment. He wondered what happened to that cheerful, fast-moving little actress of a while back.

She felt a small shiver of electricity travel up her spine. Despite beautiful eyes and a very rough exterior, she felt that there was something to be wary of around this smooth man.

"I have interviews tonight, but thank you. Don't concern yourself, Mr. Cooper. We all have a job to do and we'll do it."

He continued to stand, silently, smiling at her. But behind that smile lurked something else. An arrogance maybe? A secret? She couldn't be sure.

Victoria fidgeted. First, she had a hard time understanding exactly why Mr. Cooper thought it necessary to seek her company. Second, she couldn't believe that out of all the rooms, Buck had given him the one right smack next to hers. She liked her privacy. She'd have to deal with him more than she wanted to. And having to share the adjoining bathroom wasn't going to alleviate that. Reconditioning one of the other bathrooms on that floor would have to be one of her first priorities. Disjointed thoughts rambled through her head.

They were standing there, he calmly and coolly, she a little nervous and warm. Perhaps she was coming off too haughtily. After all, she was the outsider here. "I hope you like your room." She didn't know what else to say or why he kept standing there.

"I'm sure I will. I thought living here would give me accessibility and a good bird's-eye view of everything. Buck said everything I need is in the hotel."

She didn't miss the glint in his eye or the merely male suggestion in his voice. And women had a reputation for flirting. This man found everything amusing. Including himself.

Ignoring his teasing implication, she glared up at him. "Look, Mr. Cooper, I'm sure Buck is using good judgment hiring you to train the men. Let's face it. I'm a little angry because I was supposed to choose the man. So if I seem irate, I am. I'm almost assured you'll be just fine for the job. I'm eager to learn, too, but you'll find some of the boys a little less interested . . . a little less willing. A lot less cooperative, I'm sure. But they're good men, if a bit cocky. I think it must come along with being a cowboy."

He grinned. A wide sweep of a smile that brought an actual glint to his dark eyes. Black diamonds. "Your first lesson is to wear your blue jeans on the outside of your boots,'' he challenged.

She looked down. Her raggy, skintight jeans with the pegged legs were all the style in Virginia. And she always wore her riding boots outside. "My jeans don't fit over my boots," she informed him, irritated, but forcing herself to take it as a suggestion.

"I see that," he answered quietly and took a long time to examine them. "But out here boots aren't just for riding. They're everyday life. They protect the feet. Buy some new jeans. You might want to visit the general store here in your own town. Last time I was in there, they were well stocked on the essentials for Western living. English won't do around here."

Chagrined, Victoria had the feeling that this was going to be a run of lessons not easily learned. But she wanted to know. She wanted to do it right. She loved the West. Loved the whole idea of the wild, untamed, get-right-to-it attitude. She was determined to change from the demure Virginian she had been molded into to a full-fledged Oklahoma cowgirl.

"I'll consider it. Now, Mr. Cooper, if you'll excuse me, I have some paperwork to do." She moved to push the door against his foot, and after taking a good long look down at it, he moved and let her shove the door closed.

She'll do, Wes thought as he let himself into his new living quarters. *She'll do just fine.* He saw enough determination in her stance, in her eyes, that led him to believe she would keep at something until she mastered it. He liked her. Soft yet sturdy. There was a spark in her that warmed him. There was also a volcano of activity boiling around inside that woman, he suspected. He planned on enjoying watching it spew forth. Old Buck was used to having his way, but this woman may just be the one to hold out against him. It might be very interesting to stick around and see how this battle of the wills turns out.

Returning to his room, he kicked the door closed behind him. He walked across the worn floorboards to test the bed. Too soft, he moaned and dropped back on the quilt, tipping his hat over his face. He was tired. He could sleep for an hour or so before touring the town and making himself more familiar with the setup.

The interviews, later that night, hadn't taken long. Victoria hired two women and one man; the others didn't seem serious enough to qualify. Now, she was dirty and tired and wanted nothing but to sit in a nice hot bubble bath.

Victoria penned the word OCCUPIED on one side of a piece of cardboard and UNOCCUPIED on the other side and hung the sign from a string around the doorknob of the bathroom. Once inside, she began to rearrange things. Her towels on one side, his on the other. Her toiletries on one half of the ancient pink-marbled vanity and his on the other. After plugging the drain and pouring five capsful of bubble bath into the old chipped, claw-footed porcelain tub, she turned on the water and stripped.

She had managed to stay out of Wes and Buck's way the rest of the day. Wes had thrown up his hand a couple of times in passing. Buck's Cheshire cat smile hadn't gone unnoticed. She'd also made an appointment with the Dallas banker for later that week. After seeing to a few other important items on her list, she had gone riding and was pleased she was becoming more and more comfortable sitting Western than she had ever been riding English. Even Tonka, her gelding that she couldn't bring herself to leave behind in Virginia, seemed to enjoy the freedom. Funny, she thought, as she looked around the bathroom to make sure everything was in order, that it should feel so natural to ride Western.

Now was the time for her. A very long, languid, luxurious hot bath and bubbles. Lots of them. In this room, she couldn't hear the sounds of the tourists milling through her town. It enhanced the feeling that this really was the Wild West and she actually was a woman of the late eighteen hundreds. It was heaven. Climbing in the tub, she slid down till her chin touched the fluffy, fragrant bubbles. She moaned her delight.

When she closed her eyes, Victoria was a little surprised that Wes Cooper's face appeared in her mind's eye. But then, why should she be so surprised? Men in the West were different. And he was even more diverse than that. He was a classic. He seemed just like the brave and courageous cowboys she had watched on television and in the movies, only there was a real naturalness about him. Genuine. She had never been close to anyone quite like him.

There was one thing she noticed about all Western men. More flesh was exposed. In her world in the East, a man wore a three-piece business suit or a shirt and jeans or a jogging outfit. On occasion she would see athletic shorts in public, but in general she had never seen so much male body as she did here.

Shirts were sometimes worn buttoned only at the jeans line. Sleeves were rolled up or nonexistent, only frayed around the shoulders where they had been ripped off for convenience. Men thought nothing of leaving their chests and backs bare or exposing that area between a T-shirt and jeans when they bent over. Victoria had grown used to seeing more than usual of the male body, but now Wes Cooper was here. She wasn't sure she wanted to see more of that man's body. He had had his long striped sleeves rolled up to expose thick, muscled forearms. And hands. Big, sure, competent hands with blunt, squared fingers. She had wondered what they would feel like entwined with her own. Nonsense. She cleared her mind of him. Raising her leg in the air, she studied her toe and watched bubbles slide slowly down her ankle.

The door opened. She jerked her leg under the water, and even though she was well below the level of bubbles, she crossed her arms over her breasts.

His robe was tossed over his shoulder and he was bare chested, his jeans slung low on his hips.

"Can't you read?" Victoria sputtered, pulling her eyes away from his wide shoulders and solid chest with hair that whirled to a V and dove near the snap of his jeans.

"Both sides of the sign read OCCUPIED. I figured I'd take my chances." She was flushed and up to her neck in flowery fragranced bubbles. Her hair was damp and curled in ringlets around her face. She looked sixteen years old and mad as a hornet.

"Ohhh," she groaned and looked away. Her heart was banging away at her rib cage and she felt like a silly teenager. "I don't believe this. You could have called through the door."

"Could have," he agreed as he leaned against the door-jamb and eyed her squarely.

"Did you leave the upstairs roped off?" Victoria wanted to be sure that her new device to ward off tourists, when she wanted to be alone, was still intact.

"Yep."

Gritting her teeth, she ordered, "Good. Now get out of here, Cooper. I'm going to be a while."

He closed the door. Then she saw him move to the chair by the vanity and sit down. Before she could let go with a stream of profanity, he grinned and held up a hand to silence her.

"Buck warned me that you could be a little bit sassy. I can't see a thing, so what's the big deal? I wanted to talk to you and this is as good a time as any. Besides, you can't toss your head and walk out on me."

"I could," she parried.

He laughed. "But you won't." He briefly wondered what had come over him. He didn't usually act on impulse.

She felt vulnerable and shy. Never in her life had a man shared her bathroom. It was a very warm, uncomfortable feeling. But not totally distasteful. Her thoughts were unsettling. His thick eyebrows, barely breaking over his nose, gave him the look of a desperado. His skin was weathered and tan between that set of long sideburns. Just the size of him, wide shoulders and long legs, dwarfed her even more.

"There's a lot to be done here. Why don't you tell me what you want me to work on first?" He settled back in the chair.

She tilted her chin. "I'm certainly not going to entertain you in my bathroom. Where I come from, a man wouldn't think of . . . besides, ask Buck."

"I'm asking you," he persisted, gently.

"Why?" Because she really wanted to know the answer, she turned her direct glare on him.

"So you'll be a part of it. You and Buck are partners. He just doesn't know how to handle it, so I figured I'd show him."

He seems awfully sure of himself, she thought. *Almost smug.* "You'll make him mad," she told him. No doubt in her mind.

"No, I won't. We go back a long way, remember?" He dropped his robe on the floor.

She looked from the pile back to him. So maybe he slept nude also. She had brought her robe in, too, just to cover her till she got back to her room. Pushing the enthralling thought out of her mind, she ordered him, coldly, "I'd much rather discuss this someplace else and some other time. Now, please leave."

"You've already made that perfectly clear. I can wait. It's you who's going to get all pruned up. Not me." He crossed one booted foot over his knee. He was enjoying this.

She'd give him the information he wanted so he would leave. "The stagecoach robbery. The saloon brawl. The jailbreak. I missed the rodeo last month but I'm anxious to see the men pit their skill and stamina . . . and raw courage against the power of the animals. I don't want it to look like a circus and I strongly suspect that's precisely how it is."

"What exactly is wrong with the jailbreak?"

Growing impatient with his nonchalance, she snapped, "Why don't you just watch the shows for a couple of days? If you're half the man Buck says you are, you'll see for yourself."

"Fair enough." He found it amusing that she doubted it.

He continued to sit and look at her. It was a thing he could get used to in a heartbeat.

"I watched the stagecoach robbery very closely. It certainly needs work."

Bristling again, Victoria sighed loudly. She had been the one to choreograph that. What did the big man have to say about it? "So?"

"Thieves wouldn't run off from a woman with a derringer. Especially after she had fired the two rounds."

"Oh." Damn. It was so simple yet she had overlooked it. And the men? They were probably laughing at her behind her back.

Very annoyed, Victoria reached for the washcloth that was by her knee and tossed it in his general direction. She was glad she missed when she watched him cut his eyes from the cloth, then back to her.

She watched him rise and bend down to pick it up. Water dribbled soundlessly from the cloth to the floor. Slowly, he carried it over and kneeled down by the tub.

The audacity! The unmitigated gall! Oaf! "What are you doing?" she demanded, jerking sideways, sloshing water over the edge of the tub.

Eyeing her directly from only inches away, he smiled. "You want me to wash your back, don't you? That could be the only reason you threw this at me." He let the wet cloth dangle from his fingers.

Victoria snatched it from him and submarined it into the water. "Out," she ordered with more grit than she felt.

He glanced down at his watch and, still smiling, slowly

stood up and turned for the door. Hesitating as he reached for the doorknob, he glanced back once more and shot an amused wink her way. "Been an interesting day. Water must be getting cold." He sauntered out of the room, pulling the door shut, hard, behind him. Wes chuckled when he heard the wet slap of the washcloth thud against the wood of the closed door.

Victoria hadn't realized how tense she was until, alone again, she relaxed her muscles. She growled through her teeth. Who the heck did he think he was? So now things are more complicated than they were yesterday. Another male for her to contend with. Was there no end to the fight she would have to prove herself able to be a partner in Glory Town? Well, maybe they had a lesson to learn themselves. New resolve grew in her. It wasn't nice being somewhere you weren't wanted, and she had never been in a situation like it. She felt they could all eventually get along quite easily and happily. Didn't they realize she had a lot to offer the town? And that she didn't give up so easily? Besides, she had nothing to go back to in Virginia. Nothing but an overbearing mother who was still terribly insulted that she hadn't made her marriage to David work. Nothing but her mother's country club friends all bent on supplying her with new prospects. She squeezed her eyes shut tight. She felt totally worthless back home. This chance was like an unplanned escape route. She wanted it to work. She needed it to. With the toe of her right foot, she flipped the hot water handle on and lay back.

It was then she heard him jog down the stairs instead of going into his room as she had expected. It had been obvious that he was going to bathe and, she assumed, turn in for the night. She wondered where he was going . . . and then put the thought from her mind. It was absolutely none of her business. And neither was the beige-on-dark-brown robe that still lay in a heap on the floor.

TWO

The barn had been left to go too long. Once the host of some raucous barn dances, it now stood abandoned and from the looks of it was used for a shed or a catchall.

Tools lined the walls and the floor. Old harnesses and saddles, blankets, moldy hay, and various pieces of trash were strewn here and there. Victoria shook her head. Never had their barn and stables been in such a state. Of course, in Virginia there had been stableboys and grooms to see to such things. Out here you had your own two hands wrapped around a pitchfork and a broom.

Rolling her sleeves up to her elbows, Victoria started at the end closest to the door. Her hands had already begun to callus from some of the work she had done and from learning to work with some of the horses. Twice, one of the more stubborn mustangs had pulled the leather through her hands. She preferred the gentle company of her own gelding to some of the less disciplined mounts here, but she didn't mind it really. She found a certain amount of satisfaction in the doing as opposed to the directing. She lined the tools up according to size. The older, nonfunctional ones were thrown in the wheelbarrow. Half this stuff was going to the dump.

Not many people were awake at this hour. The sun had barely cleared the horizon, sending strong beams of light through the morning haze. The stillness was broken only by the sounds Victoria made as she moved around the barn and the early morning birds in search of the elusive worm.

As she worked, Victoria looked around, planning. Once the floor was cleaned down to the packed dirt, she would start on the stalls. They hadn't been used for horses in years but she planned on bringing Tonka up here from the new barn on the back lot. She liked that it was authentic and not a metal building with a cement floor.

They could advertise a dance for Saturday nights. Tables could be set up nearest the office, laden with pies and cakes and punch just as she had seen on TV. A not so very authentic stereo system would serve until she could find a few fiddlers and a caller. Square dancing. It would be the social event of the county. Romantic slow dances. The Western two-step. It could become a monthly event bringing steady streams of new money into Glory Town. Aside from the tourists, people from the surrounding towns could enjoy them, too.

A small anvil resisted Victoria's efforts to move it. Pushing her sleeves up farther and taking a deep breath, she bent down and grabbed it on both ends and tugged.

"Trying to give yourself a hernia?"

Without breaking her pace, she dragged the heavy iron block toward the tack room door. "You're up early, Mr. Cooper. Funny, I didn't figure you for it. Some of the men around here are as lazy as sheep and . . ." She felt the heat of embarrassment. The last time they had been together in the same room, she had been naked. A slight rush of pink flushed her cheeks.

He moved past her and lifted the anvil as if it were filled with helium. Returning, he cast her an absent smile. "Ladies shouldn't pick up anything that weighs that much.

There's plenty of men around here who would be glad to do it for you.''

Grabbing the rake, she pulled hay and straw toward the door. She watched him as he looked around and moved to one corner, then began pacing off the distance with a cocky, long-legged stride. Curious, she leaned her cheek on the rake handle and watched him.

He reached for a pad and pencil he had stuffed in his rear pocket and began to scribble notes on it. Walking to the door, he stepped off the distance to the back wall.

"What are you doing?" she asked, setting the rake against the paddock door just a mite incensed that he was here, making some sort of plan . . . in her barn.

"Measuring. I intend to set up a few classes in here. We can use the haymow for the falls. Here, I can choreograph the gunfights and practice instinct shooting. I think we need a good sharp-shooting show. That always keeps the tourists interested.'' He tested the strength of the beams holding up the loft.

Her chin tilted upward, automatically. "I was cleaning this up for barn dancing on Saturday nights.''

He nodded only half listening, caught up in his own thoughts. "Good idea. We can do all of it.''

She picked up a crushed beer can and tossed it, hard, into the wheelbarrow to make her point. "I'm glad to have your permission. And I want it kept clean.''

He made the time to take a good look at her. There was no sense irritating her even though right now he would have loved to stomp all over her queenly attitude. "Yes, ma'am," Wes agreed grinning and went on about his business. He could feel her eyes on him, at his back. He didn't mind. It had the effect of standing with your back to the sunshine on a cold winter's day.

Why did it infuriate her when he said *yes ma'am*? It was the way he said it, she decided. Insolent. He had sort of a takeover attitude, a little or maybe a lot of disregard for her even though he claimed he was here to do what she wanted. Victoria had enough of that with Buck. "Don't 'ma'am' me, Wes Cooper. If you're going to use this place, too, then the least you can do is help clean it up."

Wes turned slowly to survey the room with a lengthy look. "I was hired to teach, not sweep. I'll get some of the men in here to help."

Her fists slapped onto her hips. "Look here, Cooper. Teach, yes, not run this entire place according to you. Go on about your business. I can take care of this myself." Watching him light a cigarette, she fumed. "And don't smoke in the barn."

He looked from the cigarette in his hand and back to her. "I've been smoking in and around barns since I was fourteen. I know how to smoke in a barn." Turning his attention back to the pad in his hand, he jotted a few numbers.

"Oh, not my barn." She stared at him defiantly, the toe of her dusty boot tapping the floor.

Earlier, when Buck had explained to him that she was a spoiled brat from some rich family in Virginia, he hadn't even come close to an actual description. They stood there eyeing each other as two prizefighters might before a bout. Normally a patient man, Wes shrugged mentally. He might have to work around her but he surely didn't have to bow to her moods. He tipped his hat and was out the door, completely missing the face she made at his back.

Later, strolling through town in her new period costume, Victoria bid good day to the tourists and patted the children on the head. She loved her dress. The lace collar curled around her neck and the flounced hem swirled around her ankles. It was yellow with tiny daisies on it and lace down the entire front following the pearly buttons.

Some days she wore jeans; on others she felt feminine and indulged in the pretty dresses their seamstress toiled over for hours in her trailer. A bonnet was pertly tied under her chin and a parasol dangled from her hand. She felt as if she were waiting for the stage to roll in, bringing her husband back from business in the East. She chuckled. She could definitely get carried away with the role playing. But she also noticed it was good for her. She smiled as she looked around at her town. The ambience of this place filled her with a peace she had never known. No tensions. No pressures to perform, to be Marcia Clay's daughter. Before, there had always been some tea to attend, or a charity to work on. The life-style her mother lived and simply expected that she live also had become a hollow existence to Victoria. At exactly what point in her life she had decided this, she wasn't sure, but it had hit hard after her divorce from David. Real hard.

As she made her way toward the hotel, she spotted Wes walking out of the saloon. He, too, had purposely dressed to fool the sightseers . . . in black, with a white neckerchief flowing in the light breeze. His authenticity almost took her breath away. Colt ammunition. He wore a new Stetson with the brim turned down. A real go-to-hell hat. He looked a man to stand aside from. Spotting her, he smiled and flicked the brim of his hat with a hand snugged into a black leather gunfighter's glove.

Victoria sashayed on into the hotel and took a seat at one of the tables. Joe came over right away. "What'll it be, Ms. Clay? The usual?"

Flashing him a sweet smile, she answered, "Yes, Joe, and let me have a few of those sugar cookies, please."

A long, dark shadow fell across her table as J. Weston Cooper sidled up to it. His deep, smooth voice reverberated across the room. "Mind if I join you, ma'am?"

She smiled coyly for the tourists humming around them but said between her teeth, "Quit calling me that." And then a little louder, "Why, of course, Mr. Weston."

Joe brought her tea and cookies and set them in the middle of the table. Victoria didn't miss Wes's raised eyebrow. "Mr. Cooper, what can I get for you?" Joe asked.

Without once taking his eyes off her, Wes smiled and answered, "Sarsaparilla, Joe. No ice."

Joe nodded and left them. Victoria tasted one of the cookies she had smelled baking early this morning. It was delicious.

"Tea?" Wes queried, purposely goading her.

"It's four o'clock. And like you said, some habits *are* hard to break. Cookie?" she offered sweetly, but Wes picked up the sharpness of her look.

He shook his head. "I'm trying to give them up. So it's true that you Virginians have tea in the afternoon." He sat back in the chair and relaxed.

She looked up at him and, remembering they were part of a play, smiled again. "True enough, Mr. Cooper. What do you Oklahomans lay claim to? Plundering and pillaging?"

Without taking a moment to think, he answered. "Red Dog and poker games."

"I see. You'll have to teach me." she said, with no interest at all.

"To drink Red Dog? I don't think so. Poker I can take care of. The boys are getting together in your nice clean barn Friday night for a friendly game. Want to join us?"

He was laughing at her again. "Hardly." She adjusted her skirt. He was making her feel uncomfortable, too. Did he do it on purpose? He seemed so sure of himself, yet . . . there was something she picked up on that said he wasn't; he just wanted everyone to think so. She would strive for a decent conversation as long as they were on display for the public. "How are you getting along with the men?"

He thanked Joe for the sarsaparilla and took a long drink. "Most of them fine. What's with Nick? He have a problem with everybody or just me?"

"Oh, Nick. Yes, well, I figured he'd really resent your being here. He thinks everything is just fine the way it is. He seems to live this life twenty-four hours a day. Has nothing else going for him since his wife died some years back, they tell me. Sometimes I watch him. He takes this much too much to heart, but if it's all a man has, who am I to judge? He's been very nice to me since I arrived. He was more than willing to show me around when Buck couldn't be bothered." She dunked a cookie in her tea and took a bite. Smiling coldly, she added, "Besides, he hates it when a new man . . . a handsome one, comes on the set and turns the ladies' heads."

"I turn heads?"

She laughed and dabbed her lips with a napkin. "Don't pretend you don't realize you cut quite a figure in that getup. Even the married ones are making eyes at you."

He shrugged as he raised the glass to his lips, remembering another woman who had once "made eyes at him."

Victoria followed the glass to his lips with her gaze. "Most men like that."

"It is good," he teased, pretending to examine the dark liquid in the bottom of the tumbler.

"That women like to admire them." She knew he was playing mental gymnastics with her, but then, he had no way of knowing she knew how to play that game as well as he did. She may have been a smothered Virginia lady, one protected and pampered, but she had worked with veterans of the Korean and Vietnam wars . . . listened to them, cared about them and for them. They were a wily bunch. Stuffed full of emotions and careful who they shared them with. They were witty, capable, and sharp. She had learned to parry and banter.

"Are you divorced?" she asked, thinking that might be the reason for his indifference to his appeal.

His eyes snapped back to hers. She was blunt, and he wondered before answering her what about him revealed that to her. "Yep."

"I'm divorced, too, but I haven't lost interest in the opposite sex as your shrug would indicate."

So that was it. He seemed not to be concerned with women in general. Well, she wasn't that far off, he admitted to himself. "You weren't married to my wife. But I have nothing against women. At least not at the moment." He signaled Joe for another drink.

"It just happened and you're still hurt, right?" she guessed, somehow feeling a little satisfaction along with it.

When Wes chose not to answer her, she merely smiled. She had learned about silence, too, and how to respect it at times. "It's about time for the stage to roll in and get rightfully robbed again. The boys and I made some changes but you might still find it needs work."

"That's what I'm here for." He was wondering, now, what had possessed him to stop in to talk to her.

Used to asking questions when she wanted to know something, Victoria didn't hesitate. "Why did you quit the state police?"

His interested gaze fell on her mouth as she slipped a small sugar cookie between her lips. He wished he didn't keep wondering what it would feel like for him to be there. This lady just wasn't his type. He didn't like pushy. "It was a get-nothing-done job."

Chuckling, she asked him, "How so? Couldn't you keep up with your quota of traffic tickets?"

"Don't like cops, huh? I'll save us both a very boring conversation. No matter what an officer does . . . it doesn't change anything. The perpetrators just come back in different suits with different reasons. I got tired."

"I wouldn't think that to be true. You get criminals off the streets, save lives, assist . . ."

Glad to hear the heavy creak of wheels and the thunder of horses' hooves, Wes looked out the window. "Here comes the stage. You coming out?" he asked her as he pushed his chair back.

Victoria rose along with him and took the arm he offered her. So being a cop was a sore spot with him for some reason. She sensed he had a number of tender areas. That was fine with her. But still none of this fit. Why was he here? She answered it herself. He was here because Buck jumped the gun. Because Buck wanted to be sure she didn't go out and hire a man who would do a great job and make her look good.

After the announcement cleared the streets to prevent accidents, the stage thundered into town with "Ghost Riders in the Sky" blaring out over the grainy intercom system. The sidewalks were overflowing. Some of the children still had oversized hats and vests on that they had borrowed from some of the reenactors. They paused in their mock shootouts. Other children were either on their parents' shoulders, pulled up and propped on their hips, or swinging from the porch posts. From the looks of the smiles of anticipation, the adults were just as fascinated as the kids.

Wes and Victoria took a place on the walk where they could see everything clearly. Before long the stage was surrounded by the five mounted desperados, kerchiefs hiding their faces, guns waggling in the air. Shots were fired. The ringleader ordered the driver and the man riding shotgun to throw down the strongbox. Randy's horse reared and spun around when the metal container was thrown close to his hooves. One of the other men shouted for the passengers, all convincingly frightened, to get out of the coach and empty their valuables into a pouch he held up. It was nearly a carbon copy of the stage holdup Wes had walked in on. He couldn't see that much improvement.

Wes murmured. "Eye contact. That's one of their problems. They're watching the audience from time to time."

She nodded. They certainly were. "Hams."

"The horses should be wired up a little more. They need to get them out and work them a while before riding into town. That one looks like he's about to go back to sleep. Well, that dude just screwed this one up. He put his gun back in his holster before mounting up. I could have shot him and the leader before they knew what happened. All the men should have kept their guns drawn. A real desperado wouldn't secure his weapon until he was safely out of town.''

He was talking to himself as much as to her. She nodded. He had a good eye. A good sense of what she wanted here. She could have looked all day and known it wasn't quite right but not put her finger on what needed correcting. Secure his weapon? His terminology amused her.

Again, he arched his eyebrow and looked at her. "Well?"

She tilted her head, stubbornly. "I guess I agree with you. Have a problem with that, Cooper?"

This job was going to prove more interesting than he had ever imagined. "Nope. No problem."

As the outlaws rode off, hooting and hollering, the female passenger fainted dead away into the dust. Wes shook his head.

"What?" she asked him, thinking it was a pretty good swoon.

"Women usually lose it during the holdup, not after all the danger has ridden away. And the whole thing took too long. Should be done quicker. They couldn't have taken that much time if they were out on the trail. What if someone came up on them? Just because it's staged in town for convenience doesn't mean it shouldn't be authentic. I think the driver should have taken a shot at them. It's his job to protect his passengers and their possessions."

Still, the audience was pleased. A couple of the little kids ran off the sidewalk firing pistols she recognized as being purchased in the general store. Good.

"There's a jailbreak in half an hour, then a little before dark the cattlemen, in from a trail drive, come rodeoing down the road whooping and hollering. They jump down and sweep up some of the women into the saloon for a little rip-roaring dancing," she told him as they strolled along amicably. "The crowd loves it."

He nodded as he looked around. Keeping step with him, she slipped her hand into the crook of his elbow. That surprised her as much as him. She didn't stop to wonder why she did it. She was growing used to doing what pleased her and she liked it. She smiled to herself. Something weird was happening to her. In one instant she resented the hell out of him and in the next she wanted to touch him. Victoria took a deep breath. She'd have to analyze all this later.

"I'm going to join Lola in the saloon show tonight."

He looked down at her. "From schoolmarm clothes to wild woman garb. This I've got to see."

Yes, she had thought of that, too, but it all seemed like so much fun, she promised Lola she'd join her in entertaining the crowd tonight. "I can't join in the singing because I can't carry a tune, but I *can* carry a tray laden with glasses filled with lemonade. There's going to be a barroom brawl that needs your attention."

"What time?" He checked his watch.

"Ummm. Show starts at 8:15, so I think the fight is at nine o'clock."

They crossed the street, dodging and waving to Buck driving his freight wagon loaded down with happy passengers.

"I have to be somewhere at nine but I'll plan on catching it another night."

That was about the same time he had disappeared last night. A date? Why should that surprise her or send her spirits tumbling down a little? She didn't think of him that way. Removing her hand from his arm, she excused herself. "See you later."

All she wanted was to be busy. Wes Cooper was a chauvinist and a bossy one at that. He aggravated her. As she swept up the stairs of the hotel, she marveled that such exasperation could cause such warmth.

The saloon was filled to capacity. Lola and Roxey were dancing to a bouncy tune. Victoria cast them a small wave as she made her way into the crowd. Their costumes weren't as revealing as they could have been but this was a family show. She was glad for that because she felt uncomfortable exposing as much bosom as she did. Her fiery red satin skirt bounced over the white crinoline. Her bright red high heels tapped over the wooden floor. Victoria wore a splash of rhinestones at her throat that refracted the light and warm red rubies on her ears.

Spotting Nick at a corner table, his chair tipped back against the wall, Victoria sidled over as she had seen the saloon women do. She dearly loved this play acting. "Cowboy, you look lonely tonight."

His face brightened. Nick was a handsome man in a dark way. He was just under six feet, had square shoulders, and was narrow at the hip. He wore an unusually long, droopy mustache in keeping with his image. Though his eyes were blue, it was a midnight blue and he always seemed to have shadows beneath. He righted his chair and offered her the other one. "Sit down, Vic. You sure look perty in that dress."

Victoria was mildly amused at the ease with which he used Buck's nickname for her. Yet, there was something about Nick that unsettled her. She chalked that up to the fact that he was a very moody man. She had caught him looking at her when he didn't think she could see. She had seen him lose his temper with the other men too quickly, and she knew that he preferred the company of the horses he cared for more than that of humans.

She gracefully accepted his compliment and tried to ignore the fact that he couldn't keep his eyes off her bustline. He was just playing the part of the lonesome cowboy and doing it well. They sipped their drinks and chatted through another of the girls' songs. Looking around, Victoria could see that the tourists, more couples than families tonight, were really enjoying the show and the dancing.

Victoria watched the swinging doors for Wes. When she realized what she was doing, she took Nick by the hand and dragged him to the center of the floor. Smoothly, they danced.

Other couples came to the dance floor and Lola and Roxey joined them, leaving Tom at the piano punching out honky-tonk. Before they knew it, they were all dancing with each other. The female tourists were elated to be in the arms of dashing cowboys, and the men had no qualms about randy-dancing with saloon girls. Breathless and laughing, Victoria whirled from one partner to the other. Her eye caught a glint of light and she looked back.

Just through the swinging double doors, stood Wes. Missing a step and almost tripping, Victoria couldn't pull her eyes from him. He was dressed in a gray suit jacket over black jeans. His white shirt had three buttons undone. At his waist a huge rodeo belt buckle glinted in the light. His boots reflected the lighting with a high polish. He wore no Stetson tonight, and his hair, wavy and thick, fell outlawishly across his forehead.

Nick grabbed her and twirled her around. It was then that she realized the crowd had stopped dancing and formed a circle around them, clapping them on. Nick loved it. He yanked her to him, roughly, and then spun her away only to pull her tight against him and spin with her. He was good. No doubt about it. And she smelled whiskey on his breath. There was no doubt about that either.

From outside the circle, Wes watched. Victoria's cheeks were flushed a rosy red. Long, sleek, black-stockinged legs peeked out when Nick spun her around. Her hair, shiny and curly, bounced around her head. Wes felt a tightening in his gut and was amazed to find his palms damp. She looked beautiful and wild. When he'd first pushed through the doors, he'd heard her laughter. Rolling, throaty, and sexy.

When the dance ended, Victoria looked breathlessly toward the doors. He was gone. There was no explaining the letdown she felt. Had she been hoping he would come in and claim her for his partner?

Nick led her by the hand back to the table in the corner.

She turned her attention to him. She told herself she had no desire to be in J. Weston Cooper's arms. She had just wanted him to see her successfully playing her role . . . adding something to Glory Town instead of being an albatross as she was sure Buck must have described her.

Nick cleared his throat. She realized he had asked her a question and she hadn't heard. She turned a smile on him and, after casting one more look at the saloon doors gently swinging back in place, patted Nick's hand. "A root beer on ice would be nice."

Midnight. The town closed at ten. It was quiet except for the ever-present wind that rolled down the deserted street and played along the sidewalks, through the porch posts, leaving ghostly, red, dusty tracks.

Her home was the Donaldson Hotel. One room or ten. The entire lower floor consisted of lobby, dining room, and kitchen. In the daytime it might be teeming with tourists either climbing the stairs and wandering the re-created rooms or sitting down to a nice steak and potato meal and sopping wonderful, huge homemade biscuits through thick flour gravy with fresh apple pie for dessert. But at night . . . it was all hers.

Heavy velvet drapes lined the tall windows. They had once been a bright eye-catching emerald green. Tonight they appeared to be the limbs of a weeping willow, dull and saggy. The mantel over the fireplace supported a branding iron and over it hung a painting, slightly askew, of pioneers making their way west by wagon train and an aging woman soaking her feet in a nearby stream while her husband stood guard.

The furniture was Victorian and old, but still functional. A sizable bank loan would bring this place up. That, in turn, would bring in more tourists, drawing more money. Most of the businesses were owned by the people occupying the trailers on the back lot. They paid a small rent on the buildings and a percentage of their profits to Victoria and Buck.

But the hotel and dining room were theirs and the money from the horseback rides helped. She would like to eventually rent out rooms as she was told they did years ago when there had been a piano player and then the visitors danced and sang the night away.

They also owned the saloon, and even though they served nothing but soft drinks and snacks, there had once been a bigger show than Roxey and Lola singing "She'll Be Comin' Round the Mountain." She hoped the people she hired earlier would spice up the show. Before, there had been a cover charge and a night's entertainment, not just a small souvenir counter and a cooler filled with ice cream. All these things had to be brought back if this old town was to survive. And she was determined it would. It meant too much to her to watch it decay. And even if Buck didn't realize it right now, it was important to him, too.

It would all be so simple if she just wrote a draft from her bank and put her money to work, but that was what her mother was waiting for her to do. Trust funds and IRAs and CDs that belonged to Victoria were the result of old, moldy family money, and even at this age, she would have to get permission to move such a huge amount. Control. Some people could never relinquish it and her mother was a prime example. She was hoping Victoria would fail in this venture as she had secretly hoped she would at everything. Victoria had sensed it every time she tried something new. Her mother didn't hide the fact that she thought women should hang on a man's arm, adorn his home, and bear his children in quiet and loving peace. Victoria chuckled.

Tired after the long day but not yet ready to retire upstairs to her room, Victoria sat in an overstuffed powder blue chair in the cozy lobby, one leg slung over the arm.

She had opened the fake cupboard to reveal the television and was now snuggled in to watch a rerun of *Gunsmoke*.

Victoria had always been fascinated by the Wild West. The rough-riding cowboys and Indians and cavalry and trail drives. She had read books, fiction and nonfiction, whenever she had had the chance. Victoria knew all about Annie Oakley, Buffalo Bill, the James boys, and the Youngers. This was like waking up after falling asleep in a movie theater, finding you had somehow slipped through the giant screen to stand up on the other side. Now that Victoria had everything she needed to propel herself back to a time that enchanted her, she wanted it to be perfect.

There was a certain freedom in the Old West. Laws were tested as soon as they were made. A man's mettle was his reputation. Some of the women, outlaws and girlfriends of desperadoes, dared to be what they wanted . . . even back in those days. When she was younger, Victoria had dreamed of being one of those women. Riding beside her man, firing her gun at the law fast on their heels, hiding out at the Hole-in-the-Wall, bandages and beef already at the waiting.

During a commercial, Victoria walked barefoot back to the room behind the dining room that served as office for the CPA who came in once a week to bring everything up to date and be sure taxes were filed and paychecks written. Pulling the clipboard off the wall, she unsnapped the profit and loss statements from under the metal clip and returned to her chair, snagging a bag of chips on her way to munch on.

Glory Town wasn't in dire straits. Things were tight and had to be managed properly, but with a nice fat loan, the tourist business could be increased two hundred percent. Prices needed to be adjusted. Victoria had spent many an afternoon in Tulsa and Oklahoma City comparing price tags on T-shirts and boots, Western clothes, and souvenirs. She had compared their prices with those of a few other restaurants in town. They were selling below market value. No one had bothered to assess these things in years. She wondered what kind of a man her uncle had been. It seemed neither of the partners had a real head for business. If it wasn't for the bookkeeper that Victoria strongly suspected had gently led the men along, the place could have folded years ago.

On the television, Marshal Dillon headed up a posse hot on the heels of a gang of bandits. The gunfire drew her undivided attention for a while. Horses' hooves pounded the earth, sending spirals of dust behind them. The men rode low and bent in the saddle, hats flapping in the breeze. They cornered the outlaws in a blind canyon and slid off their horses in one smooth motion and ran to hide behind boulders, guns drawn. A volley of gunfire was exchanged. One man grabbed his midsection and, with a screwed-up face and blood dripping from between his fingers, twisted and flopped to the ground. Another took a bullet in the head, threw his rifle in the air, and fell off a small cliff, body sliding and skidding in the dust. She studied the movements and the actions. A wry smile appeared on her face. Yes, her men needed a lot of improvement.

From the books Victoria had seen, the men's pay had remained relatively the same for some years based on the take from the gate. From time to time, the odd, occasional bonus kept them going, but they would all enjoy seeing long lines at the entrance, knowing the money was going to get better. Besides, they had to be tightened up and sharpened a little. To do that, they needed an incentive. Victoria looked forward to meeting with Bill Boyd in Dallas about that loan the next morning.

Tapping the pencil on the board, she let her imagination run. Paint, lumber, new harnesses and fences. The gallows that the tourists liked to climb up on and put their necks in the breakaway noose was actually getting downright wobbly. More material for the seamstress so she could make new and better costumes instead of merely repairing the old ones. A shiny new spittoon for the saloon and a few of the new gaming tables. Pool would be good. Every man liked to do that. And flashy, silver-laden saddles and bridles for some of the horses. And some potted plants for the lobby of the hotel . . . Her mind whirled and filled way beyond her means but it was fun to dream and imagine. She knew limitations and priorities would have to be considered. But that was okay. Her town was going to thrive and simply teem with tourists. Everyone would be happy.

A commercial touting the benefits of trying the four flavors of oatmeal ended and *Gunsmoke* was back on. This scene was in a saloon. Her set wasn't far off but could use some more props.

The marshal and Festus walked down the street of Dodge City, Matt assuring his deputy that all the bad men were captured and safely in jail. The credits began to run up the screen and the theme song faded into the background.

Half an hour later, her head stuffed with plans, she turned off the TV, snapped lights off in her wake, and headed for bed. After dreaming about the legends and the mystery and the wildness of the Old West, she could now taste it and live it. Victoria planned on propelling herself into the untamed, adventurous life portrayed here. This was as close as she would ever get and it excited her. Motivated her. The hell with the people who would like to see her fail. Tomorrow would be a good day. She would make it one. It would be the real beginning of her new life here. And if that included getting along with or at least tolerating J. Weston Cooper, then so be it.

THREE

For the next several days, things ran pretty smoothly. Victoria attended some of Wes's instructional sessions but during others she was busy. Buck kept a quiet eye on her. He seemed to be mellowing just a bit, but Victoria didn't trust it. She was still a long way from being accepted.

It was seven o'clock on Tuesday and they had the usual light count of tourists. Having just returned from her trip to Dallas, jetting down and back in the same day, Victoria headed for the barn after dropping her luggage in her room and changing to jeans and a T-shirt. She was anxious to ride a while and spend some time with her horse.

As she approached the barn, she heard shooting and knew that once again Wes was giving lessons. Her gelding had been stabled inside. Hurrying her steps a bit, she swung around the corner and spotted the horse out in the paddock with another she hadn't remembered seeing. Parked behind the barn was a pickup and attached to that was a stately lettered trailer. COOPER RANCH. She bristled just a little. Flashy. Pretentious. She crossed her arms over her chest. He moved his horse down here, just as he'd said he would. It was a beautiful palomino; his white tail and mane, groomed and flowing, were velvety and long.

46

Lifting the latch on the gate, Victoria walked through, pushed it closed behind her, and strolled over to the new occupant. The horse was friendly and nosed the hand she offered him. As Victoria ran her hand along the horse's back and sides, she noticed the soft sheen. She wanted to ask Wes what he used on him and that griped her.

Hearing Wes's patient and deep voice, instructing the men on what was called a trade-off, she let her curiosity get the best of her. Giving the horses one last scratch on the ears, she left them to move into the doorway and watch.

As he stood behind a table, the men in various places alongside him, Wes placed two guns. One was a single-action .45 and the other a lever action .30.30. The targets were tacked to the new wall Wes and some of the men had made. It consisted of four-by-six's formed with a hollow section and filled with dirt. A thick sheet of metal, plywood, metal again, and more wood stopped the lead.

He asked one of the men to call "go" and in a split second he fired the .45 and, with the same hand, set it down and picked up the rifle, levered it, and fired before replacing it on the table.

It was a blur of sound and motion. Both bull's-eyes. Victoria had never seen anything like it. And judging from the murmuring and the "God's britches!," neither had the men. Pappy, Buck's aging foreman, simply stood off to one side, shaking his head and grinning from ear to ear.

Nick stepped up. "Been doin' that for years," he boasted. "It's no big deal." He grinned at the other men, confident he could follow Wes's act.

Cooper backed up and gave Nick the table. Nick fired both guns concurrently but without nearly the speed Cooper had displayed. Eyes down, he dropped the guns on the table. Nick stepped back. "I'm a little out of practice. Don't matter none. We don't have a sharpshooting show."

"We will from now on and all of you are going to get good at it. You're just out of practice, Nick. The two of us will specialize in the hand-clap draw. I bet you're familiar with that one. We'll end the show with my clapping my hands together, catching your gun between them, a holster draw, and one coming from out of your belt from behind your back. Now for instinct shooting.''

Victoria didn't miss the resentful look Nick cast toward Wes. Wes wasn't there to show Nick up, but Nick would never see it for that.

He went on with his instructions in his calm, tireless teacher-like voice. "Instinct shooting is just that. You'll learn not to take aim, just fire. After enough practicing you'll get the hang of it. Billy, would you line six of those beer cans up on the shelf?"

While Billy did that, Wes flexed his fingers and dropped the .45 back into his holster. He turned his back to Billy and told him, "Now rearrange them and yell when you're clear.''

Wes saw Victoria watching and smiled at her. Billy yelled and Wes spun, yanking the revolver from the leather. Victoria never saw him stop spinning, for the instant he leveled with the cans he pulled the trigger, the other hand fanning the hammer. He popped them all. Six cans exploded and fell at almost the exact same time.

The men whistled and hooted. "Now all of you take a turn. Simply let your instincts guide you. After you have that down solid, we'll do the balloon drop. You'll learn to hold it up above your head and drop it, draw your gun with the same hand and fire, exploding the balloon before it touches the ground." He left the men staring at him wide-eyed and walked toward her.

"Shoot?" he asked her as he came up to her.

She tilted her chin. "I've taken down my share of skeet.''

Impressed, Wes grinned and nodded. "I have a trap release. We'll have to do some of that. Want to learn this way?" He jerked a thumb back toward the men.

She did. But not in front of the boys. She could stand

being laughed at as well as the others, but she had limits. Although it galled her just a little, she asked, "Private lessons?"

He looked from the men back to her. "Why?"

"Pride. Virginia pride actually," she answered his next question before he asked it.

Nick watched the two of them instead of doing what he was supposed to be doing. Victoria saw him move to the side door and disappear.

"Have you seen Buck this evening?" Victoria asked, idly wondering why Nick didn't seem to be as interested as the other men in honing their gun skills.

Thumbing his hat back, he told her, "He was holed up in the jailhouse earlier. Much luck in Dallas?"

Irritated, she looked at him, "He discussed it with you? Next thing, he'll be making this a corporation and asking you to be one of the officers."

"I wouldn't use the word *discuss*. He doesn't like your idea much. This is Oklahoma. We don't deal with Texas banks."

She shrugged. "Buck doesn't like a great deal from what I've seen, so that doesn't worry me anymore. Is that your horse in the paddock with my gelding?"

"Yes. He's mine. I didn't think you'd mind. I don't want your horse to be lonely or the only one able to enjoy these fine quarters. Not when there's plenty of room."

"He's a beauty," Victoria admitted, at the same time resenting his takeover attitude.

"Smart, too." He opened the gate and walked into the paddock. The horse immediately came over and stood in front of him. Wes put an affectionate hand to the horse's nose and the gelding returned the gesture by rubbing his face on Wes's shoulder. "He runs a beautiful barrel pattern and I could let go of the reins and sit back, arms folded across my chest, and he'd still take the poles. He has a strong flying lead change."

Victoria stroked his fine mane and the horse stepped

back to look at her. Wes talked softly to his horse and Victoria heard the love in his voice. It was a thing she admired in anyone. She gave him one small notch on the good side of her mental measuring stick.

"What do you use on him? He shines and I can smell an insect repellent."

He walked to the fence and pulled a bright yellow carrier through it. From underneath the brushes and leads, shedder and hoof pick he pulled a bottle of his own mixture. Holding it up for her to see, he offered, "A little of this and a little of that. Does a good job. Feel free to use it on your horse."

"I will. Thanks. The supplies I brought with me have long since been depleted." She watched the smooth motion of his body as he bent and slid the carrier outside the fence again.

"Someone said you had this horse shipped all the way out here." Wes expertly scratched the gelding under his chin. The horse responded by rubbing his nose down Wes's chest.

"That's right. He's been mine since the day he was born eight years ago. We both had a time of adjustment to the Western tack and gear but we love it now. The freedom of it. The relaxed atmosphere."

She turned to go and Wes walked with her. "Have you been in the saloon since you returned?"

"No, why?" she asked, instantly suspicious.

It was his turn to shrug. "Just wondering. See you later." He turned back to the barn, obviously keeping a secret.

She went after him. "Why?"

He laughed. "I figure Buck just wants you to remember who's boss around here. And he doesn't figure it's you."

Walking hurriedly toward the saloon, Victoria felt Cooper's eyes at her back. She suspected he was laughing at her.

Pushing through the saloon doors, Victoria stopped. Off

to one side stood a big, gaudy, red, shiny mechanical bull. Dollar signs appeared before her eyes. Huge green ones.

Turning on her heels, she stomped her way toward the jailhouse. Buck was on the porch in the rocker, whittling knife in one hand, a soft piece of wood in the other. He had been watching her path and wasn't at all surprised to see her coming his way, claws bared. He chuckled low.

Baiting her, he waved the wooden object at her. "Evenin', missy. Have a good trip to Dallas?"

"A mechanical bull?" she stopped in the road, hands at her hips. Forgetting all about the tourists, she let him have it. "I go all the way to Dallas to wheel and deal for money and you're back here spending what little we do have? Where did you get it? How much was it? Will they take it back? Good grief, Buck, do you have any idea what that will do to our insurance rates? That's the thanks I get for successfully pulling off the loan."

He rolled his shoulders and stretched as he stood up. "Maybe we'd better take this conversation inside." He nodded toward the tourists and saw Wes in the background, grinning as if he could just spit yellow bird feathers.

"You bet we'll take it inside." She pushed past him and into the building. "We're partners and we're supposed to make these decisions together. Did you forget that?"

Wes went back to the barn. Those two were a pair. He was beginning to love his new job. And he could get real used to the lady boss even if she wasn't his type. What was his type? he wondered as he walked. Oh, well, there weren't going to be many dull moments. Checking his watch, he made note that he would have to leave in a few minutes.

Nick went back to his trailer. As he walked, he brooded and tried to untangle his thoughts. Everything was changing here. This Wes Cooper was becoming a real live hero to many. The women like him, the men like him. He does everything well. He cast one more bitter look over his shoulder. Vic likes him. Buck likes him. He didn't. He reached his trailer and headed immediately for the refrigerator. Antacid, straight from the bottle.

The tourists ignored the slightly hushed, but heated argument going on inside the jailhouse. But they did make way for her when, a few moments later, Victoria banged the door open and stomped across the sidewalk and stepped onto the road.

She was just in time to see Wes Cooper come out of the barn, check his watch, and head for his truck that was still parked on the back lot. Without thinking much about it, she swung back onto the sidewalk and yelled at Buck. "Just what is it that makes your Wes Cooper look at his watch all the time and then go driving off somewhere? I thought he worked here."

Buck came out and stood next to her. "He does. But I pretty much gave him his own time schedule. And I figure he's off to see his Katie. He sure loves that little gal."

Why did she feel as if she'd been hit with a rock? She knew a man like him would have a lady friend. And why should she care? She didn't. Dammit, she didn't. Just because she was beginning to really admire the man and his abilities didn't mean she liked him. Turning on her heel, she swept back down the street.

So Buck hadn't seemed elated with the news that she got the nice fat loan she went after. Too bad. Somebody had to take the initiative here. The town had come to a standstill. Even Buck realized that or he wouldn't have agreed with her idea and consequently hired J. Weston Cooper. She wasn't happy either. She wasn't happy with his childish display of ownership. They would all just have to learn to deal with it. Things would just have to eventually smooth out.

She didn't like the way she was acting. Being forced to act. Once again, as she did so often back in Virginia, she was reacting to outside influences.

Back on the East Coast, she had strived to be all her

mother wished her to be, all her husband thought she was, and all that society dictated was acceptable. Phooey. Enough of that. She had had no idea that Buck would resent her falling heir to this place, until she had arrived. Hadn't even been slightly prepared for it. The result was that she had to put on a layer of steel. It was fast becoming a heavy thing to deal with. She walked down the street nodding and smiling to the tourists and the townspeople. She was good at covering her feelings when she wanted to. Damn. Why did it have to be this way? She kicked a pebble that zinged and ricocheted under the boardwalk.

Glory Town was a special place. She had felt it the moment she stepped foot on the grounds. Even though she had made only small, insignificant contributions, the changes were evident. There had been a nonchalance on the part of the reenactors when she arrived. Everyone, including the shopkeepers, seemed bored and lulled by the monotony. Maybe some of her exuberance was rubbing off.

Alone in her hotel room at ten o'clock, she was perturbed when someone rapped on the door. Putting aside her list of priorities for spending the money, she pulled the door open.

She felt the slightest bit of unease but she chalked it up to the simple fact that she and Nick had never been alone so late at night. He had a way of looking at her sometimes . . .

Nick appeared sleepy. His eyes were deeply shadowed and he seemed a bit unsteady. Victoria didn't detect the odor of liquor, so she tried to relax as they faced each other in the doorway.

"Evenin', Vic." He lifted his hat from his head and set it down again.

"Hi. What can I do for you?"

"I was wonderin' if you'd join me downstairs for a drink."

"This late?" She glanced at the clock on her bureau. "I'm working on a repair list. How about some other time?"

He leaned on the doorjamb and politely removed his hat from his head this time. Changing his tone, he offered, "You work too hard. I wanted to talk to you about the repairs in fact."

"I see. What about them?"

"Can't we talk about it in the dining room?"

So it was his way of getting what he wanted. She needed some volunteers to do the hard labor and now was as good a time as ever to recruit. They went downstairs.

A few straggling tourists kept the staff busy. They found a table off to itself and Nick asked to see the list. "You have a lot of stuff written down here."

"Lots to do. This place has to shine."

"I don't know. Fancier it gets, the less it looks like what it is. The folks expect peeled paint and warped boards, don't you think?"

"To a point." She sipped the coffee she had insisted on, passing on the liquor Nick offered, and nibbled on the sandwich he had ordered for her without asking.

"That fancy dude Cooper thinks he's something, doesn't he?"

Alerted by Nick's tone of voice, Victoria took a good look at Nick. "He's . . . confident. But I think he'll help shape this place up."

"I like this place just the way it is. Especially now that you're here." His slow, lazy grin unnerved her just a little. He seemed just a tad too familiar. A tiny shiver ran between her shoulder blades, but she instantly dismissed it as her being too tired to have this conversation.

"Thank you."

He leaned forward, closer to her. "I'll help with anything you need done. Just ask."

Wes Cooper came through the door looking tired and

hurried. He spotted Victoria and Nick at the corner table. Nodding a curt greeting, he walked toward the stairs.

Victoria picked up on Nick's contrived exuberance when he motioned toward Wes. "Wes, old man. Join us."

Pausing with one booted foot on the stair, Wes lifted his hand in the air. "No thanks. I'm going to turn in early tonight."

Nick would have none of it. Playing the big shot, as it was obvious to everyone, he made a big to-do of convincing Wes to share a drink with them before they all turned in.

Wes cast Victoria a calm glance before accepting the offer. "Did you schedule the men to meet me on the hillside at nine?" Wes asked Nick as he sat opposite him.

Nick sat back from the table. "Nine? You said ten. I told the men ten."

"Ten's too late, Nick. I told you precisely nine so we could be finished early enough to get some roping practice in." And he had. He remembered expressly making sure this man had the instructions right. The fact that he had decided to take Nick under his wing and let him be as important as he felt he was was going to prove to be a mistake. He didn't like Nick's attitude but had been willing to give him a chance. That willingness was being sorely tested.

Victoria noticed the edge to Wes's voice, and even though she had known him only a short while, she knew that wasn't like him. He was in early from his date. Maybe things didn't go well, she thought smugly.

Wes shook his head. "Never mind, Nick. Ten is fine."

Victoria offered, "Nick, maybe you might find that making notes is helpful. I do."

Nick sat back in his chair and smiled at her. "Wes has a lot on his mind. He was just mistaken, that's all. No big deal."

Victoria caught Wes's eye. Instinct told her a man like

him made darn few mistakes and would have been quick to admit it if he had.

"I'm really tired, Nick. We'll get into the repair list another time." When she rose to leave, Wes got to his feet and Nick scrambled up.

"Good night, Nick. Wes, if you're going up, could you walk me to my door?" Victoria didn't want Nick to and for some uneasy reason she felt he was going to offer.

Wes moved to stand beside her and they both bid Nick good night.

"We'll get together tomorrow and go over the plans. We'll have lunch. I'll be free by then," Nick offered, hurriedly, following them to the foot of the stairs.

"We'll see." Victoria was glad when Wes took her arm and escorted her up.

In front of her door, he merely tipped his hat and headed for his own room. Victoria watched him go. Something was wrong.

"What's bothering you tonight, Wes?"

He was surprised by the genuine concern in her voice. With his hand on the doorknob, he looked back at her. "Thanks for asking, but I'm just tired. If you're not going to use the bathroom right away, I will."

"No, go ahead. Don't let Nick worry you. He's okay."

He walked back to stand a few feet from her. He caught the faint scent of something exotic as he drew closer. "Nick doesn't worry me. I just wonder if he's good for this town. Like you said, he takes all this to heart. I had decided to let him be my right-hand man, but if he can't keep directions straight, it won't work."

"That was very nice of you." And it was. It warmed her heart to think that this tough, in-charge man would try to smooth Nick's amplified ego, give him a chance to be what he wanted to be. She wanted him to know how she felt. "I think it might be just what he needs. Don't give up on him right away. Give it a chance. I like the idea. Maybe it will fill a void the man seems to be nurturing."

Wes thought a minute. She might be right. It might be worth giving him the benefit of a doubt if just for her. It would be one less thing she had to deal with. Her eyes looked tired and she seemed much less the steel maiden tonight. Almost touchable. He leaned a little closer. "Good night."

The aura that she sensed surrounded Wes Cooper from the first moment they bumped into each other seemed to envelop her. Her biological perception seemed to over-react. In the dim light of the hallway, his dark eyes captured hers. His sensuous mouth was close. She had a fleeting picture of it coming slowly down toward her own. Drawing herself up to her full five foot five, she pushed the door open. "Good night, Wes."

He stayed where he was for a few seconds. One. Two. Three. Her mouth went dry. She cast him a quick smile and ducked into her room. It was another few seconds before she heard the sound of his boots on the floorboards as he moved back to his room.

She sat on the bed. For the first time in years she let the loneliness that she had suppressed float to the surface. No matter how large the crowd, Victoria had always experienced a loneliness. Even married to David, she had felt alone.

She heard the door click and then the water running. Victoria shivered at the thought of the man naked, hot water steaming the room and misting the mirror. She remembered what it was like to be a wife. She missed the physical contact. She missed being held and loved by someone who cared, even if he hadn't cared in the way she needed. She could still have it. It had been her choice, she reminded herself as she headed for the door. Surprised at her reaction to merely living so close to this very virile man, she sniffed. She needed a walk.

The last of the tourists were driving off the lot. Her reenactment crew and the owners of the businesses were straggling back to their living quarters. Only the crew in

the dining room remained to clean up. Glory Town seemed
to sigh and settle in for the long, warm night.

Walking toward the stables, bathed in light from the
full moon, she scuffed her new Western boots in the dust.
Yes, it had been her decision to end her marriage to David
and sometimes she wondered if it had been a wise choice.
The guilt she carried with her was heavy. It wasn't a thing
he had done that spoiled the marriage; it was what he
didn't do and maybe, just maybe, she had expected too
much. She'd never forget the look on his face when she
told him of her decision to end the union. Hurt. Regret.
A willingness to do whatever she wanted . . . and that
had made her mad. What if she'd been wrong? If he truly
loved her, why hadn't he fought for their marriage? But
then, if she had really loved him, why hadn't she stayed
and made it work? Running her hands over her eyes, she
blew out her breath. Maybe, just maybe, that was the way
marriage was supposed to be. Comfortable. She had none
close by to study. She didn't know of any that lasted very
long.

She listened to the soft nickering of horses and walked
past the barn and beyond. The grass grew longer here.
Climbing the hill, walking through blue columbine and
around flaming yucca flowers, Victoria enjoyed the cool,
faraway call of the meadowlark. She sat when she reached
the top. Pulling her knees up and encircling them with her
arms, she let her chin rest on them.

The landscape was beautiful. All shadows and glistening
dew. Soft lights glowed from the trailers on the back lot
as families settled in.

Other women had men to lie next to, to love with zest
and take care of . . . and to have care lavished on them.
A late dinner would be on the stove. The kids would be
settled. The radio might be playing softly. He might come
up behind her and turn her into his arms for a slow, romantic dance around the kitchen. Or he could be propped

up in front of the TV with a martini and she curled up on the couch with a good book. He'd look up and wink at her. They would both think of a time coming, a little later and behind closed doors.

She knew many of those who lived together weren't married. Was that a requirement? Did marriage cancel all the ways a man treated a woman when she was his girl? Complacency. Benign neglect. She hated it.

Stretching out flat on the damp ground, Victoria watched light clouds scoot across the dark sky. The moon was virgin white on the black background. Maybe a lot of the soft, yielding woman she thought she left behind in Virginia was still with her. It wouldn't be all that bad if she didn't have to act so tough and durable to prove herself to Buck and the boys. They didn't have much use for Easterners anyway and she knew she had to show them. But sometimes it was a real chore to be so self-reliant and gutsy. She wished she had a strong shoulder to lean on. A simple piece of blue cotton denim with a man stuffed in it. A man who adored her. A night animal skittered through the grass.

She missed the men at the veterans hospital. She missed their joking and mischievous ways. She missed sitting quietly and letting them talk about the war. She yearned for their sometimes undaunted spirits and their insecurities. Most of all, she missed the way they needed her and counted on her. She would call them Sunday night. It was the time that she usually spent watching a movie with them or humming along with Jesse as he strummed his scarred and battered guitar. Even though his legs were gone, his hands could still coach beautiful music from the instrument. She could almost hear the strains of his sad, sad songs play along the wind.

A puffy cloud threaded its way across the moon, dipping her into complete darkness and then showering her with light once more. The night air was cool; the sounds were soothing. As the breeze whispered through the tall grasses, it caused a secretive, whispery sound all its own. If that was all there was in her world at the moment to offer her comfort, she would gladly accept it. There was a new excitement about her now, one she wasn't about to lose, no matter what it took.

Everything would work out. She would see to it. In his own way, Buck was doing what he thought best. Ornery as she felt he was being, it was just his way. And she knew he must miss her uncle. He had told her they had been together a long time. She resolved to interact more with him . . . show him that she wasn't such a bad person to have around.

An owl hooted somewhere in the distant night and somehow it comforted her to know she wasn't the only one out here alone tonight.

A branch of long-needle pine snapped swiftly and silently back into place. Grass bent, making no sound, under a booted foot. The old owl looked down from its perch and studied the shadowy figure of the watcher make his way back behind the trees.

"Whooooo," the old bird called, but no answer followed.

_____ FOUR _____

Later, Victoria strolled down from the hill and passed the barn. Hearing movement in the paddock and knowing that the horses were stabled inside, she moved to the wooden fence to see who was there.

Under the full spread of moonlight, Wes worked his horse. He was dressed simply, in a white T-shirt, jeans, and boots. The go-to-hell black hat tilted low on his forehead. His hair still glistened with water from his recent shower.

The horse's white mane picked up the moonbeams and bounced them back. But it was the horse's gait that caught her full attention and the way the man on his back sat . . . quietly, talking low and gently, and seemingly a part of the animal.

The single-foot. She recognized it even though she had only seen it once before. Not a natural gait to a quarter horse, it was a slow, flourishing, well-learned, and disciplined movement by both horse and rider. The gelding's neck was arched, proud head bowed. Wes, too, looked downward. The turned-down brim of his hat hid his eyes.

She couldn't pull her gaze away. Wes appeared to be dancing, dancing . . . with his horse, here in the moonlight. In the still and privacy of the night, man and horse merged. Minds and spirits were in tune.

An eerie feeling crept over her as she watched horse and rider. There was so much more to J. Weston Cooper than she had ever imagined, and it baffled her why seeing him like this revealed it to her. Granted, it had taken patience to teach the horse. It took practice to keep the animal good at the routine, and it took love for it to be performed so uniformly . . . the two of them working together, each waiting for the other's signal . . . and approval. It meant something to him. It was obvious by the calm, happy look on his face. Something that was shared only between man and beast was significant to him. The dance wasn't to be shared with others. This was a time and an activity that Wes kept just for himself and his horse. How much of himself did he keep that way? Isolated and protected.

A shiver rode Victoria's spine. Goose bumps popped up on the skin of her arms. Her sigh slipped out quietly. This had to be the most beautiful thing she had seen. It was almost supernatural. If there had been music, it would have been a Vienna waltz. If there had been an audience, it would be hushed and amazed.

Wes kept his eyes downward, one hand dangling regally at his side, the other loosely holding the reins. The slight creak and give of the saddle leather were rhythmic. The soft clop of hooves was a quick one-two. High prance, leg up, leg down, again leg up, leg down. In swift movements, yet it almost appeared as slow motion, it was body up and body down, then . . . one-two again. In carousel motion. Again.

Wes's strong legs were clamped around the horse and his booted feet rested in the leather stirrups. Mane flowing, tail swaying, the horse seemed to sense his owner's desires. Their movements continued to be made—painstakingly slow and precise.

Victoria didn't realize she had been holding her breath

until it escaped in a long sigh. A smile played on her mouth as she watched, attentively and longingly, a relationship she envied. Never in her life had she been exposed to an intimacy like the one she saw before her. She had never met anyone capable of it. Or was it she? Maybe she had been the one not capable of it.

She knew she kept her real feelings inside for too long. Strapped by protocol, tied by a society she had lived in all her life. The first and only relationships that could come close were with her hospitalized vets. And even then the specialness could only be shared on a careful and measured basis. If they all got too dependent on her and she counted too much on them, then it would be another restraining relationship and none of them wanted that. It was a wonderful kind of kinship. A bridled freedom. Right now she felt real freedom rip through her and was grateful to Wes for it. Grateful that she had come out here tonight. Glad she had had a chance to witness this.

It excited her to know that what she felt she needed in her life could be obtained. And then she took a good, long look at Wes. She had resented him right from the first. She had fought getting to know him because he was an intruder. When he'd tried to be nice, she'd be flip. When he showed interest in the feelings Buck was stepping on, she had simply batted it away. There was so much more to this man than she had allowed herself to see. She decided to change that. For her. If only for her.

"Well, hello." Wes had spotted her and it had snapped his concentration . . . and the flow of satisfaction he had been feeling traded itself for another.

Surprised he had detected her, she felt as if she'd been caught with her hand in the cookie jar. "I was taking a walk . . . I wasn't spying on you. But when I saw this," she gestured toward him and his mount. "It's beautiful. I'm afraid I've been watching for a while."

Horse and rider sidled over to the fence, the single-foot forgotten for the night. He scratched the horse between the

ears and stood up in the stirrups to flex bunched muscles in
his legs. "He's quite a horse," he grinned, proudly.

"And you're quite a rider," she added, meaning it.

He smiled at her and she felt as if it were the first time.
There was a measure of intimacy between them. They
seemed to really see each other instead of merely engaging
in the usual thrust and parry routine.

She was beautiful, showered in the light from the fat,
round moon; the staunch shadows of the town jutted
toward the black sky behind her. It was as if she had let
a shield down, one she held out in front of her like a
banner at all times.

"I could teach you," he offered as he dismounted and
leaned his arms on the fence.

She shook her head. "I don't think I could do it. I
don't know if my horse could do it."

"Sure, you both can. It'll take practice and patience,
but you'll do fine. Why are you taking a walk this late at
night? Is anything wrong?" Laying the horse's reins over
his shoulder, Wes leaned sinewy forearms on the fence.

She smiled. "I could ask you why you're riding this
late at night but I think I know. You needed to be alone
with your thoughts and yourself. I guess I needed that,
too."

"To be alone with my thoughts and me?" he teased.

She was glad for the darkness and his inability to see
that a warm rush of red came to her cheeks and that he
was totally unaware of the way his closeness left her weak.
The fence boards felt rough and splintery under her hands.
The soft, almost nonexistent brush of his lips on hers was
unexpected, startling, then warm and fiery and left her
waiting for more.

"Every woman should be kissed when she stands in the
moonlight on a night like this," he explained, his voice
whispery and skidding along her ears.

She was amazed for the second time that night. Excitement whirled its way from the pit of her stomach to fill

her. His eyes, dark in the daylight, were only shadows . . . but she felt their intensity. She was inclined to press forward and kiss him, not the feathery contact but hard, full, and sound. She stepped back from it.

"Why isn't a beautiful woman like you married?"

His question was so completely off the wall, she stepped back and tilted her head. "Why?"

"Yes, why? I can't imagine some man not scooping you up and taking you home with him. Forever."

His voice was low and coaxing. It rode along her senses and raised her pulse beat.

Lulled by the night, amazed by his light kiss, surprised by Wes's comfortable interest, Victoria sighed, letting her mind run backward. It was the first time she actually felt free to express her feelings. "Remember I was. Once upon a time."

He chuckled. "Tell me about it."

"His name is David. He's quiet, sophisticated, and peaceful." It was nice to be able to talk about David without having to be on the defensive. "I think I was always waiting for the superman I thought was inside him to break out. He's handsome, charming, and loving. But he lacked something I needed. A spark, I guess. A thrill for being alive. He was a fiery lawyer in the courtroom, but a passionless man the rest of the time. He was content to watch TV. He was happy to read the Sunday paper on a beautiful bright morning that simply screamed for a long walk or a good game of tennis. He thought a ripping thunderstorm was good for the grass but never paid any attention to the power in the streaks of lightning or got a bang at the feel of thunder rumbling the earth. He could name every star in the sky but he could never simply look up and enjoy the majestic beauty of a brilliant night. Nothing excited him."

Looking up at Wes, she was glad not to see a frown of blame, a look of impatience, one of aversion. Her mother would have looked that way and did very often. "Everything to him was just okay. The bottom line was that I was afraid I would atrophy.''

They were walking side by side with the fence in between, headed toward the gate.

"He sounds like a real monster," Wes bedeviled. And then thinking better of it, he asked, "How long have you been divorced?" He attempted to keep his amusement from dancing in his eyes. This lady had been suffering from a guilt put on her, and one she accepted. A little twist of anger for those who had done this to her tightened the muscles in his jaw.

"A bit over a year. Even that was civil. When I told him, he merely stood up, put the paper aside, and held me. Now that I look back on it, I think two friends got married. And it wasn't enough for either of us. Our families were happy with the wedding and furious with the divorce. Society had labeled us as perfect for each other. The families took it as a personal failure. He helped me pack my things, stood on the sidewalk, kissed me, and waved good-bye.''

"Fool," Wes muttered and meant it. Swinging the gate wide, he led his horse through.

Her head snapped up and she squared off with him, forcing him to stop. "What's that supposed to mean?"

He cupped her chin with his hand and tilted it so he could see better the tears that threatened to fall. "Not you. Any man would be a fool to let you out of his life.''

It took her breath away. The quiet fierceness in his voice, the thunder in his eyes. Oh, she was a fool all right, she thought. To be standing here with this man on what seemed a romantic night. She met his kiss full this time. But still he kept it light and left her wondering what more would be like.

Walking with him as he stabled his horse, she silently assessed what it was his light kiss was forcing her to feel. She hung the bridle on the peg. He hoisted the saddle on the rack. Flipping the light off, Victoria strolled beside him back toward the saloon. The light, casual touch of his mouth had her heart pounding. She felt her resentment for him surface again. He was too smooth. So sure of himself. And practiced.

"Buck mentioned my folks' ranch when he introduced us. They are having a barbecue tomorrow. Why don't you come up with me?" Tipping his head, he moved in front of her to gauge her expression in the shadows.

"I'd love to see a real working ranch." And she would. But she didn't know if she wanted to spend time with this man. She sensed she could learn a lot more about him and like him. But did she want to like him even more? She shrugged. She had found herself doing it again. Analyzing everything and making a problem out of it. A simple barbecue on a real working quarter horse ranch. It sounded like fun and it would be an education. Only she was making it a big deal. He had asked her so matter-of-factly that he couldn't be considering it a date.

"Then we'll leave at three." They walked into the hotel, through the quiet dining room, and, still shoulder to shoulder, up the stairs. At her door he paused. "Bathroom's free for the rest of the night. You can indulge in one of your frothy baths without worry of being interrupted."

"That's the best news I've heard all day," she told him and pushed the door open to her room, not at all sure she wasn't willing to take the chance of being interrupted. She caught a look at her flushed cheeks in the mirror.

Inside his room, Wes leaned against the window frame and looked out over the town. Every time he began to feel really good about himself and Victoria, a certain fact made him feel guilty. He remembered Buck coming to him, the talk they had, and what he'd agreed to. And now, despite his resolve to remain seriously uninvolved with any woman for the rest of his life, he was sinking fast. And enjoying it. He sat on the edge of the bed and pulled his boots off. Shaking his head, he assured himself it would turn out all right. It had to.

* * *

After spending the morning with Buck, arguing and cajoling and trying to be patient and understanding, they had come to a pretty good agreement about which repairs would be started first. At times Victoria felt that Buck was afraid of her. Afraid of the changes she was attempting to make. She tried her very best to allay his fears without coming right out and saying so.

A trip to the costume trailer had Victoria happy about her outfit for the barbecue.

Sally, graying hair tied back in a no-nonsense do, clucked and smiled and fitted the new mistress of Glory Town with one of her finest outfits.

In front of the mirror, Victoria whirled, the full skirt flowing in a wide circle and then swishing to a whisper around her white boots. At the ankle of each boot was a narrow leather band adorned with silver conchoes. The outfit was done in a southwestern pattern of earth colors. Brown, beige, light green. The yellow off-the-shoulder gypsy-style blouse was threaded around the neckline and puffy sleeves with brown ribbon. Her hair was pulled back and up with barrettes. Around her throat lay a turquoise satin ribbon. She looked festive and felt as giddy as a girl on her first date.

Wes appeared at her door dressed in a white dress shirt with stand-up collar and black jeans with wide black suspenders clipped behind the ever-present leather belt and hubcap-sized rodeo buckle. His belly-cut python boots looked amazingly real. He looked sharp and handsome. Taking her hand, he led her down the stairs. "Perfect," he raised her hand to his lips. "Just perfect."

That made it look like a date . . . and feel like a date. Her subconscious mind taunted her. *So what if it is a date? Is that the end of the world? Does that mean you have to have his children? Good grief. Just go and have fun.*

Joe let out a loud wolf whistle as they walked through

the dining room and Victoria blushed. Instead of walking to the back lot for the truck, Wes led her to a buckboard that was waiting by the hitch rail. She let out a squeal as he hoisted her onto the seat before he walked around to jump up on the seat beside her.

A flip of the reins, and they were on their way out of town.

"This is a wonderful idea," she exclaimed, grinning from ear to ear. "But won't we be late?"

"Dinner's actually at five."

She narrowed her eyes, "So you planned this surprise last night."

"It just sort of came to me." He shrugged. "You're always interested in seeing the real West. You'll see it today. And from the same perch they saw it from."

He laughed softly. She was beautiful and her eyes were shining. He was glad he had thought of it. And the advertisement on the side would be good for business.

The wagon rolled over the hill and down onto the macadam road. Wes merely watched as Victoria waved to the carloads of people that passed by. She chatted and he answered when an answer was called for. For the most part he just sat back and enjoyed. Enjoyed as he hadn't had a chance to in a long, long time. He had long since convinced himself that the sound of a woman's laugh added nothing to his life. He counted himself wrong.

Two hours later, they pulled down a narrow lane. Victoria was reminded of some of the Westerns she had seen on TV and expected to hear the theme song from *Bonanza* any moment. Excitement coiled her stomach. Cars were parked on all sides of the lane, and the closer they got, the more she could smell the aroma of beef sizzling in the air.

The huge ranch house rambled off to the left, low slung and white to fend off the heat. Four barns and miles of paddocks and green fields unfolded before her. Horses, all sizes and colors, grazed peacefully or ran and jumped.

She could hardly contain herself. It was exactly like a book or a movie . . . except it was real.

Wes tucked her arm through the crook of his elbow as they rode through the final set of wide, black iron gates. Guiding the wagon off to the side, he jumped down and came around to lift her to the ground. For a split second he held her in the air, her hands on his shoulders, her eyes smiling into his eyes. For a few moments, they were isolated and alone, then they were descended upon by the family and guests. Introductions and handshakes and back slaps made the full round. Victoria guessed, breathlessly, that there must have been two hundred people attending.

It was then Victoria spotted a little girl wiggling through the legs of the grown-ups, dirty white dress flying, a spoon in her hand, eyes bright and excited. As Victoria thought what a beautiful little girl she was, the child ran right smack up to Wes. Her arms stretched into the air.

"Daddy."

Wes reached down and scooped her up, twirling her over his head and settling her on his hip. The child squealed and held on for dear life. "My darlin' Katie. What have you been doing to get so dirty?" Always amazed at her beauty and humbled by her open and trusting love, Wes held her close. Pride swelled his heart.

Pleased, she held up her fist to show him the wide spoon. "Digging a hole. Cook says I can find China people if I dig deep. Wanna help me?" Then she turned to Victoria and said sweetly, "I'm four." She uncurled four fat fingers from around the spoon to show her.

"And quite a hole, I bet. I'll help you in a little while. Right now I'd like you to meet a friend of mine." After soundly kissing her soft little cheek, Wes turned his gaze back to Victoria and completed the introduction. "Victoria, my daughter."

Victoria took the little hand in hers and shook it. So this was his Katie. Relief. Victoria felt the floodgates that had been keeping her growing feelings for J. Weston Cooper at bay swing wide. She felt as if a weight had been lifted from her shoulders.

"Nice to meet you, Katie. I'll help you dig that big hole, too." Victoria's childhood flashed before her eyes. She had never been allowed to dig a hole or play in the dirt. If she had gotten a nice white dress like that dirty, she would have been in for a good scolding and a monumental guilt trip.

Wes's parents, looking young and fit for their age, made a fuss over Victoria. The guests treated her as if they had known her for years. Victoria thought she had never, even in Glory Town, seen so many Western hats and gingham blouses in one place in her life.

A band played on a newly constructed stage–dance floor as couples whirled and swayed. Lights were strung waiting for dusk. Food. Food enough to feed an entire city was loaded down on dozens of picnic tables. Meat sizzled on twenty grills. Children ran everywhere, soaring on swings, jumping in and out of small wading pools. Katie stayed close to her father, rejecting the other children when they begged her to come play.

At dinner, Wes bounced Katie on his knee, trying to cut his steak at the same time. Victoria laughed and took his plate from him. "I'll cut it. That way we can be sure we won't end up calling nine-one-one for excessive bleeding."

Katie munched on a juicy hamburger, ketchup squeezing out to roll down into the cuff of white sleeve. All the while her head was pressed back against Wes's shoulder. She would look back and up from time to time and just smile at him. He would plant a kiss on her nose or the top of her head.

She could never remember that kind of open affection being showered on her when she was little. First of all it wasn't proper to be out of one's chair while eating. Second, her father hadn't lived long enough for her to know if he would have done that. She couldn't remember. She didn't think so. Her mother would have objected, saying it wasn't proper to display affection in public.

Victoria slid Wes's plate back in front of him. As a thank you, he scooped up a forkful of salad greens and offered it to her. She wasn't much for the blue cheese dressing he had poured so lavishly over top but she opened her mouth and took his offering.

He watched as her mouth closed around his fork and listened closely as she sighed contentedly. He'd had only a brief taste of her the night before but it had rocked him. And he wasn't sure he wanted to be rocked. The last time he had been, the result had been disastrous. Well, not entirely. Wes pulled Katie close to him and hugged her. He had his little Katie and he couldn't imagine life without her.

There was something different about Victoria. Today. Today, he saw it even more. She seemed more relaxed and happy than he'd ever seen her. Even though he knew she loved Glory Town, he had picked up on certain reservations that she held close to her. Right now, she was pulling on an emotion of his that he couldn't quite name, that he hadn't quite figured out yet.

Needing to move around, to divert his thoughts, Wes set Katie's little feet on the ground and took her hand. "Now, Katie, let's take Victoria on a tour of the stables."

"I'll show her the debil stallion."

"I told you, my sweet girl, that he's not a 'debil.' He just needs special handling."

Katie looked up at her father with certainty. "Doc says he's a debil. Says he's mean and nasty."

Wes winked at Victoria. "Doc's our foreman. He's not big on diplomacy."

The three of them made the rounds of the stalls with Katie skipping out in front of them. The barns were clean, neat, and organized.

Wes disturbed a very old, mangy dog when he stopped in front of the stallion's stall. "This here's Moe." He crouched down to scratch the lazy dog's ears. "He's appointed himself watchdog and company to Skipper's Cool Cash Two, one of our studs. On down there is the Three Bars stallion. All the horses in this barn are sired by one or the other."

And each one was a beauty. Victoria took the time to see them all. "Conformation is beautiful. Strong and sturdy."

"They train well for the speed events. Good hindquarters. Not like that sleek thoroughbred of yours."

She knew he was teasing and countered, "Only part thoroughbred. Enough quarter horse to make him passable."

Katie turned back to them, a half-wild cat squeezed to her chest. The cat wiggled to get away, claws catching Katie's dress. Concerned, Victoria went to Katie and lifted the cat from her arms and quickly set it down when the claw made contact with her flesh.

Katie giggled and Wes smiled at the two of them. "Don't worry. It's had its rabies shot."

Before Victoria could retort, Katie was off down the aisle streaking after the elusive cat.

"They're used to her." Wes patted her shoulder. "Katie is every cat's nemesis around here. They won't hurt her."

"I like seeing you here in my barn, fretting over my daughter."

"Hadn't we better be getting back to your guests?" They were in the open now and Katie was climbing up on the fence, her dress blowing in the breeze, her impatient feet bouncing up and down.

"See the babies. See the babies!" she squealed.

Joining her at the fence, Victoria looked out over the fields. The foals were running and bucking while the mothers grazed in the shade of the trees.

They leaned arms on the fence. "The buckskin paint, none other like him. I call him Snake. Over there is Bandit, Vegas, and Cheyenne. The yellow mare there is Honey, that one Holly." Pointing to the others, he identified each one.

Victoria was impressed that the man knew the name of each and every horse in such a large-based stable and breeding operation. She liked a man who cared. And he did.

Wes turned to Katie and she launched herself off the fence. "Swing me, Daddy. Swing me."

Wes obliged. Kicking up dust as he turned in circles, holding Katie under her arms, they laughed and the sound of it carried out across the sweet meadows.

Victoria felt the yearnings from her own childhood drape over her. If she'd had the untethered love she saw before her, would her life have been different? Would her father have loved her with the freedom Wes loved his daughter? A faraway memory pushed to the front of her mind, but it was hazy, fuzzy, and unclear. It lingered at the edges, challenging her to remember. If her father had lived, would he have let her mother have all that control? In that very instant, Victoria learned that it was no one's fault but her own. She, and she alone, had allowed her mother to control her. It had been easier. God. It had been easier.

Katie's squeals of delight stopped the moment Wes leaned against the fence in mock weakness. She pulled his face toward hers and kissed him on the jaw. "Again, Daddy. Again."

"Time we got back." Still holding Katie on his hip, he extended his hand to Victoria.

With only a moment's hesitation, she took it.

Later, Victoria had Katie sitting on her lap while they watched Wes pitch horseshoes with his dad and two other men. All four of the men bragged and teased and laughed. What a perfectly happy family. So open. So together. So at ease with each other. So close. Contented, Victoria rubbed her cheek against Katie's soft hair. Wes's mother joined them on the grass and handed Victoria a glass of tea and Katie a small cup of milk.

"The men will be at this for hours." She smiled at Victoria. "Katie doesn't take to strangers very quickly but she sure seems to like you."

"I hope she does, Mrs. Cooper. She's a delightful child." Victoria looked around. "You certainly have a beautiful spread here. It's a wonderful place for her to grow up."

"You haven't seen the house yet, have you? Men don't think of things like that. Katie, let's show Victoria Grandma's big kitchen. I saved a whole plate of gingerbread cookies for you and your daddy and they need the icing put on for the face."

Katie jettisoned out of Victoria's lap, milk sloshing from her cup, to take Grandma's hand, pulling her to a standing position. Victoria took the cup from her, holding the two glasses between her fingers.

"Tory can help, too, Grandma?" Katie held hands with both women and swung their arms as she walked with stiff-legged, purposeful strides.

Grandma laughed. "Of course, Tory can help, too." She cast Victoria a wink.

They walked across a huge patio and through one set of the three sliding glass doors.

"Your turn, Wes."

Busy watching his mother, Katie, and Victoria ambling across the lawn, Wes forced his attention back to the game.

They stepped into a huge, gleaming kitchen. It was almost as large as all of Glory Town. All Victoria could do was gape. "Wow!"

"Big it is." Mrs. Cooper looked around proudly. "We started out in a small log cabin on the back forty with one stallion and six mares. That was a long, long time ago. The one thing Tom promised me was that someday I would have the largest kitchen in Oklahoma. I held him to it.''

The walls were painted a creamy white, the curtains were a handsome burlap-type material done in yellow, brown, and turquoise stripes. The floor was simply black and white linoleum. Three wagonwheel chandeliers hung over a massively done center island where three ovens and four stoves and acres of countertop sat. Pots and pans, gleaming copper and stainless steel, lined three walls. A huge fireplace took up the other wall.

Mrs. Cooper folded back four wooden slatted doors that opened into the dining room. Victoria counted fourteen chairs, six down each side of the mahogany table and two unique armchairs at each end. Candles and large paintings decorated the walls done in blue satin paper. "Beautiful."

"We entertain quite often now. There are several clients from out of town, buyers from overseas."

"It's magnificent." And it was. Victoria had always thought her sprawling home in the Virginia foothills was rambling, but it was a guest house compared to this. It was open and airy and not the least bit pretentious.

A thick gray carpet covered most of the floor but hardwood gleamed from the edges. They moved through another set of doors and into the living room. It was sunken, the backs of the sofas and chairs coming only to the top of the floor they now stood on. Another massive fireplace of fieldstone stood beneath a portrait of the young Coopers. The furniture was dark pine, polished to blind. Huge windows, floor to ceiling, went unadorned with curtains, exposing an expansive view of the rolling, extensive fields and barns below.

Going down the steps, Victoria stopped to admire the hand-woven Indian blankets that were spread along the tops of the sofas and hung on the walls. A warm room. Very warm. Love was here in every nook and cranny. Pictures in small Victorian frames snugged family members. Knickknacks, expensive and not, sat here and there on end tables and shelves. Huge brass lamps with night-lights in the bases sat on shiny cherry tables.

Katie was getting bored. Victoria could tell because she had quit jabbering and was chewing on the hem of her skirt, which she had pulled into her mouth. Victoria bent down to her and asked, "Where's Katie's room?"

The child brightened and ran up the steps from the living room, into a hall, and up a wide sweep of staircase, the banister just calling for Victoria to slide down. She remembered doing that at home every time she thought the coast was clear . . . and getting caught more times than enough.

Katie's room was large, too, with windows opened to the front drive. Lacy curtains billowed in the breeze. Beneath a ton of stuffed animals stood a double bed with a ballerina spread and a canopy on top. A miniature table with chairs was set with tiny teacups and a pot. Raggedy Ann patiently waited for her playmate to return and join her. Toy boxes, overflowing to the ridiculous, lined the walls papered in Disney characters.

Katie jumped on her bed and pushed a switch on a box nearby. Victoria recognized the voice. It was Wes singing "Hush Little Baby." A surge of passion pushed through her heart. What a lucky little girl to have a father so attentive and loving. And his voice was beautiful. And the fact that he had actually taken the time to record this, to be sure his little girl had part of him even when he couldn't be there, left her mind reeling. She had thought she was beginning to know this man. She hadn't even pierced the surface.

"When Daddy can't be here at bedtime, I play this. It's not as good as when he's here though. Daddy has to work sometimes." She was tapping the toes of her black patent leather shoes together.

"All daddies have to work, Katie. But I know he's here with you when he can be. He loves you very much." Victoria sat on the bed beside the sweet little girl.

"Does your daddy work all the time?" Katie asked, large eyes round and deep brown.

Victoria picked up one of the stuffed animals, a fat fuzzy bear with black eyes and a sleepy smile. Hugging it to her without even realizing it, she told Katie, "My daddy is dead, sweetheart. He died when I was a little younger than you. So see, you're a lucky little girl. Even though Daddy has to work, you can always see him later."

Mrs. Cooper watched from the doorway. It did her heart good to see Katie warming up to this woman. Wes had never mentioned her but she had seen the way her son looked at this one. And she liked her. Hope sprang in her aging heart. Maybe soon Katie would have a real family.

"I don't have a mommy." The child was tiring and she laid her head back on the animals and stuffed a thumb in her mouth. "Would you be my mommy?" The child's words nearly moved Victoria to tears.

Mrs. Cooper saved Victoria from trying to come up with an answer to that one. "Come on, little one. Let's show Victoria the rest of the house. We have guests to entertain and cookies to put faces on."

Katie made a move to take Grandma's hand, but before she did, she reared up on her knees and threw both arms around Victoria's neck and laid a sloppy, wet kiss on Victoria's cheek. It knocked the wind out of her. Such an abandoned display of affection for a virtual stranger. This child missed her mother more than Wes could know. She made a mental note to talk to Wes about it, even though it was none of her business. How could a person be untouched by the situation after spending time with these people?

And Grandma knew, Victoria thought as Mrs. Cooper took Katie's hand and patted her on the shoulder at the same time. Victoria followed Mrs. Cooper and Katie on a short tour of the other rooms, one being Wes's. She had only glanced in as they walked down the hall but that had been amusing. It was messy. Jeans hung from the bedpost;

a dirty shirt was pitched across a chair. An ashtray on his nightstand was overflowing. The bed was made crisply, patchwork quilt serving as a spread. Victoria bet it wasn't the work of J. Weston Cooper but that of his mother. He liked four pillows on his bed. She hid a smile and followed the pair in front of her. She smiled and turned in a circle, sending her skirt flying about. Skipping to catch up, she finished the tour of the house with them.

FIVE

After the tour of the house, they ended up in the kitchen. Katie hadn't forgotten the gingerbread cookies and enlisted Victoria's help in putting smiley faces on them. Aprons tied around their party clothes, the two females laughed as Victoria squeezed icing into the shape of large, wide-open eyes and Katie put freckles on her cookie face.

Mrs. Cooper left them there to see to her guests, smiling over her shoulder as she went out.

Later, Katie and Victoria went in search of Wes. They spotted him under a shade tree, hat thrown on the grass. Leaning back in a wooden lawn chair, he strummed his guitar and sang to the delight of several people who sat on the ground or lounges in a circle around him.

The day was wearing on and the sun was setting low in the sky. Streaks of orange and gray rolled over the top of fields of ripe green grass, white fences dotting the landscape and surrounding grazing horses of all colors and sizes.

Wes saw them coming. He almost tripped over the words of the song he had written recently. Catching himself but keeping his eyes on the two of them, he continued with what he thought pretty much explained his feelings.

Cool spring breezes swirling around
First grass rising through new-thawed ground
Like the budding trees and the sun's warm kiss
There's a lady who's a part of this.

Blue jeans, boots, and windswept hair
Horses, trucks, and open air
Strong when needed, yet fine and fair
To my mind, she's the finest kind of lady.

He saw only Victoria . . . and his daughter. They were hand in hand, both females' mouths going at the same time. And smiles, big smiles on their faces.

"Daddy's singing his new song."

Victoria stopped walking and listened . . . and watched as Wes sang the words directly to her.

Victoria's hair tossed with the wind; Katie's pigtails bobbed at her shoulders. A warm surge of pride and passion moved through Wes.

And it was then the thought struck him. Could his feelings, the ones that were growing bigger by leaps and bounds, be what they were for his daughter's sake? Could he be thinking of how much better off Katie would be with a mother in residence . . . and that Victoria would be a good one? No, that was impossible. He had become hardened but was not yet granite.

That disturbed him to the point where he tripped over his words and his fingers fumbled with the strings. He set the instrument aside. "Gentlemen, I see two beautiful women who need my immediate attention. I'll see you all later."

He didn't miss the admiring glances Victoria received from his friends. He didn't miss the swell of emotion that rose in him. When had all this started? He didn't know.

Was he truly intrigued by Victoria for himself or for Katie? He wasn't certain. But it was something he was going to take the time to explore. Victoria intrigued him, had interested him from day one. If all he had in mind was his daughter, he had better find out and be done with it.

Victoria let go of Katie's hand and watched as the girl flew to her father, to be lifted and put up on his shoulders. Wes let out a yell when she playfully covered his eyes with her small hands, and he pretended he was about to fall. Katie squealed, moved her hands up to his forehead, and hollered, "Horsey, Daddy, horsey." Wes broke into a sloppy gallop and ran off across the yard with her. Victoria hadn't missed the words of his beautiful song or the tone or the way he had looked at her. At her core, she felt the heat, in her stomach she sensed the flutter.

Victoria wandered through the crowd talking and exchanging hellos with a lot of people. She ended up sitting on the sidelines of a volleyball game, watching. The watching lasted only ten minutes. Hiking her skirt up above her knees and tying it, she joined in. It had been years, but it came back soon enough. It was her turn to serve and she popped the ball across the net with a powerful bam.

Dessert was being served now and in answer to the cook's triangle most everyone went back to the tables to indulge in strawberry pie, butterscotch with graham cracker crust, and every kind of iced cake in the free world. Some people refused to get out of the pool long enough to eat and splashed and swam and jumped from the diving board. She wished she had brought her bathing suit.

The last time she had spotted Wes he was again surrounded by a crowd of people, Katie jumping around at his side. They seemed to seek him out. The people. And there were a lot of important people here. She heard talk about politics, schools, and the community as a whole.

Popular. J. Weston Cooper was a popular man whose opinion was sought . . . and highly respected.

Feeling masculine hands on her shoulders, she looked around to see him standing behind her.

Wes saw she had strawberries and whipped cream on her lips. Sweet. Tempting. Inviting. Bending down, he removed them with his own mouth. The touch of her . . . No, he wasn't interested in this lady because of Katie. It was all for him. Just him.

"I didn't think to tell you to bring a suit but we have plenty of extras in the house. Mom will show you if you ask her. Ummm. That's good. Pass the pie."

All she could do was grin at him. It hadn't even embarrassed her that he would kiss her in front of all these people, small a kiss as it was. A few minutes later, Katie wiggled up on the seat between them, swinging her little feet over the edge of the bench, grinning up at them.

Late afternoon rolled into evening. The dance music changed from square dancing tunes to slow ballads. Full and sleepy, Victoria leaned her head on Wes's shoulder and let him lead her across the dance floor. On his other shoulder rested his daughter's tired little head. She was nearly asleep. Victoria was nearly in love. Her heart beat hard against her chest. The warm, loved, and protected feeling that enveloped her was so new and so long waited for. She had a lot of questions about all of this. But now was not the time for thinking. Just enjoying. She sighed and Wes pressed a kiss to her hair.

The sweet music floated all around her. Beneath her cheek, Victoria could feel the soft cotton of Wes's shirt smoothed over his hard shoulder, the muscles flowing as he moved. Wes brought his hand to the middle of her back and pressed her closer. She yearned to snuggle against him, wanted all of her body to be pressed against all of his body. Wanted him alone in some shadowy place . . .

The hayride was announced for the children over a loudspeaker. Katie's head came up wide awake and she grabbed her daddy around the neck. "Let's go, Daddy, you promised." Victoria snapped out of her daze and stepped back, smoothing her skirt.

She didn't miss Wes's amused and happy stare.

"That I did, Katie my girl," he agreed readily and forced his gaze from Victoria back to his daughter.

He held Victoria's hand as they piled onto the wagon and soon they were all leaning back against bales of hay singing "Ninety-nine Bottles of Beer on the Wall." Victoria had never been happier in her life. Wes leaned over and gave her a quick kiss. Katie giggled and hid her face in her father's shirt. Wes had hold of Katie's hand and with the other closed his fingers over Victoria's. Such a natural gesture. A sweet, spontaneous move. Victoria sighed inside to think she had missed all this. This was the way a man and a woman should feel. Between the mindless excitement should be the contented, kick-back-in-the-sunshine feeling.

Later, they tiptoed through the darkened house and into Katie's room. On her dresser, next to the small lamp Victoria turned on, was a picture of Wes and Katie and Katie's mother. She was a beautiful woman. She turned to watch as Wes pulled Katie's dress over her head and then, because she was so limp and sleepy, simply slid the stuffed animals aside and put her beneath the sheet in her underwear, pulled the ballerina spread up, and leaned forward to kiss her soft cheek. Then he sat back and for just a moment watched her as she slipped away with the sandman.

So this was where he went off to every evening. Victoria's heart swelled. He was such a good man. Gentle and thoughtful, rough and tumble.

They left Katie sleeping and walked to the head of the stairs. Victoria couldn't help it. It was just too good a banister and too good a curve at the end to resist. Gathering her skirts, she put a leg over and let go. It was a swift, highly polished ride to the bottom. She jumped, expertly, to the floor, laughing at having made at least fifteen miles per hour.

She glanced back up and saw Wes standing there looking at her as if he'd never seen her before. "Come on. Surely you remember how," she teased him.

"I was a lot younger and healed much faster."

"You break horses, jump from tall buildings, and heaven only knows what else and you won't slide down? I don't believe it. Come on before someone catches us."

He hesitated only a moment. Climbing on and holding his booted feet up in the air, he came down faster and with a heavier thud than she did. Rubbing his posterior, he laughed. "Gets hot."

Without thinking, she batted at the back of his jeans. When he caught her wrist and held her hand against the label of his back pocket, she drew her breath in. Then he took that hand and brought it to his lips, to linger there. "Thank you. My daughter enjoyed your company. I did, too."

The hallway was dimly lit by turned-down electric candelabra. It was an eerie sort of yellow light that seemed to lock them in a haze. When she looked into his eyes, she thought that she had never felt this way before. Never.

"Your daughter is a delight. You've done a good job with her."

"My folks have played a big part."

"Of course." She quivered as he locked one arm around her waist and pulled her against him.

"I know you feel it, too. You know what's destined to happen between us." His baritone voice flowed across her ears.

"Oh, I think *destined* is the wrong word." He had his fingers beneath her chin, forcing her to look directly at him. It was hard. Too much was eddying around in her mind. She was afraid they were caught up in the intimacy of a little girl's bedtime, of acting like kids alone in the house, of . . . what? She didn't know and, once again, didn't trust herself to know. She backed away from his embrace.

He glared down at her. "Maybe it is. But just the same we . . ."

Putting a hand on his chest, she kept distance between them. "We, nothing at this point. Wes, I like you but . . ." The feel of him beneath her fingertips nearly took her resolve away.

"You don't want to," he finished for her, dragging a hand through his hair and then hooking his thumbs in his belt to keep from pulling her to him in spite of her wishes.

"It's not that. I can't even tell you what it is since I don't know myself."

"You're not going to have a choice. I feel . . ." He chuckled. "Hell, I don't know what I feel but I will tell you this much. I've never had to ask a woman to . . . dammit. Let's go."

She grabbed for his hand. "Wes. I promised myself that the next time I became involved with a man it would be that I was head over heels in love with the guy. And now I don't even know if I would know love if I saw it."

"If you're waiting for skyrockets and bombs bursting in air, I don't think it really happens like that. It sort of sneaks up on you sometimes. Makes itself known in little ways. I think we're both taking all this way too seriously. It's late. Let me get you home before you make me go back up the steps and slide down again."

Relieved, she laughed and looked up the steps. "It's tempting."

"Oh no, it isn't," he said as he guided her toward the door.

After bidding good night to everyone, Victoria climbed into Wes's pickup truck. After waves and promises to return again, they headed back out the gates.

Leaning her head back on the seat, she sighed happily. "Where's Katie's mother?"

Wes was silent a moment. Now his tone was different. Resentful. "Who knows? Who cares? She calls and comes by to see Katie once in a while. Other than that, I don't know. And I don't need to."

Victoria shook her head. "I don't understand how a mother could leave a child like that."

He shrugged to ease the bitterness. "She didn't exactly leave her. I told her she couldn't have her. I explained that Katie belonged in a permanent home. She was headed off on the campaign trail with some slick politician. At least she had enough sense to realize I was right. She knows she's free to come and go here as much as she pleases. She just doesn't. I have custody, if that's your question." He yanked a cigarette out of the pack in his shirt pocket and flicked the lighter to the end of it. The cab of the truck was filled with smoke from his deep draws on the cigarette.

"I wasn't doubting that. I can see how much she loves you and it's obvious you worship her. She is so uninhibited, so free. Her laughter just rolls out and her eyes sparkle." She was remembering her own childhood. Rules, regulations . . . love but cool, cool love.

"At first a lot of people were critical of my insisting on keeping her. Mother's love and all that. My parents raised me and I like the way they care for her. She's happy." He scowled into the darkness.

"Don't be so defensive, Wes. Anyone can see she is. I think it's wonderful. So many times the children are deprived of a father's love and believe me I know it's as important as a mother's. Sharing is a wonderful answer. How long have you and Katie been back at the ranch?"

"Six months. The divorce was final over a year ago. Her mother doesn't come by nearly enough. Katie doesn't understand."

In the darkness of the cab of the pickup truck, Victoria

reached over and put her hand on his arm. "Someday she will. And maybe someday your wife will realize what she's throwing away. A child couldn't wish for a better environment. Bring her to work with you sometimes. I'll keep her company for a while."

He braked for a stop light and turned in his seat. "I'd like that. She needs . . . my mother isn't able to get out and play ball or run around in the fields . . . but you could."

"Green light," she told him, because she was very close to leaning closer and kissing that very kissable mouth. He knew loneliness, too. She saw it in his eyes if only for a fleeting second.

Wes turned his attention back to driving. She sat back, keeping her eyes on him. "Watching and being around your Katie gives me a chance to feel things I've never felt before . . . do things that were forbidden, like sitting in a white dress in the dirt and digging with a spoon without fear of punishment. My mother loved me, too, but she had very odd ideas about raising a child. It would be good for me. I had a very stiff and stuffy upbringing. Do you have any brothers or sisters?"

"A sister. She used to be a real pest, but now she's married, living in California with her husband and five kids. A brother. Career military. He should be home for a visit soon."

"I wish I'd had at least one. Pest or not."

"I'm glad you've decided to lighten up. You sure had no use for me when I first arrived. I understood it, but it still bothered me. Buck has been a good friend for a long time. He asked me to . . . offered me this job at a time when I needed something nontaxing. Right now I'm unsettled. I just need space for a while. I need to think about my goals and directions."

"Did something specific happen to cause you to put your life on hold?"

He shifted in the seat as if he was fast becoming uncomfortable. They were driving across the field and coming to a halt in front of the hotel. After he turned the ignition off and pushed the lights in, they were both enveloped in shadowy darkness. He put his arm across the back of the seat and looked, unseeingly, through the dirtied windshield into the night.

"I think it must be a combination of things. I watch my daughter grow and as she does I realize that life is passing me by. My job wasn't holding my attention. I felt Katie was losing something being at the sitter's all the time and then being alone with me in that small house in town. She needed a woman to braid her hair and get the rubber bands to stay in. She needed the smell of just-baked chocolate cookies fresh from the oven that she could help make. The police force needed a cop who could devote his attention to the job. I realized I wasn't that man the day we had some drug runners cornered down in Redwood. We were exchanging gunfire and I found myself daydreaming and thinking about Katie ending up without a father as well as a mother . . . so."

"So you quit your job and moved back home with your daughter and you feel guilty about it."

"I quit before I became too bitter and hardened. I'll be honest with you, I don't trust women. I haven't met one since my divorce who didn't have something already on her mind, an idea already formed of who her next man was to be, except maybe you. I always felt like a fly caught in a web with the big spider using a magnifying glass to see every hair on my leg. I had to make a change. And yes, I feel guilty about leaving a job I was good at just because I couldn't balance everything. I should have been able to."

"Maybe you ask too much of yourself. And then I pitched a fit when Buck hired you. It wasn't you, personally. I just wanted to show him I could do something beneficial for Glory Town by making a good selection on my own. Like it or not, he has to realize I'm here to stay."

"You have a real problem with proving yourself. No one is really doubting you but you. Buck is old and set in his ways, and where he comes from, a woman's place is in the kitchen . . . pregnant. Give him some time. That's all it's going to take is time. He'll come around." He watched her carefully, seeing a tiny little bit of apprehension.

He tucked a curl behind her ear. His touch jerked her from her calm reverie and reminded her how close she was to him. He seemed to fill the cab of the truck as he slid around on the seat and looked at her. "Personally, I'm glad you're staying. Your exuberance is catching. The men respect you. Nick worships you. Buck will stop being a threat. He's an old-timer. A dinosaur. He'll just be slow about it and never admit it out loud."

"You like him a lot, don't you?"

"Never met a simpler, kinder man. He and my dad go back a long way.

"I like him, too, but I also will never say it out loud. I don't think he could handle it. He's real. He never once tried to hide the fact that he wasn't happy with my decision to live here. We'll work it out."

He leaned forward, laying his warm mouth on hers. "Maybe a lot of things can be worked out."

Each time he had kissed her, it had been gentle and quick. It wasn't enough. She wanted to throw her arms around his neck and pull him to her and keep him there. Never had she been around a man who caused her blood to thunder through her veins or spin tornadoes full of butterflies into her stomach. She wondered, only briefly, how emotions could change so quickly. She wanted, just once, to sit back and just simply see how things would turn out if she jumped in without testing the water. But she wasn't quite ready yet.

He felt his gut contract as his mouth came down on

hers. A mere touch of her mouth had him wanting and needing more. He drew his arms in, pulling her close. He knew that all this was a purely biological reaction . . . but his heart, the one that was thudding soundly against his rib cage, was sending new, untried emotions through him. He had vowed to find a way around becoming involved with a woman again, but she was different from any he'd ever known before.

Beneath her resentful, prideful facade, he sensed a very warm, giving, and trusting lady. He'd gotten peeks of it at different times and been enthralled. But trusting . . . that was going to be a hurdle to get over. And when she found out, would she ever trust him again? He deepened the kiss, teasing her tongue with his own.

She changed the angle of the kiss, knowing she should stop. Her heart cried out for more while her brain denied the wisdom of it. Her bones melted. She wondered if she would ever stand again. Wes pulled her across his lap to cradle her head in his arms. She could feel the rough brush of his jeans against the soft cotton of her dress. She felt the hard push of his belt buckle against her stomach. He broke the kiss, only to trail his lips down her cheek, her jaw, and to taste the pulse point at her throat.

Her hands dived into his hair, knocking his hat back. She pushed at it until it rolled across them to land on the floor. His fingers were at the neckline of her dress, brushing fiery points of light against her skin. She wanted this to go on forever. David had touched her. They had made love. But nothing, nothing had ever been like this. Almost unable to breathe, she pulled away from him. But he wouldn't let her sit up. Instead he clamped her tightly against him and just watched her.

His eyes were darkened by passion. His mouth was wet from hers. Hair, usually trapped beneath a Stetson, fell across his forehead. His chest rose and fell quickly, proving his restraint. Beneath her hands she could feel the quickened thud of his heart. She idly hoped he couldn't hear hers, but it sounded so loud in her ears.

"This is more than we know it is. It's not just chemistry at work here. The first time I saw you, I felt something. I couldn't have known what it was. I've never felt it before."

Caught up by the swirl of her blood and the drowsy, expectant state of her mind and body, she continued to feast her eyes on him.

He moved his mouth to the sensitive place below her ear, coming back to her mouth to taste again and reveling in the confusion that danced around in her eyes. "We'll take some time to get to know each other if it puts you at ease. But we're going to be together, lady."

When she thought she knew what he was going to say, she was taken aback when she heard his whispered words.

"A family. You and me and Katie. And don't think I've been on a hunt to find her a mother," he said, although the doubt still niggled him a bit. "It's something else. Just something I know. I can't wait too long for you to recognize what there is between us. Don't *make* me wait too long." He crushed her mouth under his.

His last words seemed almost like a threat and Victoria wasn't at all sure she liked it. Pushing against his hard shoulders, Victoria righted herself and pushed her hair back from her shoulder.

Wes shoved the door open. Damn. So he wasn't good with words. Some things couldn't be changed. Walking around the truck, he lifted her down when she would obviously just as soon have climbed down herself. The smile was gone from her face, and he didn't like knowing he had put the frown there.

He tilted her face so he could see her better in the moonlight. "Nothing could be as bad or as threatening as that look on your face. We had a good time together. You like me to kiss you. That's all. The rest will come." He brushed his mouth across her lips and turned to walk in the hotel with her.

She wished that was all. She still felt unsteady from being in his arms, from having his mouth draw feelings to the surface that she hadn't even known existed. She let him take her hand. It fit well, seemed to belong. But once upon a time, what seemed a long time ago, her hand seemed to belong in David's. The churning in her stomach and the heat at her core were new and frightening. The anticipation, the wondering what it would be like to be in his arms, in his bed . . .

Nick had watched the truck pull onto the lot. He had remained in the shadows as he took in every movement of the passengers. His breath became ragged as he watched Wes kiss her. Now, when Wes took Victoria into the hotel, hand in hand, Nick felt sweat pop out on his forehead. He had a nasty headache. Pressing his fingers to his temples, he turned to go back to his trailer. His head threatened to split. His chest muscles tightened. Casting one more look toward the hotel, he muttered under his breath and began his long, lonely walk back to his empty trailer. Back to sleepless nights and dreams of a beautiful woman who treated him so nice. And smelled so nice, and was so soft to touch. And was in love with him. He was sure of it. If only Wes would stay out of the way.

Wes led her through the darkened lobby and up the stairs, patting the banister on his way. Victoria laughed and shook her head no.

Nick's head came up. Out of the way. Sure that was it. All he had to do was fix it so Wes wasn't here anymore. His handsome face was transformed as his lips curled back in an ugly sneer. Yes. All was not lost to him again. He would have her. And he would have her soon. He would get rid of Wes, and then she would come to him. She would be wearing a white gown, flowing to the ground, and he would open his arms. She would lean against him and he would tuck her head beneath his chin with his hand and stroke her hair. He heard her laughter from inside the hotel. Coming back to the here and now from wherever it was he went was always painful, but tonight it was so much worse.

He shook his head to clear it. "Why am I here?" he tested himself, and as it all became too clear, he wheeled and continued his trudge home, alone.

SIX

"Pull!" Thwang! Two bright orange targets took flight. They hovered on the same path for a few seconds before the discs separated and soared.

The gunfire spent the air, shattering first one target and then the other.

Eyes wide, Wes slapped his hat across his thigh. "Lady, when you say you shoot trap, you mean it. Nice smoke job. And doubles. That was good," he praised, "but can you do it again?"

"Load them up and see," she challenged.

Victoria reloaded three shells into her Ithaca SKB 700, with gold-plated game images and trigger flashing in the sunlight, and set it back against her shoulder. "Pull!"

Thinking he would be cagey, Wes cranked the target release upward, sending the orange cylinders higher and in different directions.

Once again the peacefulness of the countryside reverberated under the thunder of the shotgun.

He shook his head and smiled. "That's a nice shotgun."

She patted the butt end and beamed proudly. "Algerian walnut."

Manning the target release, Victoria cranked it downward and, watching Wes, pulled the string as soon as he got the shotgun to his shoulder.

Caught before he was ready, Wes took aim and pulled the trigger. He hit the first one but missed the second. "Cheat."

"All's fair. Go again." Changing the angle of the release, she put two more targets in the air for him.

This time he broke both of them and grinned as he turned toward her. "Three."

"Oh, a hot-dogger." Leaving the angle the same, she loaded three, one single near the top and two lined up near the bottom. *That ought to throw him*, she thought as she waited for his signal and set them loose.

The top single one pitched high and to the left. The two on the low end split and one sailed straight and high, the other to the right and low.

His body tight and positioned, he moved smoothly and swiftly, plowing through them, one, two, and three.

"Beautiful show. Again?"

He nodded, loading, and for the next ten minutes, Wes showed her his skill with the shotgun. He easily downed most of the targets with a swift twist at the waist, a keen eye, and a fast hand. Victoria anxiously waited her turn.

When he moved to the release to set up for her, she informed him, "International rules now. Doubles."

At his look, she explained. "Shotgun at your hip. Signal for release and take aim after the birds are in the air."

"All right. Whenever you're ready, Annie Oakley."

Flashing a mischievous grin at him, she positioned the shotgun at her hip. "Pull."

As soon as she spotted the discs she jumped the gun to her shoulder and swung it to the first bird and through. Never stopping the movement of the gun, she picked off one and then the other just as it dove toward the wild plum thickets that dotted the hillside.

"Damn. Let me try that."

"No way. You pull so I can show off for a while. Go

on, set it up again." She was good at this. Let them all know it. Some of the men had straggled up the hill at the sound and were watching. She had even seen some money exchange hands. She handled the gun expertly, the pride in her stance and ambition shining in her eyes.

Wes pulled and Victoria shot. Forty-eight birds bit the dust . . . in a row. She wanted fifty straight with no misses. This was when she always got antsy. And the crowd had grown. She had to make this last shot. Her arms were tiring. It had been a while since she had used a shotgun. And once she hadn't snugged it quick enough and she had taken a slam low on her shoulder. She could feel the bruise forming.

Shaking her arms to free them of the clenching muscles, she loaded two shells under and one in the chamber. A nod and he set the clay pigeons free.

The sound of her shotgun exploding was nearly drowned out by the hoorahs, whistles, and applause from the crew.

Victoria held her gun over her head and yelled Indian style. It was a very unladylike war whoop. Now, let those bullies think she was just a wimp from the East. Let them talk that one over at their Saturday night poker game. She hoped it wouldn't be long before good ole Buck heard the story. And she was sure, in a week's time, the total number of shots in a row would have multiplied to some stupendous number.

Wes walked over and shook her hand and then, dragging her into his arms, swung her around and around. The men were still cheering when Wes lost his balance and they both fell to the ground. Another, even louder whoop rose from the men.

"Now, woman, we'll try guns you're not familiar with. If you show me up with those, I'll resign and you can take over the position of head honcho to this sorry bunch of rowdies."

That sorry bunch of cowboys was disappearing over

the hill. The show was over for now. Now that the lady sharpshooter was sprawled on the grass with the big man.

"Let me up, and you're on."

Wes looked up to be sure the men had scattered and shook his head. She was beautiful lying half beneath him, fringed in blue-stem grass and cushioned by the rich green carpet beneath. "Not yet. Not yet."

The smile left her mouth as she realized he was about to kiss her. Her heart was pounding against her ribs and she wasn't sure it was from the excitement of the match . . . unless the match was his lips playing with hers, teasingly light, and then the tip of his tongue tracing their curve.

It felt good. So right. No matter that she doubted herself and doubted him. It was time to just go with it. She wanted to make him feel as she did. Running her hand up the back of his neck and through his hair, she pulled his mouth down on hers hard and parted her lips.

The earth melted away. The prickly grass that tickled her arms softened to silk and caressed her skin. Heat rolled through her as he took what she offered and returned it, hotter, harder, and swifter.

Jeans brushed jeans, cotton shirt glided over cotton shirt. He slid his hand down the satin column of her throat and across her collarbone and down, skimming across the gentle swell of her breasts.

One hand in his hair and one reveling in the hard line of muscles up and down his back, Victoria felt herself falling into a world of fire and speed foreign to her. The rising morning sun added to her fear that the field might burst into flames any minute.

So this was it. It had to be. No woman had made his blood course at such a speed. No female had ever lifted him from the bounds of earth to a place where he only drifted, aware of only the taste of her, the feel of her body melding with his. He wanted her but not only in the way a man wants a woman. He never wanted to be too far away from her to reach out and touch her. He never wanted to be out of hearing range or out of sight. She was slowly becoming part of him, the very vital, extremely important point of his reason.

He reared his head, looking at her with eyes dark and anxious. "You know, you kiss as good as you shoot, lady. Right on the mark." He thought it had to be this way. He had to want her, need her more than any woman before, because it had never felt like this. Not even come close. He was a grown man and had never known the kiss of someone he loved.

She lifted her shoulders and moved her lips over his jaw, nipping as she went. "Unless you want to be ravaged out here on the hillside, I suggest you remove your body from mine and stand up," she teased, breathless and afraid her words were too true.

"You wouldn't do that," he dared, catching her earlobe between his teeth and continuing his feast along her cheek on his way back to her lips. It was as if someone had thrown a book in front of him years ago and he had never bothered to open it. Now as the pages fluttered in front of him, he realized he had never seen the words before. What a shame she hadn't come into his life a decade ago. All that time wasted . . . the happiness lost. Not anymore.

She gave him a playful shove. "At this point, I don't know what I would do."

Because she deserved more than making love in the sunshine, where they could be discovered at any moment, he yanked her up and pulled her back into the wonderfully warm and slightly trembling circle of his arms. When they made love, and they would, the time would be right.

"Now I bring out the big guns." He smiled to himself. She wasn't even ready for the courting she was going to get. This lady didn't trust. He would teach her.

For a moment she looked confused and then he pulled her by the hand over to where he had placed his .30.30 and .357 magnum.

Standing behind her, he put the gun with the eight-inch stainless steel barrel in her hands. She tested its weight. Then with his hands and arms supporting her, he aimed at the targets he had nailed against the stands. Amazing. The feel of his body curling against her back, her bottom, and her legs. His warm breath at her ear threatened her aim and concentration.

It was a different feeling from any she had ever known. Auras merged. It was as if every piece on a chessboard was lined up just right for the kill; as if she had the last king on the checkerboard and was about to jump six of his pieces. And only the fitting of their bodies together, here in the open with prairie breezes pushing past them did this?

"Take aim and fire when you're ready, but . . . it's going to kick and deafen you at the same time. It's the long barrel. Either you can cock it and you have a hair trigger or you can just squeeze the trigger." He was about to drown in her. The arms he supported her with wavered only slightly. Blood pounded through his veins and he thought his heart might burst.

He had known she fit to him, but not how well. He had known her kisses would send him soaring, but not how high. The lilac fragrance of her hair made him want to take her to the ground again. The knowledge of that was almost a threat to him. Almost. Caution was about to be thrown to the wind. The female scent of her soft skin and the strong grip of her hands, beneath his, threatened to push him over the edge of reason. Forcing his concentration back to the target area, he nearly lost it again when she was pushed back against him discharging the first bullet from the gun.

Grin wide, she looked back at him. "Wow." She wiggled in his arms. "Let me try it on my own."

"Sure, after you fire the other five rounds first. This is called practice. Keep your arm straight, support the gun butt like this with your other hand. Look down the ventilated sight plane and plug that target . . . in the middle," he teased.

Bracing her legs farther apart, she adjusted herself straight on to the target. This time she cocked it and brushed the trigger. Right of the center. One, two, three, four more. The sixth one dead center. "Could have placed them all in the bull's-eye if someone hadn't been waving me off target." And if she hadn't felt the hard wall of his body each time she gave with the shot.

Even though the cylinder of the handgun was empty, he stayed in the firing position with her in his arms. "Have you ever been regressed? I'm beginning to think you've been reincarnated and you were William F. Cody in another life. Maybe that's why you love this place so much and just maybe why you can shoot like this."

She laughed, turning her face back toward his, his chin at the top of her head. "Couldn't be I'm just good, could it, Cooper?"

"I don't think so." He let go of her then, even though it was the last thing he wanted. Showing her how to load, he handed her the gun and stepped back.

Her jeans fit snugly over slim hips and rounded buttocks. He wanted to trace his hands over the lines. The sound of her blasting away at the target grabbed his attention. She splintered the corner of the board and then homed in and circled the target.

"I love this. Now the Winchester .30.30."

Shaking his head, he picked it up and put it in her hands. "And this afternoon I want to show you how to smooth out your riding and then in about a month we'll start the barrel pattern."

"Barrel pattern?"

"Yep. You're just the right weight to ride a horse well in that event. Ever thought of rodeoing?"

She levered the rifle, aimed, and pulled the trigger, finding the target. Again and still again. Laughing, she answered his question. "Why a month, and what do you mean smooth out my riding?" She reloaded.

"You still tend to ride English. You give too much with your legs and you almost post. This is the West. You ride smooth and easy, sitting back in the saddle and putting your weight there. You're more in tune with the horse riding Western. In my opinion, the smaller the saddle gets, the less connection you have with the horse. We're not chasing some damn fox with hounds yapping at our heels."

"Oh, we're not. That's fine with me. Since I taught you to shoot skeet International, it's only fair you teach me to ride Western well. But don't think I'll be bad at it."

"You think you're something, don't you?" he teased.

She leveled the rifle and then caught it over her arm, flipping the safety on. Turning halfway, she frowned. "No. But I want to be something. I want to be . . ."

"A cowgirl?"

"Through and through."

Taking the rifle from her, he planted a kiss on her nose. "Done showing off for now?"

"Thanks, Wes. I had fun. Don't be too hard on me when we do the riding."

"I'm going to be real hard on you. You want to be the best and I'm the one to teach you, but you'd better grow a thicker skin and get used to not taking offense. I want you to be the best, too."

"Do I do that?"

"You bristle up from time to time."

"Maybe it's the way you teach. Maybe you expect too much too soon or maybe you simply don't like a female being as good as you. I blew you away at trap."

"In your lifetime, you couldn't be as good as me."

She popped him then, good and hard in the shoulder.

"Ow. What a charley horse. I'll have a knot for a week."

When had the camaraderie set in? She didn't know but they were easy with each other. Comfortable and she liked it. She also liked the excitement that hovered around them, nudged her nerves alive, and she liked the way the man enjoyed life.

Gathering up the weapons, they headed back toward the buckboard they had used to haul everything up there. Once on the seat next to him, she stopped him from tapping the reins against the horses' rumps to start the drive back.

"You know, I can almost feel them," she told him as she looked around. Many times she had walked up this hill and many times she had wondered what had gone on, years before, right where she stood now, exactly on this spot of earth.

Wes nodded. "The Indians, the pioneers, the outlaws, and the settlers. Me too. Just about where we are now a small church once stood. It's said that the preacher taught the Indians all about the white man's god. For years they listened and believed and then the other white men showed up. The ones who wanted the red man's land and weren't willing to pay for it."

Victoria listened to the smooth story-telling sound of Wes's voice and looked out across the field trying to picture a small, poorly constructed place of worship, the preacher dressed in dark clothes and a wide-brimmed hat standing in the doorway. The breeze whispered across her face while the sun reddened it.

"The preacher was hard put to make the Indians understand that they must learn to live with the white man, especially when the white-eyes killed their buffalo and chased them off the land. For a while the little church was abandoned as both sides fought for control. After the white man won, the preacher held on to his church and waited for the Indians to return. He had faith that someday they would. Well, they didn't, until that night six years later and the old preacher heard someone at the door of the church. He opened it and there he stood. The old chief, broken war lance in hand, a party of young warriors behind him. It seems it was time for him to die and he wanted to die here, so that he could find the peace the white man's god promised and the preacher had taught him about.''

"So the preacher's sermons hadn't fallen on deaf ears as he had thought.''

"No. The old chief was brought into the church and the preacher cared for him until he passed on. As it turned out, the old Indian asked to be buried near the church so he could always be near the smart god-man. Also in hopes that if there was a heaven he would be guaranteed better passage coming right from holy grounds.''

"That's a nice story. Do you ever feel them in the town? Glory Town? I do. Like lost souls coming home. I know it was all built years ago and was never a real Wild West town, but if I were the soul of a brave sheriff who had died defending his town or a weary cowboy almost finished the trail drive and drowned crossing the river . . . someone like that would feel at home in our town. There're ghosts here. I wish I had lived in those days.''

He planted a quick kiss on her cheek. "I don't. Then I wouldn't have had the pleasure of your company or your very vivid imagination.''

A smile played its way across her lips. Lips that wanted to be pressed against his again. "Who knows? Maybe we both lived back then. Maybe we even knew each other.''

"Unlikely. I would have remembered it.''

"No, you wouldn't. But it would explain my feel for the rightness of being here. My ability to ride and shoot without instruction.''

"Ability?'' He teased. "You still ride like a girl, and the shooting, well, it could be luck.''

"You hope it is. There's a barn dance tonight. The first one that has been advertised in town. You going?''

"Hadn't thought about it. I like to put Katie to bed. . . .''

"Afterward then."

"You asking me for a date, Vic?"

She winced when he used Buck's nickname for her. She reached over and tentatively took his hand in hers. Looking directly at him, she decided to be as honest as she could be. "I've decided to open my heart and really see. For the first time. I think I only saw what I wanted to see. Maybe I never gave reality a chance before. I don't know where all this is going, if anywhere. But I find, despite the fact that I resent your being here . . . I like you. I like you a lot. Yes, I'm asking you for a date."

He grinned wide and slapped the leather across the horses' backs. "I'll be there tonight." He lifted their joined hands and kissed hers. "I like you, too, Vic. And I've got all the time in the world."

Wes put everything away and headed out to go over some more roping tricks for the upcoming rodeo with the men. And, he thought, there should be a parade at the beginning with flags and trick riding. It should look just like the real thing. When he was done with them, it would be the real thing. He just hoped he could keep his mind on the task at hand.

After spending a congenial morning with Victoria Clay, the stubborn, unwanted Easterner . . . wanted now at least by him, he wasn't sure his world could ever be the same. Life had lifted the sash on the window of what could be, and he liked it. He needed it. He craved it. He still worried that she would never believe him if he was completely honest with her and was unwilling to take the chance. He watched as she crossed the dusty road of Glory Town and wondered if in some strange way they had been catapulted back in time and no one noticed. Not even them.

The barn dance was going to be a success. Victoria stood on the sidelines and all but clapped her hands. Many local people drove out to park their cars beside the potholes and beneath new construction to see what was happening different in a very old business that had simply been there forever.

From the looks of the costumes, crinolined skirts and Western shirts and bolo ties, some interest had been stirred. It might only be from the lack of entertainment in the vicinity, but Victoria didn't care why they were there, just that they were. It made a nice mixture. Crew, tourists, and locals.

The colored lights she had strung around the inside of the barn cast a festive mood. Crockpots full of chili and trays laden with rolls and pies lined the tables. Buckets of ice and cases of pop and beer sat here and there. The stereo blasted from a corner hidden from view.

Maybe she had finally done something that would make an impact on Glory Town. Victoria watched Buck. He stood on the outskirts of the barn, looking in and around. The darkness prevented her from deciphering the look on his face as one of pleasure or pain. She headed his way.

Buck saw her coming. She almost looked smug and, dammit, he had to admit she almost deserved to. The reenactment crew was actually taking pride in Glory Town and their roles. The acts were tightening up and looking very authentic. She had done one heck of a job with this old barn. One heck of a job. But then why shouldn't she? He had already counted plenty of locals kicking up their heels and spending money. He rubbed his hands together and grinned when she approached.

"Not a bad turnout, Buck. What do you think?"

He grunted. It was too late to change his image now. He wasn't sure he would if he could. "Time'll tell."

She nodded. "It certainly will. The hot dogs are delicious. We bought the best, the big fat ones that plump in the middle. And the fries are being cooked in peanut oil. You ought to try some."

He shrugged, looking around. "Later, maybe."

He was dragging at her good mood and she wanted

none of it. "Suit yourself." With that she walked away from him, hands moving in time to the music.

Buck felt the slightest tug of rhythm in his feet and stood with his weight evenly distributed to discourage it. He wanted to dance. He wanted to get out there and do the hoedown. But then they'd have him made as an old softy and you couldn't run a business if you were a marshmallow. Right? he asked himself. Hadn't he done it right all these years? He watched as Victoria let herself be grabbed up by one of the men and kick up some dust on the dance floor. She seemed to manage to mix and mingle and still have the men's respect. Could she actually have been right all along and he wrong? No, he decided. No way.

SEVEN

The minutes moved on quickly and to a timely beat. Victoria sipped on a cold glass of cola and watched from the sideline, toe tapping to the rhythm. She was watching for Wes.

Buck was still there. That in itself disturbed her. What did it mean? Was he gauging the worth of the event? Was he trying to decide if she was taking over, playing the big-kid partner again? Or . . . could it be that pretty older lady who seemed to be smiling at him from under lashes still thick and pretty? Victoria felt the corners of her mouth curl as she watched the scenario unfold before her. She deliberately eyed Buck. She wanted him to know she was watching.

The lady was probably in her fifties. Her hair was a soft champagne blond threaded with silver. Her face was heart-shaped and her eyes were green. She had painted her lips a soft pink to match the dress that reached her ankles to top off white boots. Her nails were long and painted a rose color. Each finger sported a ring, either a plain band or one with a gemstone. She was pretty. And she was shy. She seemed to want to come over to talk to Buck. But instead she just watched him and from time to time would pull her gaze to the dance floor and clap her hands in time to the music.

Enough of this. Victoria walked over to the lady. "Hi. I'm Victoria Clay. Welcome to Glory Town."

The lady's voice was soft and rich. "Hello. I'm Emma St. Claire. It's a wonderful get-together. I've been curious about this setup since I moved here a few months ago. It's the first chance I've had to come out. I run the bookstore in Redwood. Takes up a lot of time. But I took tonight off to come out with my daughter and her husband."

Shoot. Married. Well, maybe not. "Your husband doesn't like to dance?"

"He died last year. That's why I moved out here from Maryland to be near the rest of the family. I like being with the grandchildren. It keeps me busy and I don't have to think about being alone."

Great. And an Easterner. That would teach Buck. If Victoria had a mustache, she would have twirled it. Plotting, she guided Emma toward the table supported by three sawhorses and overflowing with food. "We're neighbors. I'm from Virginia. Come on over and I'll treat you to a hot dog. I'm starving."

The woman smiled a pretty smile and followed Victoria over to the table. Buck was only five feet away. Victoria made him wait. They laughed when they both reached for the ketchup. Taking a big bite, Victoria pretended to just spot Buck. "Hi, Buck. Great party, don't you think?" She winked at him. He scowled at her.

"This is Emma St. Claire. Runs the bookstore in town. Emma, this is my partner, Buck Mitchell. Together we own Glory Town. You two have running a business in common. Oh, I see Nick. I want to talk to him about the show tomorrow." With a wave, she was off. Buck was left alone with the pretty lady. And Victoria almost prayed he would fall for her. Hard. An Easterner. It would serve the old crust right. Besides, she hated to see anyone be alone.

Wes was late. Well, not late, she reminded herself. They hadn't set a time. She berated herself for the fact that she wouldn't have a good time until he arrived. "Nick. How's it going?"

Nick looked handsome in his cavalry shirt and tight black jeans. He wore a new after-shave. One spicy and sweet. He beamed when she held out her hand and was glad when the music turned from fast to slow. "The Tennessee Waltz" played lazily along the sweet night air. He pulled her into his arms and moved to the beat.

They chatted, but Victoria didn't pay much attention. She was looking around, seeing what needed attending to. Everything appeared to be going smoothly. And then he walked through the door.

The music faded into the background. The darkness in the barn only served to heighten the desperado look about him. He wore his go-to-hell hat, brim turned down. His shirt was white, his jeans gray. He spotted her and walked toward her. She heard no sound. Saw no movement but his. And wanted desperately to feel his arms around her.

He didn't ask. He took her by the hand and led her to the outskirts of the crowd, near the wide-open doors where the air stirred and was cool. Laying a light kiss on her mouth, he pulled her to him and together they swayed.

His shirt felt crisp as if just ironed with a touch of starch. Had his mother done that for him, stopping him on his way out and insisting? After all, mothers were always mothers. And sons were always sons no matter what age. The thought made her smile.

Her hair smelled of lilacs and caressed his shoulder. He pulled her closer. Her hand was tiny and warm in his. A hand he knew could toil with a rake, restrain a leather bridle, or pump rounds from a gun. He lifted it to his lips.

"Katie says hello."

"Give her a kiss for me."

He put his fingers under her chin, lifting her mouth to his, and collected one to carry with him. "You were watching for me."

"I was not."

"You were."

"A little." She tucked her head and snuggled against his chest.

"A lot." He two-stepped her closer to the outside, a little at a time. The cool breeze wafted over them. He kept circling her until they were beyond the patch of light showering from the barn.

Nick shoved his hands in his pockets. Wes had walked in and she had merely turned to him and danced into his arms. He looked around. How many of his friends had seen that? Blatant rejection. Benign neglect. A slap in his face. His brain cells took a turn. As happened so often lately, he couldn't think clearly.

He rubbed his temple to stall the headache that was beginning to thunder around in his head, destroying his thought process. Victoria was just being nice to Wes. After all, she was his boss and they had lots to talk about. The voice in his head began to whine as it so often did. He closed his eyes. A roaring began in his head, like waves from the ocean pounding the shore, rhythmically and steadily. Unaware, Nick left the edge of reality. Again.

The sounds of gunshots and shouting rang in his ears. A stagecoach appeared in his mind's eye. It was a runaway. The driver was dead and slouching across the high seat. A small hand clutched the door strap of the rocking, bumping, headed-for-disaster coach and held on. He spurred his mount, demanding more speed. The heavy thud of horses' hooves beat at him, accelerated his pulse. He had to save that lady passenger. It was his Victoria.

Reaching the stage, Nick leaned and grabbed hold of the railings. Pulling himself from his horse, he floated momentarily between safety and death, falling and being trampled under the coach as he lost his grip. Then he heard it. Her soft cry. "Nick," and she grabbed for him. This and this alone was enough to give him the physical strength he needed to pull himself onto the coach even though it jerked and swayed and rolled at a perilous speed. He climbed to the seat and pushed the dead man out of the way. Standing, he grabbed the reins and, after some pulling and jerking, managed to stop the runaway team.

Jumping down, he opened the door and she fell in his arms. Together, they tumbled down to the dusty ground. She wrapped her arms around his neck and brought his mouth toward hers. "My hero."

Excitement rippled through Victoria as she ran her hand along the smooth ridge of muscle down Wes's back and found that she was trying to press him even harder against her.

He stopped moving. She looked up at him. In the dim silver glow from a thin slice of moonlight, she made out his features. He was dead serious. No smile played on his mouth now. No amusement lit his eyes. She grew short of patience and stood on tiptoe, bringing their mouths together.

Her gesture tore through him and almost hurt. A storm of emotions circled his gut and soared through his chest. Afraid he would crush her, he was careful not to give in to his instincts but instead reveled in the way her mouth fit to his. The taste of her. The promise of her.

Her lips, like satin, moved over his. A soft sigh escaped her lips as she changed the angle of contact. The smell of hay and feed, hot dogs, and burning cooking oil rolled all around them. All she knew was the feel of him. The eagerness and the restraint she could feel in his body. And then the air was whooshed from her as he grabbed her tight and lifted her from the ground. It almost frightened her, the force she felt in him. Almost. He would be no gentle lover . . . and she wanted it no other way.

A man should be able to take anything a woman can dish out and still remain a gentleman. He almost laughed as he set her on her feet and, to keep from taking her here and now, began the dance again. Her lids were heavy. Her lips were swollen from contact. Her breasts rose and fell quickly to match his own hurried breath.

He asked with a look. She answered with one. Turning, she took his hand and led him away from the barn. Away from the noise out into the quiet, silky darkness of night.

He jerked her to him, not wanting to wait any longer to feel her mouth under his. She wiggled away and pulled him after her. It had to be perfect. She wanted him to remember tonight. She wanted to remember it all. The night she decided what she wanted out of life. J. Weston Cooper.

The crash resounded across the night air and reverberated in the loftiness of the barn. A few shrieks and then curses followed. Wes jerked his head back and looked into Victoria's drowsy eyes. "What the hell was that?"

"I don't know but I think we'd better go find out." The cold rush of air crossed her lips, leaving them wanting his mouth to cut the flow of it off again. She felt him take her hand and pull her along behind him.

The food table was turned over. Soup and hot dog rolls and bowls of chips and trays of pies rolled to a stop nearly at their feet. One stereo speaker that had been set up on a hay bale lay face down in the sawdust, the sounds of music muffled.

All eyes were riveted on the man who stumbled near the mess. Nick swayed again, both hands holding his head. The crowd of people made way for him as he tried to grab something to hold on to. Victoria saw that some of the women had food and drink splashed on them. Two of the men brushed the remains of chili from their shirts and jeans. Lord!

Nick flailed around, groaning low in his throat. Wes ran over to him. "God, man, are you drunk?"

Nick swung at him. Wes ducked and then moved in. Not only the crew was here, but the public. Something was definitely wrong with Nick and he had to get him out of here as quickly and quietly as possible. Wes grabbed him and spun him around, locking him in a hold.

But Nick was strong and wild. He elbowed Wes and came around with a quick left hook, taking Wes by surprise and sending him flying across the floor. A woman screamed and was quieted by her husband. Some of the other men moved in to assist but Wes was up and charging forward. With one swift punch to the jaw, Nick was rendered unconscious. Two of the men took Nick and carried him from the barn. Victoria stepped forward and tried to help right things, but the evening was spoiled. People moved toward the door.

Rushing in, Victoria joked, trying to ease the chaos. "Well, folks, the dance next month probably won't be as exciting, and when you get the bill for your dry cleaning, send it on to me. It has been a real pleasure to have you here and I hope to see you next time." The crowd was amenable. They chatted with her a while, not even noticing that her hands twisted together nervously.

She turned on her heel. It was time to find out what had happened.

Buck was escorting Ms. St. Claire to her car along with her family when he saw Victoria come out of the barn and look around. "They took him to the hotel. See what's going on. I'll join you in a minute."

Victoria expected to see Nick sprawled on the sofa, but instead he was sitting up in a chair in the parlor talking to Sally, who had stayed with Wes to find out what the story was. She had bustled the other men out and on their way and then simply plopped down in a chair opposite the two men and waited for an explanation.

"It was hot. I lost my balance. And then everybody

started hollering at me. I don't like to be hollered at. Howdy, Victoria."

She continued on her way in and sat next to him. "Are you all right, Nick? You were holding your head like you had a migraine." She felt his forehead for fever and found none.

"He doesn't remember a thing," Wes told her as he lit a cigarette and she picked up a decided edge to his voice.

"I think you should see a doctor, Nick."

"I'm fine now. Thanks to good ole Wes over there. Just took charge and brought me out here. Wes and me, we're good friends. Have a few secrets just like friends do, too." He laughed.

The hair on the back of Wes's neck prickled. "I'll walk you back to your trailer to be sure you're all right." He stood.

Nick laughed again. "Don't worry about me. I can take care of myself. Been doing it five years now. Until Wes came along and now he makes sure I do things right. Got to be the best. That's what he preaches, you know."

"Let's go, Nick. It's time the ladies here got some rest."

Nick looked from Sally, who sat quietly with a worried look on her face, to his beautiful Victoria, who waited patiently, concern in her eyes.

"Aren't you going to tell Vic the real reason you're here?" Nick challenged Wes in an overly friendly tone of voice.

Wes yanked Nick to a standing position and started prodding him toward the door.

Nick glanced back at the women and leered. "No. I mean the *real* reason you're here."

Wes tipped his hat to the ladies and shoved Nick through the door.

Sally stood up. "Well, I don't know about you but I'm tired. Don't worry about the mess. Some of the men have gone back to clean it up."

Confused, Victoria walked Sally to the door. "Whatever happened to cause Nick to fall like that isn't normal. I think he should see a doctor."

"Don't worry, honey. This has happened before. Nick isn't, well . . . Nick hasn't been the same since his Annie died. Every once in a while he goes off. No reason, no explanation, and he never remembers. It doesn't happen often and he's such a nice guy. I think it just gets to him once in a while, being alone and all. You're good for him. He likes you. He'll be fine. Good night, honey."

Victoria stood in the dimly lit room and let her mind run over the events of the evening. No. Nick's actions weren't normal. And what had he meant when he said he and Wes had secrets? And the *real* reason for his being here? What was that all about?

As soon as Wes walked back into the hotel and found her half asleep in the chair, he picked her up, as he had done countless times with Katie, and took the steps easily so as not to disturb her too much.

She roused and wrapped her arms around his neck, snuggling against his solid chest. "Nick okay?" she murmured.

"He's fine. Don't worry. And the townfolk? They'll forget it by the time it comes around next month. No harm done." He booted the door to her room open. He could smell her there. In the air, in the bedspread as he laid her down. Flowery. Intoxicating.

She kept her arms around his neck as he tried to straighten. Smiling, he knelt on the floor beside her bed. "Good night," he said and placed a light kiss on her lips.

Victoria strengthened the kiss when she pulled him closer and harder to her. She whispered, "Don't go."

An energy, a potency, and a concentrated force jolted through him. Two words. Two small, softly spoken words altered everything. He had thought he was being smart to leave her be after the events of the evening. But he had judged wrong. He kneeled down on the bed and she stretched her arms out for him. Taking her hands, he drew her up and to him. Kneeling together, bodies locked, he sought to please her in every way. He placed hot, moist kisses down her neck, where her scent was so sweet. He made himself go slowly, forced himself to be gentle. The passion that rode through him demanded attention. Instead he turned that attention to her. He laid her back, gently, on the bed. After feasting his eyes on her shadowy form, knowing that tonight she would be his, belong to him only . . . he leaned forward and went toward her waiting arms.

In Wes's arms earlier that night, Victoria had come to terms with her distrust of her judgment and him. They belonged together. A strange alliance. A joining of two souls brought on strictly by fate. He had been there all along. She had been searching the entire time. Miles and tempo had been between them. But no more. No matter what happened in the light of day. No matter what happened as a result of rhyme or reason, tonight . . . this night they would be together. The part of Victoria Clay that had always been cautious, always bent to the rules of whatever dictator prevailed, pushed it all aside and just became the woman who wanted to be in the arms of this man.

She was growing weak. His hands, his mouth. The sound of her name on his lips. Songs were written about love. Poems, novels, but nothing could ever come close to the age-old ritual of loving. Still she waited, anticipated, lingered, and tarried. She wanted this to go on forever. Then the urgency sped through her and she moved her hands to the snap of his jeans.

Losing himself in the taste of her skin, heated and moist, sweet and slow, seeping, his mind reeled. Never had a woman flowed into his pores and raced through his blood like this. Never had a woman meant so much to him. Her happiness, her sorrows, her joys, and her dreams. She was pouring into him and becoming a part of him, blood, guts, and heart. Finding the buttons to her dress, his fingers worked them open. His mouth found the sweet, delicate form of her breast and tasted. She bloomed beneath his mouth, his fingers.

He left her breast to roam, slowly, so slowly. As he explored her body with his tongue, he felt her ripple like silk in the wind. He learned her taste, her texture, the sweet aroma of passion and heat.

Victoria ran her hands through his hair and pressed him closer to her. So this was making love. This was being loved. Not the methodical mating of male and female but the coming together of man and woman. His hands branded trails as he removed her clothes. Then his were gone and flesh pressed against flesh. His strong limbs mixed with her supple ones. Her heart raced, sending her blood speeding and leaving her light-headed. She felt him pull back and she reached for him.

Bringing his hand to her mouth, she kissed it and tasted his palm with her tongue. Hard knuckles brushed the smooth skin of her cheek and she kissed them. In the darkness she felt rather than saw his eyes darken and watched as the shadow of his head moved toward her once more. His mouth was at her throat, her breasts, and down her stomach. All the while his hands explored, cherished her, made her feel revered and breakable. Bringing his mouth back to hers, she tasted him once more, investigating with her tongue as she left the kiss to find out what he tasted like elsewhere.

His shoulder, his chest, the inside of his forearm. Her hands ran over his hips and down his muscled thighs. The play of his body under her touch delighted her. This strong, handsome, take-no-bull cowboy was subject to the feelings her hands and her mouth could bring him. She watched as she ran her fingers along his body, watched the muscles contract, his breath quicken, the way he moved toward her for more. He was wide open and in need of the way she felt in her heart and in her mind. And it mattered to her.

He had promised himself he wouldn't take her quickly. She deserved better. His body screamed for more. His mind, his heart made him take his time. He wanted to please her. He wanted to know that every move he made brought delight. His possession of her body and hers of his had to lend to the opening and freedom of their hearts. The blending of their souls. But as they rolled together, discovering each other's bodies, he felt his control slipping.

In the smoky, hazy, eerie land of lovers, Victoria reached for him, pulled him closer to her, wanting to feel him beside her from head to toe.

He stretched his long, hard body on top of hers and she felt the thrill of it rip through her. The anticipation of being one with him, being filled with him. Heat whirled and fire pushed her toward him. Lifting her hips, inviting him . . . demanding him, she craved to be one with him.

Perspiration sheened them both. In the play of light shadow on dark shadow, he could see the desire in her eyes as she looked at him. He could see the love. Most of all he could see that. Could she see it? Could she feel it when he touched her? Could she trust it? He wanted to be sure. He needed her to know.

She was liquid beneath him. Volcanic. He felt himself slipping close to the edge. Sliding along on hot ice. Control was melting away. Lifting slightly, he felt his heart soar as she opened for him, eagerly. Joining her hands with his, he put them over her head and nuzzled her lips with his. "I love you."

His words rocketed through her. Almost unable to breathe, she smiled and mouthed the words against his lips. "And I love you."

Eyes open and on each other, he poised, touched, and slipped inside her, slowly . . . so slowly. A completeness. A oneness. A purely unexplainable peace filled her just before the fire backlashed through her and jettisoned her to a place she'd never known before. He tightened inside her, she closed around him. Insisting. Arching, twisting, she reveled; floating, sinking, she cooled. Drowning, she submerged only to dive again; spiraling, twining, soaring, she thrust herself against him.

He was lost and glad for it. Gone. Everything he had was now hers. As he held himself back, as he drew the pleasure nearly to the point of exhaustion, a new and unknown power and surrender played with his foggy mind. His heart pumped to the point of bursting and yet he wanted to please her more. For each move that brought her delectation, it brought him joy. For every touch that brought her delirium, it brought him frenzy. He pulsed, at once, with wild excitement and gentleness. Every time she breathed his name, he was empowered. Every time she moved her hips up to meet his, he thought he was close to death. One he wouldn't shun.

They rolled, they twisted, the gentleness he promised himself he would give her, gone. Her fingers bit into his hips as she pushed against him. Fury, a storm of passion hovering and then streaking, pounding, and crashing.

He caught her mouth with his and held her still. Their bodies joined and committed, found a world of heights and depths, of fire and ice as together they catapulted over some unseen, unexplored wall into a universe that consumed them.

_____ EIGHT _____

Glad she had thought to pull on her cotton shawl, Victoria watched the sky change from light gray to fiery orange as the sun pushed its way upward. The first glow of color for a new day. She drew in the slightly chill air and kept walking. This was a beautiful time of day and really the first time she had ever been outside the moment Oklahoma night turned into Oklahoma day.

Wrapping the ends of the shawl around her fingers, hands outstretched, she turned several circles; the hem of her skirt heavy with the dew of the tall morning grass, she got more than slightly dizzy. Jogging up the hill and over the top, she laughed out loud. No one was around to hear. No one was near to see her let loose all those things pent up in her for so long. Running, she headed for the stream that bubbled and rippled along its way at the bottom of the hill. Pink smartweed waved in the breeze alongside yellow mammillaria.

Once there, her mother's voice in her ear saying "You'll only catch cold and have to spend boring time in bed," she slipped her shoes off and held them dangling from one hand. The water was ankle deep and icy. It felt wild and was crazy. She walked down the middle of the stream, squealing and talking to the new morning as if it were her friend. "Yes! I can walk on water. I know where all the rocks are." Giggling at her own foolishness, Victoria lifted her face to the glow of the warm sun.

It was from the top of the hill, astride his horse bareback, that Wes spotted her. Reining the horse to a stop, he watched. Pushing his hat back on his head, he smiled. He had interrupted her private time. He shouldn't sit here and watch as she played, childlike, in the stream. He shouldn't, but he was damn well going to do it.

He had never met anyone like her. She was intense one minute and perfectly silly the next. She could smile happily or scowl with the best of them. She had a spitfire temper and a suspicious and distrusting mind at times. And she could be giving. Last night, he had seen it and felt it. Thinking of her, lying in his arms . . .

His horse nickered and Wes quieted him with his hand on his neck. He didn't want anything to distract Victoria from the enjoyment she was finding in the new day. He watched as she caught the hem of the back of her skirt and brought it through her legs and tucked it in her waistband to pull it up safe from any more drenching as now she was jumping in the water, sending splashes of it shooting in the air. Wes smiled and a warmth he had never known filled him. It nearly made up for the restless night and slight headache.

Unable to resist, he urged his mount down the hill. The pair walked behind her for a full minute before she heard them and, startled, yelped. "You scared me. How long have you been out here?"

Grinning, Wes swung his legs. "Long enough." Then guiding his horse beside her, he offered his hand. "Ride with me a while."

After losing at least the last half of a good night's sleep over this man, lying in his arms being swept away with passion, was it safe to join him on the horse this morning? She took his hand and he lifted her, settling her in front of him. It was the strangest sensation she had ever experienced. Gravity pushed her body back against his. Full against his. The slow rock of the horse's body as he picked his way through the rocks and then over the open field only amplified the hardness of his chest and thighs against her. She looked down at the hand that loosely held the reins a few inches from her stomach. Competent hands.

They were good hands. Large with blunt fingers. She remembered the feel of them on her face, her body. Bringing her soul alive, forcing her to feel all she was afraid to feel. They were rough hands, yet smooth. Cool, assuring, and warm . . . confident hands that had done many things. Hands that had held a gun . . . a tiny little girl . . . made a horse dance under him and fluffed the flattened fur on a teddy bear . . . and made beautiful love to her.

They were silent for a while, the horse picking his own path. As the wayward breeze lifted her hair, Victoria could feel Wes's breath at her neck. As the sun rose higher in the sky to warm her skin, the man at her back warmed her heart.

Because he needed to know, Wes said, "Tell me what you used to do on a day like this back in Virginia."

She let her mind zero back to the East. To a morning like this one. "I'd ride Tonka early. Usually Mother and I would join her friends later and ride again. I went to the veterans hospital almost every day just before noon. So many of them need assistance to eat and hospitals are always understaffed. I stayed till three or so depending on the needs of the day." Remembering, she sighed. "Then there was always a dinner or a party to go to. My mother was big into social events and she belonged to many clubs that used any excuse to party. After my divorce from David, her friends were always trying to match me with one of their relatives or a long lost friend. I guess most of my attention was lavished on my horses and my veterans. They never expected anything of me."

"Buck mentioned the VA hospital but I didn't think you were so involved."

"It's all volunteer. I have the time and they need the help. Besides, I love those guys. Such spirits. Such strength. Some have lost it for a while but they get it back. Most of them." A sadness washed over her when faces flitted across her mind's eye of ones she'd lost.

Her giving, her caring touched him when they lived in a world so caught up in the me generation. "What'd you do for them?"

"Anything that needed to be done. Like I said, some need help to eat. Some need letters written or phone calls connected. I ran errands, like shopping for their girlfriends or wives and kids. I take some of them to therapy to encourage and bully and hoorah. Whatever is called for. The physical needs are sometimes much easier to care for than the emotional. A lot of the time I'm simply listening and hearing stories no one should ever hear let alone live through. Scars. Deep, deep permanent scars. Some of these men will never be fully functional again. Were you there, in Vietnam?"

"Yes. But I wasn't in combat much. We were on the perimeter and only involved in small skirmishes. I spent a lot of time in the bush, on edge, alert to the point where I thought I could hear my pores opening and closing. Snipers were a problem. But there were plenty of other guys who had it a lot worse. Huge firefights that lasted for days and nights . . . and bombings."

She pictured him, slightly disabled sitting in a corner, tormented and in mental and physical pain. Shaking her head, she said, "I take the guys in wheelchairs on walks around the hospital and sometimes I'd take them out to the house and have them sit on the porch beside me in the rocker. There was this one man. A special one. I learned a lot about myself from what he told me. My emotions, how deeply I can care, how strongly I can feel. We'd sit for hours and he'd tell me, teach me. What it was like to be in war. And I would look at him and try to imagine him there. That body. That mind. Those hands. That heart. Then and only then did I learn about the human spirit. And love. We talked about everything. And laughed, we could make serious things funny. My friend . . . my friend gave me all that. What a gift it is.'' She missed him.

Bringing herself back to the present, she drew a deep breath. "I guess I was just a person who cares, who wants them to have a real friend while they are in the hospital. It takes just a little effort to make a change in someone's life or outlook. I think I've helped a few.''

"I'm sure you have. You miss them. I can hear it in your voice.''

"I sure do. I'll go back and visit. Of course, it won't be the same but—I guess when this opportunity came along I became selfish. But then again, maybe I seek my freedom as much as they seek theirs. They were happy for me. All of them. But when it came time for me to leave, some cried. I cried.''

He hugged her then. He simply lifted the arm that had been dangling at his side and wrapped it around her . . . and left it there.

After another few moments of silence, Wes nudged the horse in the sides and the three of them were off across the field like a streak of lightning. After the first jolt, Victoria grabbed a handful of mane, tightened her legs against the horse's sides, and held on. Her hair flowed back as they rocketed past the trees and through the grass. In response to Wes's slight move forward, she bent her body to fit his and with eyes cut against the wind, her laughter rolled out over the air. Fast, faster, the horse thundered, the sound of his hooves muffled against the grass. Wes's body was hard and arousing. His arms kept her safe and his heart beat in time with hers. Every inch of their bodies was touching, moving in time to the horse's hoofbeats. Friction building fire. Confidence building confidence.

Exhilarating. Thrilling. Breathtaking. The world whirled away from them in a blur as they seemed to leave the hard, packed earth for the soft weightlessness of the atmosphere. Wind streamed through her hair and carried her laughter up and away. It was fantasy. It was reality. It was a dream. Together, two humans and one animal, mutually forged in a world of speed and pleasure. Unafraid, completely trusting Wes and the horse, she let herself go. Complete abandon. No fears, no doubts. No mooring ropes. Freedom. She loved it. The wind dragged across her ankles and up her bare legs. On they went.

When Wes slowed the horse to a trot and then back to a walk, she turned and planted a kiss on his chin, noticing for the first time the stubble of a night's growth of beard.

He pulled the horse to a halt beneath the tree and dismounted. Turning, he held up his arms and she slid into them. Taking her shawl, he spread it on the ground and took her down with him.

"Do you always ride so early in the morning?" she asked, her lips close to his.

"Only when I can't sleep." She could feel the vibration of his voice in his chest where her hand rested.

She grinned, knowing he couldn't see it. So with only a thin wall between them, both had tossed and turned the rest of the night away. Somehow that made her smug. "Did you feed the horses already?"

"All taken care of. The men and I are meeting at ten to go over some of the rodeo skills. I feel like having a great big breakfast. Want to go back and see what cook has on the stove?"

She didn't want this to end. Ever. "Okay. You need sustenance before you start your hard day's work. I know that much about cowboys."

He chuckled. "But you have a lot more to learn. And I'm just the man to teach you."

She circled his neck with her arms, looking up at him through a wide sweep of dark lashes. "Teach me."

Still moved from the night before and fired up from their ride across the grass, Wes cradled her in his arms and touched his lips to hers. He was almost afraid it wouldn't be there again. But it was. Stronger. Vibrant. Potent.

Lying still when all she wanted was to hurry him, she waited as he tasted her, traced her body with his hands. She didn't object when their lovemaking became ardent. She had never made love in the shade of a big old tree before.

He took his time and relished her. She watched the emotions cross his face and smiled when he tucked his head to nuzzle her. Like young lovers, never before together, they tested, experimented. As her heart soared with a happiness never before known, she saw it in his eyes, too. Last night it had been too dark to see. This morning it was bright and clear. Slowly, their clothes were cast aside.

Not once did Victoria worry about being seen. The horse would warn them of anyone approaching, which was a long shot. And besides, she couldn't have prevented their coming together. It just happened naturally. It was a freedom she had never allowed herself to experience.

When he covered her with his body, it was as if she were coming home. A strange mix of the comfortable and the unknown. One of expectations and surprises.

He filled her. A complete union, the feelings as new as if they had never been together like this before. Arching toward him, murmuring his name, she exploded with more love and heat than she ever thought possible.

He was home. Each time he drove hard into her and rode closer to completion, he wondered at it all. Never, never had he loved someone as much.

*   *   *

Later, much later, he kicked his gelding into an easy gallop and they headed toward Glory Town.

Victoria leaned back into him. She hoped he would think it was the momentum of the gallop but it was her. She wanted to feel his long, lean body supporting hers. It would be nice to know what it would be like to have a man to lean on, mentally and physically.

Glory Town was just stretching into the waking hour. People stirred here and there. They rode to the barn, through the gate and inside. The first thing Victoria saw shot ice water through her veins. Her horse wasn't in his stall but on the sawdust-covered floor of the barn. Stall door open . . . feed room door open. Two and two added up to death.

"Oh God. He's down. Didn't you lock the doors?" It was more an accusation than a question as she jumped off his horse and ran to hers. Tonka's breathing was labored, and after putting an ear to his stomach and hearing silence, she knew. Colic! The dreaded word among horse owners.

Wes was beside her. "Of course, I locked the doors. Do you think I'm a fool? Horses are my job. Get him up."

Her groan was almost a cry. "You really screwed up this time and it's liable to cost me my animal. Damn. Call the vet."

Her mind skimmed over all she knew about colic. Any time a horse ingested too much of something it wasn't used to—lush green grass, alfalfa, or too much grain—it ferments before it can be digested, forming gas in the intestines. Unless the blockage can move along the insides and out . . . the internal agitation causes extreme pain. And if the horse lies down and rolls to relieve the suffering, it can twist the intestine, closing off any hope of passing the blockage. The horse dies. In a matter of eight to ten hours, the animal is gone. A long, painful death.

Panic threatened to pour in but she held it at bay. Running for a lead shank, she returned and clicked it on his halter. It took some coaxing, but she had the horse on his feet and walking as Wes dialed the vet.

He had locked the doors. He was no greenhorn. How the hell could she assume this was his doing? Because he was the one who came in early and fed and took his horse out for a ride. He was the one. Hanging up, assured help was on the way, he hurried to the refrigerator and pulled out a syringe. Sticking the needle in the bottle of Banamine, he withdrew 100 cc's. Holding the syringe up to the light, he flicked the air out of it and rejoined her in the arena.

Walking on the other side of the horse, Wes injected the muscle relaxant in hopes that they had found him soon enough. Time. Time would tell. He felt his gut tighten up as he stood back and watched Victoria walk the horse around the barn in a wide circle. It was going to be a long, long day. "Let's hope we found him early enough. If the Banamine relaxes the muscles and the blockage is small, we'll be all right."

"Vet coming?" she demanded as she passed him.

"Right away." Even though he understood her tone of voice, he didn't like it. "I didn't leave any doors open."

"Hardly matters to me now. Walk him while I run back to the hotel and change." She needed her jeans and boots on. Not looking at Wes, she handed him the lead, and after patting her horse on the side, she took off at a jog. She wasn't going to lose this horse simply because someone was careless. Dammit. Dammit. She wouldn't.

It didn't make any sense that Wes would be that lax, she argued with herself, but, she continued the silent battle, he was the only one in there. But he's been around horses all his life. Hadn't she mentioned to him that she didn't like the feed room being accessible from the main arena area? Many a time the horses were set loose inside so they could run in and out of the paddock area at will. He had assured her it would be all right, and guess what? It hadn't been.

Returning to the barn, she was relieved to see the vet's car parked outside. Running inside, she stopped. They were tubing him now and a bucketful of fluid was coming from the rubber tube in his nose that tapped his stomach. Squelching a squeamish flow in her own, she marched up and helped hold the gelding still.

"I'm sure you know this only relieves some of the pressure. If he hasn't already rolled and twisted an intestine, we have a chance of saving him. Later this afternoon, we'll know more. You know the routine. Walk him fifteen minutes, rest him thirty. Walk fifteen and rest. Don't let him go down and, for God's sake, don't let him roll."

"We know, Doc, and thanks." Wes turned to Victoria. "Doc is leaving us more Banamine."

Victoria offered, hopefully, "I heard a little bit of movement in his gut when I first got him up. Maybe he'll do okay."

The vet stripped off his rubber gloves and put the hose and bucket away. "We'll see. I've done all I can for now. I'll come back," he looked at his watch, "at six. If you need me before that, don't hesitate to call."

Victoria knew what that meant. If the horse went down and couldn't get up, if he rolled . . . it was time to put him down. When the pain got so bad . . . no, she wouldn't think of that now. Just walk.

She began circling again and watched Wes walk out with the vet. Both men were about the same age but the veterinarian was small and wiry with sharp features and short legs. They mumbled quietly to each other as they walked, and soon both men were out of sight.

She rubbed Tonka's nose and talked reassuringly as they walked. Step. Another. Another. She felt the horse falter a little and talked louder to him, tightening her hold on his halter. How much feed had he eaten? How much water had he drunk? How bad did his stomach ache? Those questions whirled in her mind. Checking her watch, she led him to his stall and clipped the lead off. Locking him in, she went to the feed room to look.

The lid from the rubber trash can Wes had installed to hold the high-protein feed was slid aside. The can held fifty pounds. Nearly half of it was gone. There was no way a horse's system could take a deluge of feed that way. Whoever had coined the phrase "eats like a horse" didn't own one. A horse's food was measured and the fields it grazed in were monitored. She groaned and kicked the can. Slamming the feed room door shut, she locked it securely. Too late.

Watching the time carefully, she brought Tonka out again and they started their trek. She stalled him once more and got him out again. Wes came in, his hands laden with bologna sandwiches, cans of cola under his arm.

"Eat something," he coaxed. "I'll walk him."

When she just stared daggers at him, he set the stuff on the top of a bale of hay. "It's going to be a long damn day. You're going to need energy. That horse is going to need you." Frustrated and angry, he scowled, "It's up to you."

He was right and that grated her even more. She handed over the lead and sat down, mindlessly forcing the food into her system. Wes talked to the horse and kept him moving. When the time was up, he stalled him and joined her on the other bale of hay. Biting into a sandwich, he waited while she popped the top on the cola and took a swig. He hated her silence. And the pain in her eyes.

Hours. Long, tiring hours passed. Buck and the boys appeared in the barn now and again offering to take a turn walking. She shrugged them off. "He's my horse. I'll walk him." J. Weston Cooper miraculously showed up at regular intervals to inject the muscle relaxant, only to disappear quietly again.

Wes had given up offering to spell her and busied himself elsewhere for a while. But now he was back. It was four o'clock and Victoria was exhausted. He watched from the doorway. The two of them were dusty and he could see traces of tears swiped away by the streaks on her cheeks. It pained him to see her this way. They both knew how it would probably turn out, but they also both knew they had to try.

Victoria was counting. In her mind, she ticked off the numbers. Seventy-one, seventy-two, seventy-three. Anything to keep from thinking about all this. And the rhythm she set in her mind kept both of them paced. She tripped and went down on both knees. She pounded a fist against her leg and felt the animal at her side go down on his knees. She looked at him, his head near hers, his eyes pleading with her to do something. "We can't give up, Tonka. We can't. Get up." She pushed herself to a standing position and yanked the lead to get him up.

The horse coughed and grunted but came up and walked when she did. It tore Wes's heart. He stormed over to her and took the lead. "Rest. I don't give a damn if you go back to your room or collapse in one of the stalls. But rest." He shoved an open can of ice cold cola in her hand.

She blinked her eyes and stared at him. A weak laugh escaped her lips. "I don't think I've ever prayed so hard in my whole life."

She dragged herself over to the hay and slumped against it. In two seconds, her eyes were closed and she was asleep.

She awoke with a start, her heart pounding against her rib cage. When her eyes cleared, she looked first at her watch—6:20—and then at the two men working on her horse. The vet came around from the rear of the horse and stripped off his rubber glove. When Wes looked at him hopefully, the vet just shook his head and began to put things away.

Victoria ran over to him. "Well?"

The vet breathed a heavy sigh. "I can put him down now or you can give him another couple of hours. I couldn't find anything with the palp and nothing is moving through the intestines yet. I can give you some strong pain medicine to give him. Once again, it's up to you. He seems to be a fighter.''

She rubbed her damp palms against her thighs and looked at Wes. He nodded. Directing her words to the vet, she answered, ''We'll give it a little longer. We may just luck out.''

In a daze she walked and prayed, listening for the sound that would mean things had worked their way through his system and he would be fine. But the heavy cache of fear that laid in the pit of her stomach and squeezed her heart was always there. The clock ticked on. She put one booted foot in front of the other. Talking, always talking to Tonka, she walked with him.

The horse nickered very little now. His stomach was bloated and tender. The minute she stopped walking, the horse made one turn and fell down, exhausted.

The boys and Buck were back again, offering to take turns walking the horse. She shrieked at them as she snapped Tonka on the rear with the riding crop to make him get up again. Fear and heartache made her unreasonable. ''Get out of here. He's mine. Get up, Tonka. Get up.''

Buck watched her and muttered to himself, ''Looks just like her father.''

''What?'' Wes sided Buck.

''Nothing,'' Buck dodged and moved away.

Wes shook his head and went out with the boys. He couldn't stand to watch her, tears streaming down her face as she had to hit the horse to make him rise again. But he knew if it was his horse he would be doing the same thing. No one who loves a horse gives up very easily. He walked to the phone and dialed the vet. It was time.

Just as Wes entered the barn, the horse staggered and staggered again. With a snort and a sigh he fell, heavily. Victoria jumped to hold his head down to make rolling harder, but the animal, in his pain, kicked his legs high and rolled halfway. Wes ran and slammed his body over the horse, glad he had the syringe of pain medicine ready. He punched the needle in the horse's hide and injected some relief.

Her voice filled with more agony than the horse was experiencing, she looked back at him. "It's time, Wes. Call the vet."

"I did. He's on his way."

She soothed the animal, as she lay half against him. "You'll feel better soon now, old boy." The pain medicine kicked in and the animal lay quieter, his breathing ragged and quick.

They lay there. The three of them. The animal in total distress; Wes and Victoria sad and resigned. She ran her hand across the horse's cheek and laid her face beneath his ear. "It'll be okay real soon. Go to sleep, Tonka." Her voice shook and Wes reached to touch her shoulder. She shrugged him off.

The vet arrived armed with a huge syringe. Handing the tube to Wes, he fitted the needle in the artery at the horse's neck.

Victoria had no tears now. She sat with the horse's head in her lap, petting him, crooning to him. The horse looked at her, eyes filled with pain . . . and love. Wes felt his breath snag.

"He'll go right away," the vet explained as he injected the life-taking medication, "but it will take a full fifteen minutes before his heart stops beating."

The horse never made another sound, merely drifted away in the time it took for Victoria to draw a deep breath. Though the animal no longer lived, his eyes remained open and vacant. When Wes offered her his hand, she ignored it and continued to sit with the animal's head in her lap and stroked and rocked while death took over. The relief that flooded through Victoria came out as silent tears that rolled slowly down her face.

Wes and the doctor left them there, knowing it was time they needed alone.

She walked from the barn half an hour later. Wes waited, leaning against the fence, his foot propped on the bottom rail. He chucked the cigarette he had just lit and smashed it out. He walked toward her.

She stopped him with a hand she held out. "I need a bath and some sleep."

He matched his steps with her own. "You need to eat. I'll bring something up to your room."

"No."

"Yes."

She stopped in the street, tourists milling all around. She didn't care. Dammit, she didn't care. "Leave me alone. It's your fault he's dead. Yours. Get away from me." Even as she said the hurting words, she hated herself. She hated everything right now. She hurt so bad. She ached. She felt sick. Let him feel the same way! That horse died because someone was careless and she knew it wasn't her.

Grief made for erratic actions, Wes knew. But her words cut him with the swiftness of a razor. The unfairness of her assumptions riled him. They both needed space right now, and instead of the closeness they could share, he gave her that space and felt a wedge driven between them with more pain than he had felt watching the horse die.

She sensed eyes on her as she dragged herself through the hotel doors and up the long stairway. Her feet seemed leaden and her heart ached. Once in her room, she leaned against the door and simply slid down to sit on the floor. The big tears came then. When she was alone. Sobs racking her body, she let her grief loose.

She pulled her boots off where she sat. Then, forcing cramped legs to work, she rose and stripped the rest of her clothes off, leaving them in a trail across the floor.

When the bath had filled, she slid into the warmth and let
the cleansing water work kinks and pains from her body.
Victoria wished it were so easy to do the same for the
heart.

Wrapping a towel around her tired body, she walked
toward the bed, only slightly feeling the burn of two big
blisters she had worked on her feet. Without pulling the
quilt down, she fell across the bed. No tears now. She
was dry. She was wrung out completely. Exhausted, she
gave way to the sleep that she had pushed away for so
long. As the sun set, Victoria closed her eyes and fell into
the dark pit of a dreamless sleep.

Her door creaked slowly open. Nick walked quietly to
the bed and sat down next to her, easily so as not to wake
her. His hand moved to stroke her hair, lightly. Don't
wake her. The smooth glow of moist skin above the towel
beckoned his hand but he didn't dare. Not now. The time
would come when they would be together. He could wait.
The towel covered her bottom but her long legs rested
against the bed. His poor Victoria. But she would get over
it and now she would know that Wes wasn't the man for
her. Surely, now she would know.

He picked up the hairbrush that lay on the table next to
the bed and held it in his hands. Toying with a necklace
carelessly thrown on the dresser, the rubies she wore so
often at her ears, Nick enjoyed. In the light of day, he
wouldn't dare do these things. But at night . . .

Opening the door to her closet, he ran his hands over
her clothes, caught the scent of her from the traces of
perfume lingering there.

A man had to win his woman's love. In the time frame
that Nick lived in, his mind talked to him. Told him what
to do. And if winning didn't work, then he should take.
The sound of the breeze picking up outside her window
caused him to walk to it. He looked up and down the
street of Glory Town and smiled. In the daylight, horses
and cowboys, bandits and the law would fill that street.

In his head, as always, he heard the strains of an old song. The strum of a guitar and the restless stirring of a cattle herd bedding down for the night.

Looking down, he could see himself. Strutting down the middle of the town, guns strapped against his thighs. Coming from the other end was Cooper. They would face it off. Twenty paces and draw. He grinned as he saw Wes facedown in the dirt.

Victoria moaned in her sleep and shifted a little. Dropping the curtain back in place, he turned his gaze to her. It eased the dull pain in his heart to watch her. It allowed him to keep his eyes open without hurting. He loved her.

He sat a long while with her, and as the room deepened with night, he got up. He lightly touched the third finger of her left hand where he could picture his wedding ring. A smile curled his lips beneath his droopy mustache. And then the terrible sadness of the day shot through his heart. The horse had died. The horse had suffered. His heart ached and a sick feeling filled his stomach. Then a pain shot through his head and he reached up to press his fists to it. It was worse this time. He reeled with the sharpness of the attack and almost fell to the floor. A single tear slipped down his cheek. The slicing effect of pain eased and he turned to creep from her room.

_____ NINE _____

J. Weston Cooper stared out the window. The last of the tourists had gone. Night had taken over Glory Town. And it was damn-well welcome. Resting a hip on the windowsill, he wondered. Who was responsible for leaving the stall door open and the feed room door?

He had racked his brain and come to the final conclusion that he hadn't been careless. He had gone over every step in his mind and he remembered, clearly, latching Tonka's stall and locking the feed room door.

So now what? Find out. And then what? Whoever did it didn't mean to. Suppose it was just one of the kids around who wanted to ride Tonka or was just curious as to what was behind the locked door? It was just something they would have to put behind them. But could she? There had been hate in her eyes when she had looked at him. But then there had also been times when she looked at him with gratitude, with hope. And with something much, much more.

She needed time to recover. He remembered the first time he had lost a horse. He had been twelve. The scars were still there. Every time something like this happened he asked himself why he was in the horse business. And then he remembered. The good times outweighed the bad. She should know that, too. Maybe she did and he just had to give her time to work it out.

A lone figure darted across the road and disappeared into the shadows toward the back lot and the trailers. Alert, Wes watched but then chalked it up to his overactive nerves at the moment. It was probably just one of the men, late and trying to get home before the little woman got behind the door with a rolling pin raised over her head.

Tired, Wes kicked his boots off and laid across the bed. Sometime today he realized how desperately he loved the woman who slept in the bedroom next to his. When it had happened was elusive, but it was definite to him now. *I love her.* He rolled the words around in his mind and it scared him but not by much. He thought he had been in love before only to find out he had made a tragic mistake, one a little girl paid for. This time he would make sure everything went right. Positive. But he would have to be patient. Give her time. So much was uncertain in her life. He wanted to offer that certainty. Be a constant. *And suppose she's not interested after a while?* his mind questioned him.

Dammit! She will be, he told that off-part of his brain. *She'd have to be or I couldn't feel the way I do now.* The best move he had ever made was to put a sudden stop to the direction his life had taken. Otherwise, he would never have had the chance to meet Victoria. He'd slip away early in the morning and bring Katie back with him. She wouldn't give Victoria time to mourn around all day. And that was what she needed. Not him right now, but his daughter.

He wanted to open his door and then hers. He wanted to go to her even if she were asleep and lie down on the quilt beside her, pull her to him, and cradle her head on his chest. She needed him, even if she didn't realize it. He would hold her . . . just hold her. Let her cry it all out. Or let her swear and curse and stomp and scream. He wanted to be with her now. He needed to be with her.

Turning on his stomach, he closed his eyes, forcing the scene from his brain. Her tormented eyes haunted him. Her teary face saddened him. He slept, tense and fitful.

Katie stood on tiptoes to reach the doorknob and then turned it, jerking the door open. Smiling back at her daddy, she marched right up to Victoria's bed and shook her.

Who dared disturb her sleep? Opening her eyes, she took a moment to focus. A foot away from her stood a grinning little imp, long-legged gray rabbit under one arm. "Katie. Hi."

"Daddy brought me." She pointed to the doorway. Victoria followed that little finger and saw him, looming giant-like in the door frame. Becoming aware of her near-nakedness, she took hold of the end of the quilt and rolled, pulling it with her.

"What'd you wanna to do today?" the child asked, her face all aglow.

"The question is, what do you want to do?" Victoria slid backwards and leaned against the headboard.

"Well, Daddy said I should take you to town and buy you a new dress." Katie pulled herself up on the bed, legs dangling. "He said we women liked to do things like that."

"He did, did he?" She looked at Wes, not sure how she felt about him just now. Her stomach was still in a knot. He stood there so sure of himself. So tough. So confident.

He removed his hat. "Nothing like a day of shopping to chase away the blues, my mother always said."

Moved by his gesture, but not ready to let go of her doubts and anxiety, Victoria turned a weak smile back to the child. "Well, Katie, I suppose I could use a day in town. But what's poor Daddy going to do all day without you?''

"Oh, he's coming, too. He said he's going to take us out to lunch.''

Lunch? Right. But it was sweet of him to think of getting her away for a day. Or was it his guilt rearing its ugly head? God, could she really blame him? He was sure it wasn't carelessness and he ought to know. He'd worked with horses all his life. Fresh pain rolled over her and she shoved it away. Pulling Katie in her lap, she planted a kiss on her round cheek and then patted her on her ruffled butt.

"Then scoot and let me get dressed. We'll make history in this town, partner.'' After the two of them promised to wait downstairs for her, she got up and got dressed. Looking at herself in the mirror, she looked closer. Dark circles shadowed her eyes. Her skin was pale. Dragging a hand through her hair, she turned and walked to the window. As she looked out, it seemed like any other morning. The world hadn't stopped just because her heart was broken.

Outside, Victoria climbed in the back of the pickup and held out her hands for Katie. Wes laughed and scooped his daughter up and lifted her into the truck. As he drove away, he heard their laughter over the hum of the engine. Peace filled him. Something. Some instinct told him it would be all right. It would all work itself out.

Redwood was a nice town with a sprawling mall on the outskirts. Victoria found more pleasure in buying Katie the new overalls and sneakers than in allowing Katie to pick out a dress for her. Katie's tastes ran toward the bright. Victoria ended up leaving the store with a sundress done in daisies. Not understated little flowers, but great big yellow willowy ones with bright green leaves. Katie loved it. It meant a lot to Victoria.

Despite the fact that Victoria and Wes found a delightful little French coffee shop right there in the mall, he gave in to his daughter's preference for fast food. Katie feasted on the burgers and fries while Wes and Victoria shared bits of chicken and a large chocolate shake. They talked of silly things and made jokes for Katie. Wes noticed that Victoria kept her eyes from lingering on his for too long.

They decided, after prodding from Katie, who was getting spoiled rotten in one day, to go to a movie. The usher commented on the "lovely family" as they made their way down the aisle, arms laden with popcorn, greasy with butter and gritty with salt, balancing huge cups of cola.

Katie sat between them, proud as a peacock with two tails, and looked from her dad to Victoria and back again. Even she didn't miss the fact that halfway through the movie Wes slid his arm over Katie's chair to toy with the sleeve of Victoria's blouse. Wes wanted to talk to her. To hear the soothing tones of her voice. Wanted to see the light come back in her eyes. He waited.

Sometime during the day, Wes had acquired a bag. It was getting dark and Katie was half asleep as she walked when Victoria noticed it. "Didn't Katie get enough? You had to stop and get her more."

"This is for you, but you can't have it yet. Are you two riding in the back of the truck on the way home, too?"

"No. We haven't got the strength to hold on, and when you get home, Katie and I might have flown off with the wind and you wouldn't even know it in time to look for us. We'd be carried off to the Land of Lost Boys and never be seen again."

Katie laughed and crawled up in Victoria's lap. She was asleep before Wes made his first right turn out of town.

"So, what's in the bag?"

"Wouldn't you like to know?" he answered smugly.

"I would." She smiled into his lazy eyes.

"Later. Did you enjoy the day?"

"Yes. You accomplished what you set out to do. I didn't think of . . . all day. Hardly. It was sweet of you."

He grunted. "I never thought of myself as sweet. I don't think I like that."

"Wes. I . . . I don't blame you. I said some pretty mean things to you yesterday but . . ."

He patted her shoulder and let his fingers slide down her arm to twine with hers. "Let's not talk about it. What's done is done. Whoever . . . Whatever happened to cause that tragedy . . . we might never know. It's over. It's part of the risk you take any time you deal with horses."

They rode the rest of the way in silence. Arriving in Glory Town, they decided Katie should stay in Victoria's room for the night since she was already soundly sleeping. "Where are you going to sleep?" Wes asked slyly.

"The bed is big enough for both of us," she answered smiling.

"Mine?" he teased.

"No, mine, for us girls."

Turning the bed covers down, Victoria laid Katie down and tucked her in, clothes and all. When she turned, she slammed into Wes, a solid barricade of cowboy. He corralled her in his arms, and before she had time to think, his mouth crushed hers. A deep, dark kiss. One that didn't ask but demanded. One that didn't hide the fact that he wanted her and wanted her now.

Sinking against him, her body relaxed. She knew she was melding to him like hot candle wax, but didn't try to stop it. Magic. Sorcery. Necromancy. His hands, his mouth worked her away into a world of hallucinations and sleight of hand. Nothing was defined. Nothing was as she'd seen it before. Absolutely nothing was as she'd known it before. Together they seemed to disappear . . . away into a glowing darkness, lit by embers, filled with heat and haze.

He reared his head, reveling in the passion he saw in her heavy-lidded eyes. Needing to taste her again, he trailed his lips up her throat, behind her ear, and across her cheek, only to slam into her mouth again, tongue seeking tongue, teeth grinding teeth. Sweetness and fire. He had never guessed the whole of it. His stomach muscles coiled and knotted as his arm banded around her waist, one hand cupping the back of her head.

Where had the depth of this emotion come from? As it tore at his doubts, it built his knowledge. They were meant to be together this way and every other way. Fate had seen to it that they both knew what they didn't want before they tasted what they did.

She was liquid nitro in his arms, sliding like mercury through every pore in his body. He could never be the same again. Never be without her. She had slipped into his system and could never be washed away. He would never let that happen. Branded. Scorched. Wes called on all his control not to take her to the floor right now.

Pulling her trapped arms free, she wound them around his neck and stood on her tiptoes for more contact. His body was hard and strong and she felt his heart pound against hers. Wild. Out of control. Or was it very much in control, guiding and seeking, affixing and finding? Her breath gone, she pulled away from the kiss.

His eyes sparkled darkly in the dimly lit room. There was naked passion in his eyes. He wanted her. She couldn't mistake that. Was it because it was a good and natural thing to happen between a man and a woman if they cared enough about each other? No, she judged a man like him didn't take such things lightly. And she wanted him. She couldn't deny it. Body, mind, and soul, she ached for him. The old doubt niggled its way into her brain and she leaned her head against his shoulder. She hated the doubt. Despised her reluctance to simply accept things and say yes. Yes. This is what I want. This man is who I want to spend the rest of my life with. It was right there. Under her palms, waiting.

His lips were in her hair, at her temple, and trailing down. He rubbed his mouth against hers and then left it, wanting more to kiss the pulse point at her throat. He pushed her blouse aside and moved his warm, moist, seeking mouth over her collarbone and down.

Her breath snagged and she became all too aware that this was going to go too far with a child asleep close by. Remembering well what it was like to make love with this man, she gently pushed him away and rested her forehead on his chest.

"Make love with me, Victoria. Come to my room."

His voice was husky and low. He brought his fingers up under her chin and forced her to look at him. What he saw there disturbed him. "You still don't trust, do you? You or me?"

"Either. I can't think clearly when you're kissing me. The other night . . . it was beautiful and it made me want to spend every waking hour with you. You do things to me, Wes. You make me feel . . . I've never felt this way before but . . ."

He blew out his breath and moved away, pulling her toward the door and away from his sleeping daughter, afraid they would wake her, and he didn't want anything to stop their conversation. "I've been looking for something in my life. Until now I couldn't identify it. Right now I'm holding it in my arms." He pulled her back into the circle of them and held her there.

"I . . ."

He put his fingers to her lips. "Shhhh. Don't talk. Just listen. Really listen to my words. I've been mixed up. Off track for so long, it just hit me all of a sudden from out of nowhere. I do love you, Victoria. I can wait for you to realize it's the same with you. But not for long. Do you understand? Not for long."

"I've been wrong before, Wes. I'm scared of making the wrong decision. Making love isn't all there is to a relationship. I don't know that I can go on without you if anything goes wrong. Men and women make love all the time without cementing promises. I won't have it handed back politely. I won't love anyone who won't love me back. Totally and without question.''

"You got it.'' His mouth touched hers once more, only lightly this time, only hinting of what would be. "I feel the same. I gave my love once but it was never handed back politely. It was ripped from my chest and thrown in my face. I have a hard time with pride, Victoria. Like I said before, I won't ask again. You'll come to me all on your own. It has to be your decision. All or nothing. But if I don't like your decision, well then the rules might change. Sometimes you can't see what's in front of your face unless someone opens your eyes.''

She wormed her way out of his arms before there would be no turning back. Instantly, she felt the emptiness, the cold incompleteness come back. Like pieces of the same puzzle turned sideways, they eyed each other. Only their hands touched.

She wanted more than anything to take his hand and guide him down the hall. But something stopped her. She hated it, but something made it impossible for her to tell him that she was afraid. Afraid of not knowing herself. Afraid of not knowing him. Always too cautious in life, she was only now learning to spread her wings and fly. She didn't want to fly blindly into the side of a mountain . . . and die.

"If only I could be sure . . .'' Her words sounded stupid even to her ear.

"I'll see to it you're sure. One way or another, lady, I'll see to it.''

A charge ran through her body. She knew he meant what he said. She knew he could melt her and seduce her to the point of no return. She remembered, all too well, how willingly she had gone with him before. Into that beautiful place only lovers go. Lovers. A smile curled her lips. She was grateful he wasn't pushing her. He placed a very conservative kiss on her cheek and left her standing there.

* * *

It was only nine o'clock. After taking a cooling walk, Wes headed over to the jailhouse to talk to Buck. Tomorrow was the first bank robbery that had been practiced over and over. A few last details and it would be all set. He had already measured the change in the men. He had his fingers crossed that all went well in the morning. It would add to their self-respect and be the first real step toward the completion of their education.

Not able to sleep, Victoria slipped out of bed and into the new sundress, deciding to see if Wes was still at the jailhouse jabbering with Buck. It would please him to see her wearing the dress his daughter had picked out for her. And she wanted to please him in some way. Plus, she felt an irrepressible urge to be around him. Only near him. To look, to savor.

"Do Not Forsake Me, Oh My Darlin' " piped softly and twined into the background from carefully concealed speakers. During the gunfights they blared the legends and increased the suspense and tension. While the stage was being robbed, the speaker touted the lawlessness of yesteryear. Tonight the sound simply took Victoria back a century into a beautiful world. She smiled and took a good look at the sky, crowded with bright, twinkling stars, and thought of all the women in years gone by, buried now beneath the grass, who looked at this same sky and felt love.

Going the back way because the dress was certainly not period costume, she approached the jailhouse from the back. Upon hearing the men's voices, she slowed down to sneak up on them. When she heard words that turned her blood to icicles and her mind to fire, she froze.

"Buck, I'm serious. She can't ever find out under what circumstance I took this job. She doesn't trust anyone now and she never will again if she hears the truth."

Buck snorted and poured himself another drink. "Wes, that's bull. Victoria knows me. She'd understand that at first it was just a job to you. One I sorta twisted your arm to make you take. Didn't even tell you my new stubborn Eastern partner was a woman. Just to discourage that partner and send him packing.'' He laughed. Buck laughed. She couldn't believe it.

Her skin prickled. The hair at the base of her neck stood on end. Air, there seemed to be none, trapped itself in her lungs and refused to budge. Her brain buzzed from the lack of it. Backing up, she never heard Wes's next words. She didn't want to. Enough was enough. So it was all a hoax. A cruel trap they had all fallen into. A cold, penetrating wave of reality washed over her heart and nearly stopped it. Vicious emotions tangled and began a slow weave of disbelief through her. She doubled over as pain racked her body and her mind.

A clean cut with a knife, a blow from a weapon. Nothing. Nothing could compare to the wrenching actuality of his words. Just when she was opening up, inviting . . . Double-crossed. Sold out. Deceived. Hoodwinked. And by J. Weston Cooper. The man she imagined herself in love with. Just her rotten luck. Or was it just the way life is? All the rest, all the good stuff was just made of fairy tales. Buck. She could believe it of him . . . almost expect it. It never left her mind that he had to feel cheated finding out that the other half of Glory Town was hers, not his. But Wes? When she was on the verge of letting the walls down and believing? Trusting?

As she ran the back way to the hotel, her mind tumbled like leaves in the wind. A sham. All of this was a sham. But how could it be? It couldn't be. But she heard it clear as day. They were in on a plot, together, to get her to go home. Was killing her horse part of the plan? No, not even Wes could be so cruel. Did he set out to make her look foolish with the guns and riding? Was wooing her and making her feel things for him a way of getting her off guard? That didn't make any sense. Nothing did. Running, she didn't see the man making his way toward the back lot and plowed right into him.

She sent him sprawling and tumbled on top of him. Nick, not believing his luck when he realized who was in his arms, smiled. "All you had to do was holler. I would have stopped. You didn't have to snowball me." Then he saw her and something snapped inside him. That same something that had been stretched tight since the first day he'd seen her. "Vic. What's wrong?"

He could see the tears she didn't even know she was shedding glisten on her cheeks in the shadows. Something in his heart turned cold. Like a stone, it weighed heavy in his chest. Standing, he offered her his hand.

Disoriented, Victoria looked up at the man from her seat on the ground. Cool air returned to her lungs and she let him help her up. "I guess yesterday's events just got to me, Nick. Sorry I knocked you down."

"Well, I'm not. Come on back to my trailer with me. I have some whiskey. It'll brace you up real good. Come on."

"I can't. Katie is asleep in my room. I'm afraid to be gone too long. She might wake up and look for me."

He took her hand. "The dining room then. You'll be right there. It's the least you can do after throwing me to the ground like a bull steer."

Suddenly, like a wave of water building and crashing to the shore, she didn't want his hands on her. She didn't want his support, his friendliness, or his help. A sob tore from her throat. Claustrophobia set in and she thrashed about searching for air.

Nick didn't back away. Catching her arms and pinning them to her sides, he forced her to calm down, to listen to the soothing sounds coming from his throat. She fought him. He held tight. Finally, breathless and weak, she slumped against him.

They stayed like that for a measured period of time.

She fragile and shaky, wavering. He strong, stalwart, and staunch. He stroked her hair and kept talking to her.

His words floated to the back of her mind as fragments of Wes's words crowded in the forefront. "If she hears the truth. Can't ever find out." And Buck's "Discourage the partner. Send him packing."

Wes had, just a little while before that, held her in his arms and professed to love her. And she had wanted to believe him. Oh, how she had tried to believe him. It was too much to think about. Too much to deal with. She wanted relief and this man who kept her bound tightly to him was offering it to her.

Trying to clear her mind, she let him keep his arm around her shoulder to guide her. How much was a woman supposed to take in one forty-eight-hour period? It was funny, terribly funny, how all her excitement and exhilaration of the past weeks could turn to exasperation and desperation. Her mind swam. She needed the arms of a friend, badly. But she didn't have any. Not here. Not in this godforsaken Wild West town that she had come to love and think of as her own. It was too much. Too damned much.

Nick led her to a back table and got her settled in a chair. Then he returned with two whiskeys and the rest of the bottle.

She sipped hers and then gulped it. Pouring more, she looked at it and knocked it back. What the heck?

"Easy there now, girl. You'll end up getting drunk."

"I don't care. Maybe that's what I need."

"Maybe what you need is Nick." He reached across the table and lifted a curl, tucking it behind her ear.

She recognized it right away. Nick was being seductive. What the hell was this? A full conspiracy? Was the whole darn reenactment team in on Buck's special little payroll? Get rid of the Easterner. Get rid of the woman any way you have to. Though her head was spinning, Victoria stood up and glared at Nick.

Though it was Wes she wanted to punch, she got very close to Nick's face and whispered, "Leave me alone. Go away. You're all the same. You're all hoping I'll go back . . ."

He grabbed her wrist and stood up, coming around to haul her to him. "No. You belong here. You light up this town. Before you came it was dark, so dark sometimes I couldn't see. But now, now that you're here . . . you're never going to leave."

Victoria looked at Nick. For the first time, she really studied the way he looked at her. His eyes were dark and nearly desperate, and dangerous. Spinning out of his grasp, liquor woozy, she headed for the stairs. Crazy. She had crossed the line. She'd gone around the bend and didn't even know it till now. That's the only answer. As she climbed the stairs, she fought to think clearly but sense evaded her. Only slashes of pictures darted across her mind. Only fragments of sentences typed their way across her brain like newspaper headlines. She laughed. What was next? A straitjacket? A room with rubber walls and attendants with no ears and huge bald heads that shone in the light or something equally bizarre? You have just entered the Twilight Zone . . .

Waking up was very painful. Her head throbbed. Her eyes felt swollen and tight. Her jaw ached from clenching her teeth all night. The fact that a fat little hand was poking her, prodding her to wake up didn't clear the cobwebs for several seconds.

God, what a nightmare. "Morning, Katie. Did you sleep well?" She certainly hadn't. As she pulled the warm, soft little girl against her for a hug, something was trying to push itself to the front lines of her brain cells. Yes. That was it. Wes. The turncoat. Traitor. Benedict Arnold. Her heart broke. And then the sharp pieces stabbed their way through her system. She flopped back down on the bed, willing her body to feel. Nothing.

It was as if her body had traded itself for Styrofoam. No emotion seeped out through the little white holes of her existence. She was only an entity with her brain trapped on top.

As her feet touched the floor, determination thudded into her gray matter. Bullheaded and pious men. She'd stay. Just long enough to make them wish they had never heard her name. Never laid eyes on her. And after she made them the sorriest bunch of cowpunchers to exist on earth, she'd leave. Back to her vets, back to her friends . . . and what? The constricting life at Twin Forks where her life was being squeezed from her? No. Not to stay but she would go somewhere. Glory Town could go to hell. She'd open her own town and put them out of business. Yes, that was an idea. See, all she had to do was think clearly. And to do that she had to keep some distance between herself and J. Weston Cooper. Damn.

She couldn't believe that she could begin to love a man and then find out he was deceitful . . . or had he really, truly come to love her? . . . No. She wouldn't analyze it. She would go on instinct. As Wes had taught the men, she would come out with both guns blazing and let the chips fall where they may. No play-acting. No guesses. No more wondering. She'd been a fool once before, but it would never happen again. *But he loves me,* her mind cried. *Hah!* her brain answered. Taking a deep breath, she smiled at the little girl waiting for her and thanked whatever gods watched over fools that all emotion was replaced by cold, startling anger.

"Well, Katie. Let's you and me mosey on down to the dining room and see what Joe is serving for breakfast. Did I say that right?"

Katie giggled and Victoria took that as a yes. Pulling on her jeans and cotton shirt, she jammed her feet into her Western boots, blisters be damned. Victoria dressed for battle.

Dazzled. That must be it. And thrown by the death of

her horse. Excuses. Excuses. She was a bad judge of things. Now she had the proof. And she was going to swing it by the tail.

She took Katie by the hand and they literally marched down the stairs to the dining room.

"Your daddy's first staged bank robbery is being rehearsed at nine. Watch me throw a monkey wrench in the works."

Katie looked up at Victoria and asked her, "What's monkey works?"

Victoria threw her head back and laughed. A cold, calculated laugh. *Watch. Just watch,* she thought as she smiled at the sweet little girl. "After breakfast I want you to stay and help Joe. I'll be back later and we'll do something. Okay?"

"Okay."

As she ate, she plotted. Everything was supposed to go smoothly just because "big man" had choreographed the scene. By now everyone must be in on the joke. Get the girl to leave town. By sundown. Ha! After today they would be praying for her to leave. She could play the game, too.

"Joe. Look after Katie for me for a while, will you?"

"Of course. After I dry these few dishes, me and Katie will go down to the barn and saddle that new pony her daddy bought her the other day. I'll keep a good eye on her, don't worry."

"Thanks, Joe. I won't be long." No, this would take only minutes. A short amount of time to put things in order.

TEN

She stomped out into the glaring sunlight. Victoria looked up on the roof, shading her eyes with her hand from the sun. Yes, good old Nick was there preparing to be shot down, to act out his spiraling fall from the building. She had seen it plenty of times and he was good. She toyed with the idea of moving his air-filled mattress, just a few inches one way, but shoved it aside. She couldn't get much revenge if she was going to have to spend the rest of her days behind bars for murder, although at this point she knew she was capable of it.

She moved quickly. She had no problem finding the tools to build her revenge. A hammer. Screwdriver. Three potted cactus plants. A trip to the kitchen netted her a half-full can of shortening. She checked to be sure she had a pair of handcuffs swinging from her belt and that her gun was loaded with blanks.

Running to the barn, she swung around the corner only moments before the men filed in. In the prop room, she slashed slits in the bottoms of the money bags. She grabbed the crowbar and was running out again unseen. At the bank she was able to quickly complete her work. She pried two boards off the walk and then set them back so they appeared to be stable. Placing a few cactus plants strategically made her chuckle. She tapped the bolts from the door loose so that it would take one swing open but probably not the second. Tying a rope around one end of the porch post, she coiled it and hid it for later.

Most of the other reenactors not involved in this skit gathered around to watch the results of Wes's hard work.

Eight men were involved in this show, two on the roof because the band of desperadoes was expected and was to be ambushed. Two men were in the bank and four were holdup men. She knew Wes would cross the street and watch from a good vantage point to pick up any mistakes. She hoped he saw every detail.

When he walked down the road to take his place, just seeing him squeezed her heart. But she pushed the feeling away and took a place close by. Larry and Jeff took their places inside the bank as tellers. Tim joined Nick atop the building. Wes signaled and the action began.

From the west, the desperadoes rode up, guns drawn and bandannas covering their faces. Dismounting, they whipped the reins in a circle over the hitch rail, looked this way and that, and then dashed into the bank. Victoria held her breath when one of the men teetered over a loose board but relaxed when he simply pounded on into the bank.

Now she had only seconds to act. It didn't matter at this point that she would be seen. No one could stop the chaos that would follow. She pulled the loose boards up and tossed them aside, leaving enough of a space to trip them yet not wide enough to break an ankle. Then she stretched the rope across the walk and let it lie there. Running around the horses, she smeared great gobs of shortening on the saddles. Back beside the porch post, she held the end of the rope with one hand and her revolver with the other and waited . . .

In five seconds the men backed out of the bank. The door flopped aside and down with a loud crash. The men jumped, startled, but recovered right away. After all, they were actors and nothing should stop the scene. Firing their pistols, they made a break for the horses. The first two men stumbled on the missing boards, fell, looked around confused, but righted themselves and went for their mounts. The last two men sprawled into the dust when they tripped over the rope she wrapped around the post and drew tight, cussing when they rolled into the cactus pots and picked up some spines. Victoria's wicked laughter rolled across the air.

And then again, she laughed as the two men swung into the saddles only to slide almost off the other side. The play money finally worked its way through the bags and fluttered out and up on the breeze. While the men struggled to stay in the greased saddles, the horses circled and skittered in confusion. Victoria jumped toward the two men sprawled on the ground and handcuffed them together. Working her gun, she killed the two on horseback and then ran into the street to fire at the men on the roof. She plowed them unexpectedly. Nick laughed and took a dive to his mattress. Tim holstered his gun and merely stood, guffawing and holding his stomach muscles at the hapless group below.

Both hands raised in the air in triumph, she turned to face Wes and Buck with a bright smile on her face. Confusion. Anger. The reenactors dusted themselves off and lined up. They waited to find out what this was all about.

Victoria heard one of the men lose his seat in the saddle and hit the ground with a thud and a four-letter word. She leveled her gun at Wes and Buck and walked slowly toward them, gunfighter-like.

"Bang bang. You're dead," she said and stopped fifty feet from them.

Both men were still stunned and speechless. They stood staring at her, waiting and watching for her next move. Neither man could decide just what it was he was witnessing.

Victoria advanced again a little slower. "All you high-riding heroes are the same. Egos. Giant glass ones. Come one, come all. I've got a story to tell. About a town full of traitors and pious little people who thought they could band together and get rid of the gutless creature from the East.''

Wes took a step toward her, a smile creeping across his mouth. This had to be a joke. Buck shook his head and hooked his thumbs in his belt.

Victoria stopped Wes from coming one step closer when she fired her gun in the air. "One more step J. Weston Big Man Cooper, the teacher, the cowboy . . . the turncoat and I'll blow your cocky head off. See, I can play the game, too. Only this time, I almost wish the blanks were bullets so I could shoot you in the butt.

"Thought you could hire ole Wes here to scare me off, did you, Buck? Low, underhanded snake. You made a fool of me, all of you." She waved the gun around to include everyone. "Well," she laughed, "now we're even. You should see yourselves. Well, I can stay and make your lives hell since I own half of this, half of you. Or I could demand that my half be bought out or have this place sold. Or I can fire all of you and get a new crew. But you all would like that too much. Then I would be exactly what Buck wants you to believe I am.''

"Now listen, missy," Buck began.

"No, you listen. I came here eager and willing to learn. Anxious to fit in and be a part of what I thought was a nice but weird family. I liked you. I liked all of you. But worse, I trusted you. And then you hired Wes to get rid of me, discourage me. How dare you? All of you were in on it. All of you." She swung her hand in a wide circle. "And you all betrayed me." Her heart was encased in steel and the coldness it splayed throughout her system threatened to make her sick.

How the hell did she find out? Who told her and what did they tell her? Wes turned to the small crowd and quietly asked them to disperse. They did, but some were very reluctant. They wanted to see how this turned out. Whatever it was. They were at a loss as to what Victoria was talking about. But it was obvious that Buck and Wes knew.

Nick disappeared. Tim climbed down from the roof.

Wes walked to Victoria. He had never wanted her to find out. Didn't have any idea how she had. But he damn sure was going to be certain she knew the whole story. "Point taken. Now, let's you and me and Buck go to the hotel and sit down and have a talk. You've had your laugh at our expense."

She holstered the gun. Tears burned behind her eyes but she refused to let them fall. This little joke of hers hadn't lent itself to the satisfying result she thought she would feel. She merely seemed more the fool. Anger jumped in to protect her.

"No more talk. None. I'm out of here. I just wanted you all to taste the bitterness of being the court jester before I left." She jerked her arm from Wes when he moved to pull her near him.

His dark eyes sparked dangerously when he reached to stop her again. "You seriously think I'll let you walk away from here, from me, without a fight? The middle of the street is no place to talk about this."

His eyes. What she saw there . . . or wanted to see almost cast her resolve aside. A flash of memory of the two of them, tangled together in ecstasy, feverishly uniting in the act of love, made her face burn. The remembrance of their soft words and contentment as she lay with her head on his chest almost broke her heart. But now her heart was lead, only a heavy, emotionless weight beneath her breast.

Buck sided with Wes. "Wes is right, Vic. Once you understand . . . you don't know what you think you know. For once in your life listen to me."

She shook her head. "The choice isn't yours. Not anymore. I wouldn't believe a word you said, either of you. So back off and . . ."

The sound of defeat in her voice, the look of weariness in her eyes scared the hell out of Wes. A desperation sliced through him when he realized just how serious all this was. He had to set it right. It couldn't all go for nothing. He didn't want life without her.

"Fire! Fire! The barn's on fire." The cry split the air and it seemed the dispersing crew took flight all at once like a gaggle of startled geese.

The three of them turned in unison half expecting this to be another joke but instead saw the black smoke billowing and spiraling from the roof of the old barn.

Terror froze the blood in her veins. Victoria's heart clogged her throat. "My God. Katie's down there with Joe to ride her pony."

Wes grabbed her arm. "Katie's down there?" She didn't miss his look of disbelief and then panic before he was off and running, followed by everyone within earshot.

Shock and horror kept Victoria rooted to the spot for several seconds before she was able to make her feet go. Running for the phone to dial nine-one-one, she prayed and damned herself for not keeping the child with her. This was her fault. It hit her as she hung up the phone and started back toward the barn, running for dear life.

She prayed someone would wake her up and it would all be some cruel nightmare, but as she approached the fire scene she knew it wasn't. The heat. The sparks zinging toward the sky. The dazed and broken voices of the people moving everywhere around her told her it wasn't.

The old boards and the stacks of hay fed the fire quickly. By the time Wes slid around the corner, the doorway was engulfed in flames. The wind was coming from the opposite end of the barn and had the front end blocked with searing heat and smoke. The townspeople coupled hoses and some lined up starting a bucket brigade from the water troughs but the fire was quickly getting out of hand.

His heart pounded in his head. His little girl was inside that hell pit. He had to get to her. Some of the men were jerking on the side door. The metal was hot and smoke hindered their movements. "Katie!" Wes ran to the end that was still free of flames and tried to pry the boards loose with his hands. "Katie!"

Victoria remembered the crowbar and turned back. She returned wielding it like a sword. She pounded at the boards with it. Wes jerked it away from her and stuck it between two slabs of wood. The boards creaked, split, and finally gave way. It was hot. Incredibly scorching. Sweat streaked his face and plastered his shirt to his body. Smoke blackened them both as they tore at the boards. More men came and pried and hammered at the wood. Incredible heat pushed at her as they made the opening wider. The men shoved her aside.

Choking and coughing, hands bleeding from splinters, Victoria slumped against the fence and prayed. Wes's horse was the first to find the opening and he thundered out. Wes bolted through the same opening, into the gray, airless building. The fire roared like a train engine. Wes didn't come out. He had disappeared into that blazing inferno of hell and he hadn't come out.

In slow motion, like an old movie flickering on the screen, the cold, hard reality of what was happening made its way through her shocked brain. Wes. Katie. Her entire life was in that barn. In that fire that tauntingly promised to take them away from her.

A new strength surged into her veins, reinforcing her. She got up running. Pushing her way past the men and into the barn, she screamed Katie's name over and over in the darkness only to gulp and choke. Somehow, remembering fire rules, she fell to the ground to crawl, knowing there would be some air there. The hole they had torn in the end of the building had created a backlash and the flames licked at her. She snaked along frantically.

"Wes!" The only two people in the world whom she loved more than life itself were in here, dying. Oh God, dying. She heard wood give and crash to the ground. Freezing, she waited to be justly crushed beneath the falling timbers. A new shower of sparks singed her hair and burned her skin like sparklers on the Fourth of July.

She should never have let Katie out of her sight. Hadn't Wes left Katie with her? But no, she was too hell-bent on revenge. "Katie," she screamed, her throat raw and her voice cracking.

Vaguely Wes heard Victoria's cries and he damned her for coming in here. And then he found them. Relief flooded through him, threatening to slow him down. They were slumped together in the back stall, unconscious. The pony was down. Grabbing Katie like a rag doll and dragging Joe by the collar, he began making his way back toward the opening. Flames licked at his clothing and the heat baked his skin. Thick black smoke cut his air off completely. Knowing his lungs would burst before he could get the bodies out, he forged forward . . . toward the opening. Timbers creaked and snapped as they swayed and crashed down all around him. With each movement, new molten heat reached for him. Any second the building was going to collapse. Katie and Joe in his hands, his mind flew to Victoria. She was still in here somewhere.

Outside, the fire trucks arrived and hooked up. Trained and detached, the professionals ran their routine. Drowning what was left of the building, they fought the stubborn flames. The hiss and snap sizzled in the air.

Wes nearly stumbled over Victoria. So glad to feel that he had the child in his arms, she groped around until she had Joe by the collar and yelled, "Get her out." She pushed at Wes's leg. "I'll bring him."

Wes hesitated only a second. His child. His baby was going to die if he didn't get her out. And the woman he loved . . . he reached down with his free hand and tried to yank her along. But with the added weight of Joe . . . "Go! Go!" she screamed and he bolted for the hole in the wall, his daughter held tightly in both arms.

"Go. Go!" she shouted after him. Victoria crawled and pulled, snaked along and dragged. If she died, it would only be right. She had acted like the spoiled, stupid child they had all thought she was. But not Katie. And not Joe. He was heavy. She managed to drag him only an inch or two at a time. She heard him moan and it encouraged her. Fortified, steeling herself to the pain, she squeezed her eyes shut against her own sweat and forged on. And then Wes was back and others were with him.

Blessedly, hands were reaching down, many, many of them. Unconsciousness wanted to take over as they pulled her and then Joe through the hole. Air. Cool air. She gasped and it ran down her throat and into her lungs, burning almost as badly as the smoke. Water. Wet. Frigid. The icy, cold spray of it dribbled down her face and onto her clothes.

As she was carried away from the scene, she fought to clear her eyes enough to find Wes. She did. He was running. Running for dear life, clutching his daughter in his arms, her head, arms, and legs flopping like the big gray bunny she always toted and held even now, toward the waiting ambulance. Rescue workers ran alongside administering oxygen. Victoria covered her eyes hoping if she couldn't see it all, it wouldn't be happening. But when she dared to look, the barn was fast becoming a heap of cinders. Joe was hurt and was being loaded onto a stretcher. Katie might be dead. Victoria prayed to die.

Bright lights. Burning lights. Voices. Smoke. Fire. *Katie! Oh God, the little girl . . . have to get to her. My responsibility. My fault. She can't die.* The noise rushed to a deafening roar. Her brain shot messages to her limbs to move but they wouldn't. She fought. Sirens filled her head and red and blue lights flashed behind her closed eyelids. She was suffocating. She opened her mouth to draw in air, but there was none.

Crash. Sparks. Flames. Darkness. A tunnel. Long and cool. Someone said her name, slowly, over and over. A hand. The hand of someone she cared for stroked her. She moved toward it.

Opening her eyes to stark white and a glaring light hurt. She drew her hand up to cover her eyes and found it was stiff and sore. *Katie! Joe! Wes!* Terror stilled her heart as she remembered. She began to tremble. Opening her mouth to speak, she felt as if she had swallowed a cat with its claws bared. "Katie!" she croaked.

Then she was in his arms, being pressed against him as he said her name over and over. He rocked her and thanked God and fought the tears that threatened to spill.

"Katie" was all she could say when she had so many words she wanted him to hear.

At the weak sound of her scratchy voice, Wes wept. It didn't matter that Buck stood behind him. It didn't matter that cowboys don't cry. He held her and stroked her and let his fear and desperation flow from him. She made it back. She was alive.

Head bowed, Buck turned and walked slowly toward the door. His hand on the knob, he turned and looked back at them. What had he done? He had never intended any of this to happen when he prepared the fake will . . . when he figured a way to . . . A single tear slipped down his age-roughened cheek. He yanked his hat down a little lower and crept quietly from the room.

To quiet her, he talked to her in a soothing tone. "Katie is okay. A little shaken up. They have to keep her and Joe here a few days for observation but they're fine. And so are you." He kissed her forehead, her cheek, her lips, and her hands. "You tore your hands up pretty good. Splinters and a few stitches. Your lungs are still battling with the smoke but in a few days you'll be right as rain. And you can come home."

Home. The word struck her like a baseball bat to the gut. Home. Where was that? Certainly not Glory Town, where she had caused so much trouble. Certainly not the old Wild West town she had cared about and then hated. She held tight to the man she loved so desperately and began to steel herself against what she knew she had to do.

She had caused too much hurt. Almost death. If there had ever been a minute chance that they could be together, it was gone now. Gone. Vanished. And by her own hand. There was nothing left for her now. Nothing. She couldn't be the person she wanted to be, pretended to be. It didn't matter that she loved Wes. That she loved Katie. It couldn't matter that they loved her. She was no good for them. Never could be after this. How could she live with the knowledge that just because she looked for revenge she had turned Katie over to Joe while she proved a point? Katie had been left with Victoria. That is where she should have stayed.

Victoria looked at Wes. The traces of tears were gone now. Dark shadows traced under his eyes. One hand was bandaged and she could see his arm was burned. His skin was smudged black. Lines of concern creased his forehead. He was exhausted . . . and lost. He appeared relieved. There was no look of blame. No hate in his eyes. But he must feel it. She had endangered his child. She had been irresponsible and stupid. But then he had tricked her. Manipulated her. And maybe laughed at her. She pushed his hands away.

"I want to be alone, Wes," she cracked. "Leave me alone."

If she had hit him with that crowbar, it would have hurt less. "Leave you alone? Not ever again. No. I'm going down the hall to see Katie in a few minutes, but then we're both going to come back and stay with you a while. Because Katie and Joe were overtaken by the smoke and fell to the ground, they were saved the worst of it. It seems as soon as we made the hole in the back wall, air coursed in to them. They're both okay."

He looked at her as if those words were all it was going to take to convince her that things were as they were before. She closed her eyes to his look. "Get out."

Stunned, Wes picked up her hand and pressed it to his lips. Too much. It was all too damned much. The nightmare run to the hospital in the back of the ambulance watching them work on his little girl. The knowledge that Victoria was back there somewhere. He had seen them pull her through the hole. Seen her gasp to draw in air. But what condition was she in? How badly was she hurting? The agony had cut through him even in his dazed state.

Now she was telling him to go away. Shaking his head and realizing everyone was just too emotionally charged to make sense, he bent down and dropped a kiss on her cheek. "Lady, I've got some things to say to you and not you or anybody is going to keep me from saying them. I never betrayed you. Not like you obviously think. You'll hear me out. But right now we've been through a rough time and I understand. This isn't the time or the place. Victoria, don't look at me that way. I almost lost you. You were almost killed."

"Me!" She struggled to sit up and slid back down on the cool sheets. "What about you and Joe? And my God, what about Katie? You think this is all about me? You're crazier than I thought. Get out and stay out. There's nothing to talk about." Her body was racked with a coughing spell and her throat burned like hellfire.

He stroked her back and waited till she settled. "This is only making you worse. I'm going to sit with Katie for a while but I'll be back."

Taking her hand in his, he lifted it to his lips and laid his mouth on the only spot that wasn't bandaged. She squeezed her eyes shut trying to block the look in his eyes and the pain in her heart.

Walking to the hallway, he asked the nurse to make sure Victoria was comfortable and then moved one door down and slipped inside to see his daughter.

She was asleep. Pale and sooty, she lay so still beneath the white sheet. God. He could be looking at her lying in a pine box. Satin all around, little ruffles. He closed his eyes and quietly murmured, "Thank you, God." He shook his head. He couldn't dwell on what could have happened. He would go crazy. Stark raving mad. His Katie will be fine. Joe will be fine. And his Victoria had run into the flames to save them both. *Everything will right itself,* he told himself as he settled in a chair and laid his head down on the bed next to his daughter's tiny hand that he held so gently. Cool. The sheets were comforting and soft and he was so tired. So damned tired.

Alone. That was what she deserved. Alone and empty. When Wes left the room, he took all the life with him. She hurt. It hurt to breathe. But the real hurt was deeper, sharper, more lethal.

Looking around the bed at all the wires and tubes she was hooked to almost made her laugh. So much to keep her alive when she felt so dead inside. Betrayal. The word kept floating around in her hazy brain. The original burst of energy she felt now quickly left her limp and hardly able to move.

Misery. She had never known the meaning of the word until now. Anguish. Distress. As if there were some magic to protect the suffering, she closed her eyes.

Hearing the door swing open, she looked for Wes but instead a very businesslike nurse came in and injected something in one of the tubes that fed her veins. Victoria watched her walk back out again.

If he never came back to look at her, to talk to her, it would only be right. Her eyelids were so heavy. Her chest hurt. But if she closed her eyes, if she gave in to the pain in her heart and body . . . she might never wake again . . .

A shadowy form moved slowly toward the bed. "Who . . ." her mouth seemed stuffed with cotton and her lips wouldn't form words.

A warm hand reached out and touched hers, tentatively. It felt good. Contact. Loving, gentle contact. But it wasn't Wes. She knew his touch so well. It wasn't his voice. "Who . . ." Clouds clogged her brain as drug-induced sleep forced her to give in.

The pain subsided. Thought processes shattered. Light faded. The arms that were wrapped around her made her feel better. The voice, low and consistent, lulled her. She snuggled deeper into the embrace and a low sigh escaped her lips. Darkness took over.

Nick moaned and brought her lax body closer to his. He wanted to tell her. He wanted to tell her but if he did she wouldn't like him anymore. He couldn't risk it. But he had been so bad. It was all for her. All for her. He rested his cheek against hers, pressing his mouth to hers. Brushing her hair back, he reveled in the softness. His headache was better now. The nurses wouldn't let him in before. He had simply waited. Then Wes had left and he didn't ask anyone this time.

The sight of her lying there. Machines connected. At first nothing registered except her and then it all became so painfully clear, one at a time. Wes should have been more careful! Hadn't he found a pack of cigarettes by the barn? Victoria had warned him not to smoke in her barn. He had heard, being only steps away that day. A pain ripped between his temples but he didn't take his hands off Victoria to press his palms against his head. Looking at the ceiling, waiting for relief, he found her fingers with his.

The bandage made him look sharply down, only causing the knife in his head to slice even deeper. Wes had almost killed his Victoria. He hated Wes. Wes had to go away.

And Nick had to make him. Her fingers tightened on his only slightly but enough to make him look back at her. Kissing her eyelids, her cheek, he murmured, ''All right. All right. Nick is here. Your Nick is here.''

A passion stronger than the pain racked his body. His muscles contracted, threatening to stop his heart. He couldn't stay here. He couldn't let Wes know he was here. She snuggled even closer to him and the gesture brought tears to his dark eyes. He wanted to stay. He wanted to soothe her all over. He ran his hand down her arm and brought her fingers to his lips. He had to go. Right now or they would discover him. He would come back, when they had taken the needles out. He could move her then and he would come back and take care of her.

Kissing her fingertips, he slipped from the bed and laid her hand gently back against the sheet. He studied her sleeping face for a long time. No one had a right to take her away from him. No one had a right to do that. A low sound started in his throat and made its way to his lips. The pain in his head stabbed through him like Morse code. Dot. Dash. Ice pick hard and hot, the distress threatened to force him to his knees.

Holding his head, he made his way across the room toward the door. Stumbling once, he went down on one knee. Off balance, he righted himself and bumped into the wall. He used it to find his way out.

The flames licked at her dress. The heat burned her face, her eyes. Dark, swirling clouds of smoke forced their way down her throat, choking her. Opening her mouth to draw air, she only sucked in more smoke, yanking away any air left. Flailing arms and legs, running, lungs expanding and contracting. Katie's face, laughing and then crying, eyes wide open and scared and then closed and still. So damned still. She heard Wes's voice calling her, directing her away from the terror, but she couldn't move. Nothing responded to her movements. Nothing.

She saw Wes running away from her, carrying Katie and that stupid rabbit. Wait. Take me, too. I'm dying. That's good. I should die.

Burning. Burning up and curling into a ball of blackness, Victoria fought. The voice became soothing, like a light sprinkling of cool water. She moved toward it, fighting through the fog and hell to get to it. Her throat hurt but she screamed his name. "Wes."

His head flew up from where he had nodded off. Grabbing her flailing arms, he threw himself over her body to keep her from yanking all the tubes and needles out of her limbs.

She pushed up and out of the nightmare like a diver coming up to punch through the water after a deep jump from the high board. There was air there even if it did scrape her throat and bring tears to her eyes. A small light on the bedside table was clicked on. Clearing her vision, she made out his form. He was poised over the bed looking to be ready for anything that might happen next. He looked scared, tired, concerned, and beat. Totally beat.

He scooped her up in his arms and held her. "It's okay. It's over. It was just a nightmare. Relax, Victoria. You're safe. Everyone is safe." He held her as he had Katie and prayed.

He offered her water from a straw and she sipped. It was golden and as good as ice cream on a warm, humid day. Now that she was fully awake, the guilt, the terrible dread of what happened pinned her to the mattress. She tried to move as far away as she could from the man whom she had hurt and who had hurt her.

Not understanding, but permitting, Wes sat back in his chair. "Can I get you something to eat? More to drink?"

She rolled her head back and forth on the pillow and looked away from him. He didn't like that at all. He didn't like the trapped look in her eyes or the desperation he felt in his gut.

He shook his head. He wasn't a begging man. At this

point, what he was or wasn't didn't enter into it. "Don't turn away from me. Not now. Not when I need you so much."

Nothing mattered. Nothing. "Failure," she muttered.

"What does that mean?" He moved his chair closer and took her bandaged hand in his.

"I've failed again. Washed out in Virginia society because I refused to live each day as the townspeople figured I should. They thought my volunteerism was notable until they figured I was too attached to the veterans and spent way too much time with them. It wasn't proper, the things a young lady would see there. Then I failed to catch the rich, acceptable husband my mother expected me to after David and I split up. I really messed up with David. I could have stayed. Maybe I was wrong. Maybe . . . I should have stayed."

Tired, Wes swiped a hand over his face. Patience and understanding. She was probably out of her head. She wouldn't even remember all this when she was better. All he had to do was hang on and be patient. That's all she needed. But he was so tired and she shouldn't be feeling this way. He resented it. "And been unfulfilled all your life. No one is expected to live a life as a lie. No. You haven't failed at anything."

"Failed Uncle Henry, whoever the hell he was . . . I've never even seen a picture of him. Every time I mentioned his name to anyone here, I would get a warm smile and a pat on the back . . . and nothing. Screwed things up. And then you. I almost got your daughter killed trying to get even with you. Damn you." She squeezed her eyes shut against the tears that wanted to fall and opened them again.

The muscles in his gut contracted. "Close your eyes. Go back to sleep. It'll be morning soon and you'll feel better."

She tried to pull her hand from his. He shouldn't be consoling her. She should be dead.

"I love you, Victoria. Sleep now. We'll have all the time in the world to talk this out, later." He brushed his cool hand over her forehead and pushed her hair away from her face.

"Don't love me, Wes. Don't. You don't have to play the role now. The jig's up. The worms are out of the can." Her words were slurred as sleep fought to take over. "I'll never believe another word you say. You lied. Buck lied. Everybody lied."

Wes propped his chin on his hand and watched her. "I'll love you, dammit. Don't tell me not to." He was glad when her words became only murmurs. Her breathing eased and she drifted away. Everything he ever wanted was there in that hospital bed, hovering between living and dying. Oh, not physically. But mentally. He wouldn't let her go away from him. He wouldn't let her broken heart keep them from understanding and working things out. He felt the perspiration break out across his forehead. But this was so important. Vital. And the human spirit was sometimes so fragile. Hers had certainly been put to the test.

As much as his battered mind and body wanted sleep, he didn't close his eyes. He watched over her. The cowboy and the Easterner.

Dawn was breaking. A thin stream of gray light forced its way through the slats of the blinds. Stiff and sore, Wes stood up and walked around the room, stretching his sore back and stressed limbs. He looked back at Victoria. She was quieter now, resting.

Peering through the blinds, he watched as the city came to life. So different from Glory Town. Miles of traffic stretched along the highways. Rigs bound for other states lined the edge of the truck stop. In homes along the way, bacon sizzled in the pan, coffeepots dripped their miracle aid to coping with the ensuing day. Kids raced around the house getting ready for the school bus. Mom popped a load of clothes in the washer and checked the calendar to see if PTA was meeting tonight. Mundane things. To some, drudgery. But at this point, all J. Weston Cooper wanted was to go back to Glory Town and deal with the niggling little problems he faced every day. Things that might have proved boring now would seem so very welcome.

As she hovered between drug-induced sleep and wakefulness, Wes reached under the bed for the bag he'd brought home from town. Pulling out the soft white teddy bear with the big brown glass eyes and the sewn-on smile, he set it next to her on the pillow and sat back for a little while longer. He'd have to leave. He had to see to Katie. He knew his parents were with her but he had to be there, too. To hold her hand. To watch for her beautiful little smile.

Victoria would continue to drift in and out of consciousness as she had done the past twenty-four hours. Soon, it would all pass. And the time to set this mess right would arrive.

ELEVEN

Seventy-two hours in the hospital gave Victoria too much time to think. Enough was enough. She changed into her jeans and shirt that Wes had brought this morning when he and Katie had visited.

Things had been stiff between them. She hadn't allowed him to get too close. She couldn't. It might stop her from doing what she knew she had to do.

Still numb, she moved methodically, folding and packing what few things she had to take home. Home. The word pounded through her head. Her fingers went to her temples automatically to work the pain away. She had stopped taking the medication sometime during the night. She needed a clear head. Needed to proceed with her plan and not let anything interfere. Especially not Wes. Wes, who was coming later this afternoon to take her back to Glory Town. She wouldn't be here. Her heart ached. Once again she had royally botched things up.

She couldn't get the picture of the two of them out of her mind. He anxious to get her home and in familiar surroundings and stronger. She . . . knowing there was no sense going over any of it again. Over the last three days, he had tried, time and again, to get her to discuss what

she had overheard. She'd listened to his lame explanations
. . . no more.

But she would never go back to Virginia. Not to stay
anyway. Her mother's enjoyment of her failure was more
than she wanted to put up with. She did feel the need to
be around some of her friends at the veterans hospital,
though, and the thought was in the back of her mind to
go there. Spend some time unwinding. And then do what?
She slammed the hairbrush into the case. Twice she had
embarked on a way of life only to find out it was the
wrong way. And twice it had been her fault. What was
she doing wrong? She picked up the fuzzy white bear that
Wes had given her during the first night. Sweet. How
could he be so sweet, so genuine, and at the same time
be playing a game? A cruel game.

She felt rather than heard someone enter the room.
Turning, she was relieved to see Nick standing just inside
the door, hat in his hand.

"It's nice to see you up." He thought of the hours he
had spent close to her while she slept. He didn't like that
she still looked pale and drawn. It hurt him. He wanted
her looking pink and healthy and full of hellfire as he'd
seen her before.

"Hi, Nick." Her fingers were still stiff and sore, so she
took her time making sure all her things were together.
Idly, she wondered why he was here. Surely Wes would
have told him he was bringing her back there soon. Little
did he know she planned to be far away by this afternoon.

"Wes sent me in to get you."

"Oh. Why?" She tossed her toothbrush and paste into
the valise.

"Said something about Katie, a doctor's appointment
he had forgotten . . . I volunteered to pick you up."

Strange. Nick was almost whispering. His voice husky.
She turned to look at him. He looked . . . tormented was
the only word that came to mind. "Are you all right?"

He smiled and moved closer to her. Closing the top on

the suitcase, he sat on the edge of the bed and kept his eyes on her. "You look better. If I could only tell you how it made me feel to see you. To see you lying here." He looked at the bed and back to her. "Needles stuck in that soft skin of yours. Skin burned from the fire. He shouldn't have done it. I even heard you warn him about it before."

"What?" Totally confused now, Victoria moved to the window.

"Wes. He shouldn't have been smoking in the barn just before he went out into the street to watch the bank holdup."

"How do you know this?" Dread drilled down her spine and perspiration rolled down her back.

"I saw him. And I found a pack of his cigarettes he must have dropped."

Now her head spun. "Wait a minute. Are you telling me," she walked to the end of the bed and held on to the cold steel railing, "that Wes caused the barn fire? Look at me, Nick."

He tilted his beard-stubbled chin and looked her square in the eyes. He shook his head in affirmation, a deep sadness in his eyes.

She saw him wince and reach for his head. Assuming he must be having one of his migraines, Victoria became concerned. "Nick. Is your head hurting? We can probably get something for you here."

Blinking, he got up and walked closer to her. "I'm just in a hurry to get you home. Ready?"

Now what? And something was very wrong. Very wrong with Nick. "I'm not leaving yet. The doctor wants me to wait until he makes his rounds at four. That's why Wes wasn't coming until after five."

Nick seemed slightly confused by that information but he recovered quickly. "We can come back tomorrow. Let's go. You have to be in a hurry to get out of this place. Besides," he pressed his palm to his forehead, shook his head, and let his hand drop. "Let's go." He clamped a hand around her wrist and dragged the valise off the bed with the other.

She followed him. She would simply have to devise another plan. It would be easy enough to slip away later. She needed time to digest this latest information.

The air seemed to clear Nick's head and lighten his mood. It was as if he had forgotten any of the conversation they had had back in the hospital room. He rounded his truck and opened the door for her, helping her and moving her gently.

Tired, she let her head drop to the back of the seat. Wes caused the fire. How he must be feeling. *Never mind*, she told herself. *Everyone was safe. Everything was all right*. She was out of this. All of it. Turning her face toward the cool spray of the air-conditioner, she closed her eyes, the lids still gritty. She felt the truck move and listened as Nick turned on the radio, tuned it in, and set the volume down low.

She hadn't realized she would be so weak. Her limbs felt disjointed and her mind grew fuzzy. She smelled food. Onions, mayonnaise, salami. Nonsense. She was still befuddled from the past events. Trapped in another world. The gentle rocking motion of the truck as it made its way back toward Glory Town lulled her into a half-sleep.

Crazy figures ran helter-skelter in her brain. All hazy. Gray. Nothing clear. Something pressed on her chest and made breathing difficult. Voices. Loud hysterical tones amidst the jumble of colors. Fire orange. Smoke black. She felt the heavy moisture of tears and fought to pull herself from what she came to realize was but yet another nightmare.

The truck had stopped. Nick was twisted around in his seat so he could watch her. From his relaxed position, Victoria guessed he had been sitting that way for some time. Not hearing any of the usual sounds of Glory Town, she looked out the window and waited for her vision to sharpen. Green. Glory Town wasn't green. Leaves turned, branches bowing to the wind, warning of an upcoming storm.

"Where are we?" Perplexed, she struggled to sit up and look around.

"Where we should have been from the beginning."

No more low, quiet tones. Nick's voice was full and deep and confident.

There was no town here. Only one dilapidated dingy shack with a sagging porch. Fear stabbed into her. All the suspicions she had had from time to time about Nick's mental condition came to full stand. *Don't panic*, she told herself as she asked, "Why are we here?"

"Rest. You need rest. And care." He reached down and grabbed a sack that rested at her feet. "I brought food. I came up here earlier and stocked what else we'll need."

Necessity gathering all her brain cells to work, Victoria fought back the bitter taste of distrust. "I can get all the rest I need at the hotel. Take me there, Nick."

He shook his head slowly, back and forth. "No. Wes is there. And when he is around, you don't even see me. And I so want you to see me, Vic." He reached over and threaded his fingers through her hair. "You need me, not him. I know how to care for a woman."

His mood was too bright. Too happy. He'd left the realm of reality. There had been plenty of times she had suspected that Nick was much too far into Glory Town and the role he played. Sometimes he seemed too twisted, too mixed up, too intertwined with the droopy-mustached character he portrayed. Muddled. She had sensed that he took it for real. And her role for real, too.

"I'm sure you do, Nick. That's not the point. I want to be at the hotel. I have work to do. I have to see about the insurance. See to the cleanup. To Katie." The thought of that baby threatened to force tears too close to the surface.

"Sure. In a few days. Right now, I'm going to see to it that you rest and get completely better." He jerked the door handle and opened the door. As if he read her thought to slide over and start the truck, he reached back in and slid the keys out of the ignition and into his jeans pocket. She watched him saunter around and pull her door open. Not waiting for her to climb out, he picked her up and pushed the door shut with his foot.

Placing a small kiss on her cheek, he carried her to the shack. Fighting was useless at this point. She had a clear head. She would talk her way out of this. Maybe, just maybe, he would pull out of this frame of mind all by himself.

Inside, the shack was shadowy but she could see the gleam of the clean sheets on the big bed in the corner. The table was set with nice white china and dull silver. It was a scene out of Stephen King's mind. All else in the room was in dirty disarray. Dust danced in the few sun rays that made their way through the cracks in the walls. Old dusty boxes and crates were piled in one corner. An ice chest sat against the wall. It was clean and she guessed filled with beer or pop. He set her in the chair closest to the wall and put the bag in the center of the table.

"I come here sometimes, when I don't want any people around. Annie and I used to come up here before we were married to . . . well, to be together." His eyes glinted as they caressed every inch of her face. "Annie would like you. She wouldn't mind us being together now that she is gone. She wouldn't have wanted me to be alone all these years. I sure miss her." He removed his Stetson and idly dropped it on the dirty floor. In his right mind, he would never have done that. It was sacrilege. She swallowed her fear.

At the sight of his moist eyes, Victoria decided to change the subject before he started thinking she was his Annie. "What's in the bag, Nick?"

She didn't care. Where was Wes? He wouldn't miss her

for hours yet and he would never guess she was here. Wherever that was. Lord, what else could happen on top of everything else?

He brightened again. "Subs. I'm hungry, too." He reached in and dragged out two soggy sleeves of food. Then he proceeded to meticulously unwrap, cut, and arrange the cold-cut sandwich on her plate as if it were sweet and sour venison over wild rice. She could only watch in amazement as he walked to the cooler and removed a full bottle of wine and two chilled glasses. He whistled as he moved about and she sighed. She didn't ever remember Nick whistling. Wine poured, he seemed to suddenly remember the bag of potato chips he had stashed in the unhinged cupboard and dashed to get it.

Seeing the opportunity and without taking the time to think, Victoria bolted up from the table and headed for the door at a dead run.

He was in front of her, dangling the red and white bag of chips in seconds. "We're not finished yet. After we've had some time together, I'll take you back. Don't try to run away." His eyes darkened and he brought his mouth to her lips for a slight kiss. "Don't try to run away again. I'll get mad. I don't like it when I get mad."

She let him lead her back to the table and noticed that the hand that held hers was cold and clammy and shook a little. This wasn't Nick. This was whoever he thought he was. Best to play along, for now.

Wes kicked over the nightstand, causing the nurse to jump back cautiously. "What the hell do you mean she left with her brother this morning? She doesn't have a brother. What kind of place is this that lets just anyone leave with anyone?"

The nurse, remembering her stature, grew tall and narrow as she admonished him. Looking at him over the rim of her glasses, she sputtered. "You just look here, Mr. Cooper. Control your temper, or I'll call an orderly. This is a hospital, not a prison. And if we spent all our time checking out who patients left with, well, we wouldn't have time to do our jobs.''

Wes looked around the empty room, eyes shooting darts in every direction. ''The lady's been through hell. Hell! Dammit! You know that. The sawbones was supposed to check her at five.''

''As well he would have, had she been here.''

Furious, Wes stomped from the room. Her brother. It was Nick. He had her. After their talk this morning he should have guessed it. He was a fool. An old, stupid, trusting fool. And now she was in danger. Wherever he had taken her, he would . . . because he . . . God, Nick wasn't right and Victoria was out there, somewhere, with him. He'd never forgive himself if anything happened to her.

Jogging across the parking lot to his truck, he jerked the door open. Stomping the gas pedal to the floor, he feverishly tried to figure out where he would have taken her. The first place to check was his trailer on the back lot but he knew already that it would be futile. Still, he might have left a clue. Careening around the corner on two wheels, Wes drove. And swore. Viciously.

Finding Nick's trailer door unlocked, he entered. It was empty. Neat as a pin . . . but devoid of human life. Looking around, Wes made his way to Nick's bedroom and then had to brace himself against the doorjamb. There, covering one wall and half of another were pictures of Victoria. Victoria walking, Victoria riding, Victoria shooting skeet, Victoria smiling up at Wes. He remembered that day. That was the only way he knew that the faceless male form that stood beside Victoria was himself. Nick had scratched the face away. Wes walked over and examined the pictures closer. With the tips of his fingers, he touched her face as it smiled out at him. He felt the nausea rising.

Obsession. He had seen cases of it before while on the force. Madness. Anything could happen. Anything. Rifling through Nick's place uncovered no clues to where they might be. It crossed Wes's mind that they could be on the road, rolling farther and farther away as he stood there. But where? They had four or five hours' head start. He wouldn't hurt her. He thinks he loves her. Even repeating those lines in his mind didn't convince him. The first thing to do was get an APB out on his truck. He'd get the employment records and find out his license number. Then he'd talk to Sally. Nick talked to Sally a lot. Maybe he would have said something to her that would be a lead. He needed a lead, or he would lose his sanity completely . . . too.

Victoria forced herself to eat. All she wanted to do was lie down on that bed and sleep. How could she still feel so tired? How could she think of getting on that bed? Nick hadn't taken his eyes off her since they had arrived. He had finished his sandwich now and had simply leaned back in the chair to watch her, to smile at her.

"Eat more, Vic. I want you strong and healthy real soon. When we go back to Glory Town, we'll run it together. We'll tell that new guy to hit the road. We don't need him. You and me. We can do it together. Annie and me, we planned and planned. Someday we'd do this or that. But that day never came. I'm not going to waste time again. Not now that I've had a second chance to love someone. You're so beautiful, Vic. You treat me so nice."

"You're a nice man, Nick." *When you're not spaced out like this. Dangerous.* She couldn't be sure. It was there. It had always been there. Lurking just beneath the surface. She had felt it sometimes. Sensed it.

The human mind was at once fragile and steely. Nick seemed to be in some sort of a balance mode. When he was tipped one way or the other, she couldn't trust what would happen. He had said he was going to take her back to town, hadn't he? Maybe she should be cool and try to relax. Wait him out. Cooperate. To a point, she decided. To a very fine point.

Licking mayonnaise from her finger, she put a hand to her stomach and sighed. "I'm full. It was nice of you to think of all this, Nick."

"I've been thinking a lot, lady. You make me happy. The way you smile at me. The way you listen when I talk. After we're married, we'll have lots of babies. We'll spend a lot of time just like we are now. Sitting together, talking."

Married? The stage of his fantasy was much wider than she had imagined. She had to find some way to pull the curtain on this play, but at the same time she couldn't force it. "You have it all planned out. Nick, you never even asked me what I want."

His eyes darkened and he leaned forward. "I know what you think you want. You think you want J. Weston Cooper, super cowboy." The tone of his voice became slightly menacing. "He has you fooled with his sharp good looks and his skills. I've seen you two with each other. He has you fooled. That's what it is. Women don't know what they want. Just like Luke had Annie fooled. But I fixed him and then I fixed her." Satisfied, he sat back.

Words flew around in her head like insects blinded by flame. Fixed. Luke. Annie. His wife was dead. She had never heard how she died. She had just assumed she had been ill. And Luke, she never heard of him. She wanted to scream. Had he killed his wife? No, impossible. Someone would have found out. He's crazy, that's all. And crazy people say crazy things. *Oh God,* she prayed. *Let that be all this is. Nick is too nice a man to have committed murder. Isn't he?*

"Yep," he began again and looked directly at her. "I made it look like Wes set the barn on fire by his carelessness. Left a pack of his cigarettes out there. It was easy. And just like leaving the feed door open. People will find out and they won't want Wes in town anymore."

Ice formed in her veins followed by a flash fire of anger. Nick did it. Nick caused her horse to die a slow and painful death. Nick set fire to the barn. It was his fault that so many people were hurt. In his mind he justified his way to get to her. Oh God. The room seemed to twirl. Nausea filled her stomach. She tried to concentrate on his words.

"You'd turn to me. Come to me. I knew it. See, now you're here. It was easy. It was hard to undermine him with the other men. Given a little more time, I would have. But it doesn't matter anymore. We're together." He reached over to toy with the collar of her shirt.

He was sicker than she guessed. He would stop at nothing. She had to figure out a way to get out of here. No one was coming. No one knew where this place was. Desperate, she looked around. She'd have to time it right and make another dash for the door. It was the only way. Maybe after he fell asleep, she could get the keys to the truck. It was something to hold on to. And she needed something, crucially.

Pushing her chair back slowly, she smiled. "Can we get some air, Nick? I like to sit on porches. We can sit on the step and watch for the sunset." Playing along was the only answer right now. She had to act out the game. Drawing on all the strength she had left, she rose. She felt a bubble of laughter catching in her throat. Not once since she arrived at Glory Town did she wish she were back home in Virginia, propped up on her feather bed reading a good book and waiting for Ginger, her maid, to bring tea. She did now.

It was as if he had never spoken the dark words. His eyes brightened and he came around to assist her from her chair. When he clasped his hand around hers, it was dry and steady. Hers wasn't. Together, they walked to the sloping porch and sat, side by side, on the top step.

The fresh air revived her somewhat. Where was Wes? What was he thinking? How would he ever find her? Birds twittered in a nearby tree. Rustling in the brush suggested some wild, free thing ran there. Victoria envied it.

The view from here wasn't all bad. The old shack sat atop a knoll with a line of trees at the far end. Soon the sun would be setting behind those trees. First a pale gold, then as the sun sank lower, a hazy red. It would appear the woods were on fire. She almost wished they were. What would happen after dark? Would he expect her to stay here with him . . . in the one bed cocked in the corner?

She shivered and he mistook it for a chill. He put his arm around her shoulder and rubbed his hand along her arm to warm her. She studied the swirling stitch pattern on the toe of his boots. Felt the too familiar brush of denim against her thigh and was reminded of the strength this man possessed. It would almost be easier to lean into him and give up. But she straightened her shoulders; that wasn't her style.

"It's almost dark," Wes raged and paced the jailhouse and ignored Buck's sputtering.

"Sit down, boy. You've called in his tag number and they'll send Sally down here the minute she gets back from town. There's nothing else you can do but wear a hole in the damn floor."

"Not enough. Not damn-well enough. In the few short weeks we've known each other we've been to hell and back."

"You'll get through it. You both will. You have to." The aging man wiped his brow.

Wes's head flew up and he laughed nastily. The sound of it scared Buck.

"Words of wisdom from you. I could almost be really ticked off with you, Buck. If . . . Damn."

"Don't worry, I'm taking my share of the blame here.

It was a harebrained idea, bringing you two together. Two hotheaded, stubborn people. How'd I know all this was going to happen? Now stop that damn pacing."

"I can't. If I sit down, I'll take off like a rocketship."

"What else can you do? They could be anywhere. You want to be headed off in another direction when we do get word? Sit down."

Wes stalked even faster.

"I don't think he'll hurt her. No, I don't think he will. I figure he fancies himself in love with her. She'll be able to handle him if she's careful." Buck offered consoling words in his own way, not believing one of them. He had made a bad judgment call. Keeping Nick at Glory Town might just prove to be the worst mistake he had ever made. And he had made plenty in his lifetime.

"Careful," Wes exploded. "Careful. Lord, she was half dead just three days ago. Where the hell is Sally?"

"Shopping. You know these dames when they get it in their heads to shop, they shop. All day. Calm down. The shells in your belt will go off. Here. Take a slug of this."

Wes downed the whiskey without tasting it and set it back on the table only to watch it teeter and fall to the floor. He should never have left her alone in that hospital. But how the hell was he ever supposed to dream up a kidnapping? How was he supposed to know that Nick would take her away? The woman he loved was in the hands of a madman. Pictures formed in his mind that tore at his gut. Pictures that scared a man who couldn't be scared.

If he couldn't do something soon, he would blow apart. His fingers itched to get around Nick's throat and squeeze. But it was his fault. Wasn't a man who loved a woman supposed to keep these things from happening to her?

Buck got up and looked out the door. The tourists milled around the dusty street and up and down the shady boardwalks. Happily, they watched and looked around. They experimented with roping and riding. The children seemed all round-eyed and a bit overwhelmed with the reenactors who were at this moment portraying the gunfight at the OK corral. Billy and some of the boys were giving kids rides on their horses at the other end of town. Everything seemed normal. Nothing was.

He saw Sally hurrying toward the jailhouse. He hesitated telling Wes she was on her way for fear he would rush into the street and start shaking the information out of her. And what if she didn't have any that would help?

TWELVE

Wes heard Sally before he saw her.

"What's all the fuss about? Wendy said for me to get up here right away. Some kind of emergency." She held her new hat on her head with one hand and picked up her long skirt with the other.

Wes pushed past Buck and grabbed Sally by both arms. Buck pushed them inside the jailhouse. He didn't need the whole of Glory Town in on this. God forbid anyone would figure out what an old fool he was. What havoc his good intentions had wreaked. He understood Wes's panic and fury, for it matched his own, but Glory Town had to go on as usual.

Wes waited, impatient while Sally arranged herself in a chair and looked up expectantly. And a little annoyed.

"Victoria. Victoria's missing from the hospital. Since earlier this afternoon. From what information we can get, Nick picked her up. But they're not here."

Sally's eyes grew grave. She heard the restrained panic in Wes's voice. She reached up and grabbed at her new red hat as it slid from her head to the floor. Idly she picked it up and began rotating it in her hands.

Testily, Wes grabbed her shoulders and shook her. "What?"

"You'd better sit down, Wes." When she realized he was still standing in front of her waiting, she used a sterner tone of voice. "Wes. Sit down."

Irritated, he jerked a chair over and straddled it, pulling it up close to her. "Talk," he ordered, none too gently.

"I was going to say something to you about all of this but with everything that's been going on . . . and I thought I could be way off base with this . . . Haven't things become complicated? First that child's horse dies and then the barn catches on fire with poor little Katie and Joe inside. It's almost as if fate isn't smiling on us anymore. Maybe if you and Victoria got married and started raising a passel of kids. You know we've all been talking about that and . . ."

Wes growled low in his throat. "You're rambling, Sally. Get on with it."

"Okay. Okay. My bet is that Nick took Victoria out of the hospital with the idea that they would set up housekeeping together." She sat back a little to be better able to gauge Wes's reaction to that bit of news.

His eyes widened and then narrowed to dangerous slits. She rushed on with her story. "Ever since that nasty business with Annie, well, I told you Nick has a hard time sometimes . . ."

She paused. She felt as if she were somehow betraying Nick.

"Well, he has a hard time telling the difference between reality and fantasy. It's never been serious before. Almost a joke really. Thinking he really is a cowboy and this is really 1870. That things can simply be settled with a gun and without regard for the law. That he can just do whatever he wants without using logic. When he'd talk like that, I would just listen and pat his shoulder. What else was I supposed to do? He's harmless."

"Harmless?" Wes roared. "He took her."

"Was harmless," she corrected herself and then looked to Buck for help. She didn't like the edge to Wes's looks or the way he seemed ready to spring into action and choke something. "I hardly think he dragged her out of there stuffed inside a laundry bag or anything as dramatic. Surely then the hospital would have seen something weird going on. She probably went with him willingly enough."

Buck asked Sally as gently as he could, "Do you have any idea where he could have taken her?"

"Sure. But I can't tell you till you hear the whole story. I don't want that man hurt. He won't hurt her. And Nick's become, well, sort of like my kid and he trusts me. He tells me things. Some I don't believe. Some I fear are true."

"You'll tell me where they are or . . ." Wes controlled his temper only because he knew he would get nowhere fast if he didn't. He'd have to trust Sally's judgment. He'd have to wait.

"All right, but I have to start from the beginning. Move back, both of you. You're smothering me." Both men exchanged an exasperated look and gave Sally some space.

She looked at Buck. "Years ago, when Nick and Annie first came here, I liked them instantly. With our trailers backing up to the same lot, we became friends and neighbors as well as co-workers. There's a life all its own on the back lot that neither of you knows exists. Family." She eyed him squarely and added in a near whisper, "You know how important family is."

Buck grunted and shrugged his aging shoulders. "I know you all are close out there. That's exactly the way it should be. Go on."

"I was maid of honor at their wedding, you know. She was so beautiful and he so handsome. They had been seeing each other only a few months when they decided to get married. They were happy. Well, Nick was. Annie was a dreamer. She wanted more out of life. This was okay for now, but she had delusions of grandeur about the future. She eventually wanted out of Glory Town and Nick could never understand it. But I saw trouble brewing between Annie and Nick right off. Just after that Luke fella came aboard."

Buck and Wes looked at each other, perplexed, and back to her. "Luke?"

"Yeah. Luke, Luke . . . I can't remember the rest of his name. Fancy roper. Fast-talking dude with pretty eyes and the way he looked from the back, broad shoulders and a cute butt. He took a liking to Annie and she flirted with him a time or two. Nick found out and was furious."

Wes made a motion for her to hurry up with her story, his hand making circles in the air.

She took a deep breath and continued. "Annie's interest was purely silly. She never took any man serious except her Nick. She worshiped him. Still, she wasn't beyond looking at a fine man. Smiling at him. That's when I found out how jealous Nick could be. That streak of envy was nasty. It's the only thing about Nick that's, that's maybe a little on the dangerous side."

"I need a drink," Buck muttered and walked back to the door, still within earshot but able to look about his fine town. He tried to find some solace in the daily routine. Some sanity.

"Be quiet," Wes demanded. "Hurry up, Sally."

"He took Luke out behind the water tower and beat knots on his head. Beat him up bad. And Luke was no little fella either. Nick told him if he didn't leave Glory Town he was coming after him to rearrange his face. Luke left. Most of them perty men are all saunter and no guts. Anyway, he confronted Annie with her flirting and teasing and she admitted it but said that it was only a game. He yelled at her, screamed, and threatened to punch her lights out. But he didn't. He wouldn't hit a woman. He was just that furious. She was backing away from his tirade when she fell over something. He didn't hit her. She came to my trailer that night, blood spurting from where her tooth went through her lip. After she cleaned up and wiped away the tears, she admitted to me that she had been wrong and Nick only right. She was his woman.''

"God's britches. This is the twentieth century.'' Wes took his Stetson off and wiped sweat from his brow.

"Not to those two. This was their home. Their way of life. I think that's why he clings to it so. Don't think too bad of him. He never raised his voice to her again and she never looked at another man. They were happy and so in love. And then . . .''

Wes ripped the chair out from under himself and threw it across the room and yelled. "And then what?''

"She got pregnant. She wasn't supposed to. Doctor's orders. Some female problem. But Nick wanted a family. A big one. Remember the night the ambulance came, Buck? She had started to bleed. Bleed bad. Nick had her in his arms and had come running over to my trailer, beside himself. Scared silly. He kept talking and crooning to this near unconscious woman. We got her to the hospital but it was too late. She died. And the damn doctor had the nerve to ask Nick why he let her go against his orders. Nick looked like he'd been dunked by a bronc. She had never told him. Of course, he felt responsible since he had pushed her into starting a family. It was his fault, he thought. He blamed himself. For weeks after we buried her, he simply sat and stared into space. That's when the headaches began. That's when I saw part of him slip away and out of control at times. I worried, but over the years it never amounted to much. Glory Town and the action here are what saved him from going stark raving mad. He used to talk to me about killing her. Sometimes the self-imposed guilt was too much for him. He'd snap. He'd go somewhere else in his mind . . . Glory Town. The *real* Glory Town. And then he'd cry and then he'd twitch out of it and not mention it for months. More and more, I saw him live here, in this pretend place, and think it was real. All of it.''

Buck felt his old heart grow weak. He'd always kept himself apart from the others. He was a boss, and business and friends didn't mix. Besides, a lot of people had passed through Glory Town and he hadn't thought of that many of them again. If he developed a certain fondness for some along the way, he kept it to himself.

Wes felt perspiration roll down his spine. Unbalanced. Grieving. In need of a woman. In need of the feeling a woman left a man with. He sympathized with Nick's problem, but that didn't make him feel any more confident that he wouldn't hurt her in some way if he remained out of control for too long. "Where are they?"

"I don't know this for sure, but he and Annie used to go up to that old line shack. You know, Buck, the one about twenty miles up in the high country. To be alone. To plan their life. To dream. If he has her, he took her up there." She grabbed Wes's shirt sleeve as he swept past her. "Go easy on him. He's talked to me about Victoria. He worships her. Don't push him into doing something stupid."

Wes nodded. One look and Buck sided him. They ran to the truck and jumped inside.

Trying to head off disaster, Buck muttered, "Boy, I know what you're thinkin'."

"I don't think you do," Wes grumbled darkly.

"You go chargin' in up there and there's no tellin' what he might do. When we get up there, let me go in first."

Wes turned the key in the ignition and popped the clutch, tires spitting rooster tails of dust behind the truck.

Buck put his hand on his arm. "Promise me, boy."

"You want to stay here, Buck, I'll turn around and drop you off. I promise you nothing."

"Sally knows Nick better than any of us. She says he won't hurt her."

Wes swung the truck onto the macadam road. "Which way to the line shack, Buck?"

"West." Buck didn't like the tone of Wes's voice or

the reckless way he handled the truck. A bull charging into that shack would only cause alarm and confusion. He could render Wes unconscious. He almost chuckled to himself. Those days were probably over. Wes was a strapping, powerful *young* man. He tried to settle back in the seat. It would all have to wait. He'd have to play it by ear.

Nick and Victoria. It was getting dark. Wes tried not to let his mind conjure up pictures he couldn't stand. He couldn't stop them.

"Come on inside, Vic. You need to get some rest."

The chill had her bones aching but she was reluctant to go in that shack. Nick stood up and took her hand. Pulling her up off the step, he slipped his arms around her waist.

The breeze played with her hair, swirling it around her shoulders. He brushed at it and the gentle touch of his warm fingers, the intimacy, caused her to shiver.

"See, you're cold. You'll feel better in the morning and then we can talk. We can plan. We can dream about how nice our life is going to be. And how many babies we'll have. I've seen you with Katie. You're so good with kids. Me and Annie," she saw the wince crease his forehead and then disappear, "we never had time to have little babies, but you and me . . ." His lips brushed her temple. Her pulse beat jumped, but not from passion, from fear. "And together we'll run Glory Town."

He was a strong man. She could feel it in the muscles that roped his forearms, in the solidness of his chest. His heart beat steadily beneath hers. She had to keep from screaming. She didn't want to do anything to pluck this man's strings. But the sound of her scream was loud in her head and trapped in her throat, strangling her.

They went inside the line shack. He moved to the corner to light a lantern and set it on the table. It showered the isolated dwelling in an eerie yellow light. Victoria swallowed the bitter metallic taste of fear. The dim light only served to set the mood of dreaminess.

He unbuckled his gun belt and threw it on the table. Loaded? She'd bet it didn't contain the blanks used in the shows. Nick pulled his belt from his jeans and tossed it away. Pulling his shirt out of his pants, he unbuttoned it and dropped it to the floor. His bare chest only proved his strength. Scared he was going to shed all his clothes, Victoria hurriedly reached for her bag. She needed to change. "Wait outside while I change to my night clothes, Nick."

He laughed then and shook his head. "Don't be afraid of me, Vic. I'm not going to force you into anything. Besides, you're still feeling bad. After we're married we'll . . ." His eyes traveled the length of her and back again. "After we're married. Just for now, I'll turn my back."

She dropped on the bed. "I'm too tired to change."

He walked to the table and, with his heated gaze on hers, turned the knob to douse the light.

He followed her to the bed and the creak of the old springs railed through her like nails on a chalkboard. He plumped the ratty pillows up against the shaky headboard and sat back against them. Pulling her to lie against him, he sighed contentedly.

He had his arm wrapped around her like a steel band. Her head rested on his chest. His heartbeat echoed in her head like the gong of a clock's chimes, ticking away the minutes, reminding her of her isolation. She'd wait. She'd wait until he fell asleep and then she would be able to slip from his embrace and out of the shack, into the night. It didn't matter what was out there or how far away they were from anything. She'd just run and run. She'd be free.

"Vic?"

His voice was soft and she almost felt sorry for him. "What?"

"Tell me this can work out."

She became instantly alert. Was he coming out of the

other world and drifting back into reality? She wasn't sure where she wanted him.

"This isn't the way . . . or the place to talk about this, Nick." It was so dark. Her eyes were open, yet she could only see the haziest of forms in the room. She couldn't see Nick but she could feel him, hear his breathing. His hand moved slowly through her hair.

He pulled her closer to him. "I reckon it isn't . . . but it doesn't matter. We're here. And here we'll stay for a few days."

Remaining quiet, Victoria now hoped that Wes didn't find out where they were. Nick sounded resolved. Nick sounded dangerous. She closed her eyes and tried to relax. Nick's hand rubbed, easily, gently up and down her arm. He began to hum some Western tune she couldn't put a name to but recognized. He'd slipped into never-never land. How did he see things from there? Surely there was no rationale in the state this man was in. *Oh God. What's going to happen next?*

Buck ordered, "Cut the engine here. We'll walk up." Wes had already shut down the motor, pocketed the keys, and begun the sprint up the hill toward the building.

They saw the outline of the shack in the moonlight. The night was still. No sign of life other than Nick's truck parked beside it. No night birds sang their song. No animals rustled in the brush. Even the wind had lessened to a whisper. Wes realized he was holding his breath and let it out in a fury.

"Calm down, boy. You're going to screw this thing up," Buck whispered, a hand on Wes's arm, jerking him to the ground beside him in a clump of trees.

For the first time in his life, his analytical mind failed him and his gut emotions took over. "We'll storm the place. You from the back and me from the front."

Buck shook his head. "Just like the damn cavalry. You *have* been in Glory Town too long. If you weren't in love with her, I'd sure be disappointed in you. We don't know if he's armed or what. Let me sneak up the hill and see if I can get a look inside. If he spots me, it might not panic him like seeing you would. You stay here, hothead.''

"There's no light on in there. How the hell are you going to see anything?''

"This old man's got eyes like an owl. Stay put.'' Buck felt Wes's turmoil but he knew one of them had to keep a cool head.

Wes sat. If he didn't, he'd be up there like a shot, pushing his way through the door, pounding Nick into the ground and grabbing Victoria and going home. She'd never get out of his sight again. The fact that she had been cool and aloof after the fire only attested to how deeply all this had affected her. So much had happened to her in the last few days, she was beginning to buckle from the weight of it all.

He watched as Buck's shadow snaked its way, too slowly and too quietly, up the hill. Instinct moved to take over. His nerves crackled. This went against his nature.

Charging in was his way. But in this instance, maybe this time Buck might be right. And if his actions ended up hurting Victoria in any way . . . or if his lack of action . . . damn. He began his climb.

Nick was asleep. His breathing had evened out and his hold on her relaxed a little. She'd wait. Just a little longer until he was deeply asleep and then she'd make a run for it. She forced her eyes to remain open even though her body cried for sleep, her mind yearned for release. Did she dare make a slow dive with her fingers in his pocket for the truck keys? She moved her hand to the edge of his pocket. He stirred and nestled into the mattress a little more, banding her even tighter to him. No matter. She'd go without them.

Buck creeped along, not wanting to disturb any night

creatures that might raise a fuss. Knowing that the old porch on the shack would creak under his weight, he made his way around back in a wide circle. Closing in on the building, he targeted the window on the left.

Crouching down under it, he raised slowly. Nothing. "Eyes, don't fail me now," he muttered to himself. He kept peering in until he could make out shadows and forms. They were on the bed. Together. For an instant a silly thought formed in his brain. What if she had come up here willingly with Nick? They certainly looked comfortable enough from where he stood. What if he had read the girl wrong? Nah. He shook his head. Then what if he had already forced himself upon her? . . .

He'd throw open the back door, grab Vic, and be gone before Nick knew what happened. He straightened, prepared himself for the impact with the door, and then moved. At exactly the same instant, he heard the front door crack and slam open. Damn it. Wes hadn't waited. He lunged for the back door.

Confusion. Total. Confounded by the darkness and not knowing where anything or anybody was, Wes stood silhouetted by what little moonlight there was.

Victoria, startled, panic pounding in her head, leaped from the bed toward the shadowy form she knew was Wes. Her knight in shining armor. Her hero. Buck jumped on the bed, and before Nick knew what was happening, Buck was on him, pinning him to the mattress.

"Git," he hollered to the two standing by the door. "I'll bring Nick down in his truck."

Strengthened by adrenaline rushing through his veins, Nick shoved the old man to the floor and dove for his Victoria. Wes shoved her outside and cheerfully drew back a fist and punched Nick in the face.

Wes heard Nick's animal-like growl as he righted himself and jumped Wes, arms flying, fists pounding. He fought like a cornered bear, and as Wes fell to the floor after one of his stunning blows, he swore and launched a new attack.

Buck found the handle of something heavy and approached the two figures. Hoping he had the right head under aim, he swung hard and heard the decided thud as it made contact.

At first all went quiet. The men stood still as statues. Then Nick slumped to the floor in a heap. Buck let out a whistle between his teeth.

Buck wrapped Nick's wrists together with an old rope that had been hanging from a nail on the wall. "Get her out of here, Wes."

Wes and Victoria could hear Nick's confused struggles and yelps of protest as he came to. Wes didn't want to leave the old man alone and then remembered Buck. He could take care of himself.

Safe. In his arms, she nearly collapsed. As he helped her to the porch, she remembered Nick's gun belt thrown carelessly on the table. She wanted it out of there just in case it was loaded with live bullets. She wrenched herself free of Wes's grasp and lunged back in the cabin. As she felt her way to the table, grabbed the belt and slid it off, she heard Nick call her name. She stopped. It was such a cry, a plea for her to help him. A tear slipped down her cheek. Then Wes was there, yanking her outside. Lifting her in his arms, he carried her down the hill.

Free. She hadn't known how precious a thing that was until they were in Wes's truck. He gathered her in his arms and pressed her close to him. "I thought I might lose you. God, Victoria, what happened? How did you get way out here with him?"

She couldn't tell him that her plan was to leave anyway. Because it still was. God help her, she had to leave Glory Town for good. For Wes's good. For her good. She alone had been responsible for Katie and she had endangered her. How could he ever really love her again? If he ever did? After what she heard outside the sheriff's office . . .

would she have ever been sure? He'd go on with his life. He had his parents and his daughter.

What would she do? "It's over, Wes. I'm so tired. I need to sleep. We'll talk tomorrow. Just don't hurt him."

He pushed her away from him. "Everyone is so worried I'll kill Nick. I just might. He can't simply take what he wants. Who he wants. Did he hurt you?"

"You hurt me. He didn't hurt me. He's the one that needs help. Not me."

"And damn lucky Buck saw to it that I didn't get my hands on him again."

He gathered her in his arms but he could feel restraint instead of the yielding he needed. He kissed her lips, her cheeks, her hands because he needed the contact. He pushed her away from him so he could see her in the lights from the dash. She wasn't smiling. She looked pale and drawn and tired.

Wes turned in the seat and started the truck. She relaxed against his shoulder, reveling in the feel of his strength and solidness. Her heart shattered, splintering through her like sparks from a fire. They weren't good for each other. He deserved more. And maybe she did, too. She had never been able to give what was needed to make her marriage to David survive. She had never been a source of pride to her mother. She remembered the way Wes looked running with Katie toward the ambulance. Remembered the dark circles of sadness beneath his eyes during her hospital stay. She had almost killed his daughter. She wondered if she'd ever be happy again. And where would she go . . . her eyes closed. The gentle, safe rock of the truck lulled her to sleep.

Wes took one hand off the steering wheel and put it around her shoulder. She slumped against him. He felt the hand clenching the steering wheel begin to ache. He loosened his grip and tried to relax. He was never going to let her out of his sight again. He'd come too close to losing everything that meant anything to him in the last few days. Katie and Victoria. Determination furrowed across his brow. Taking a deep breath, he kissed the top of her head and willed himself to believe everything was fine. He had her back. He could feel the warm softness of her body as she leaned against him. It would be this way from now on. No one and nothing would change that.

_____ THIRTEEN _____

He didn't take her to Glory Town. Even as she hung suspended between wakefulness and deep sleep, she knew it wasn't Glory Town. It was the ranch. He was carrying her through the darkened rooms, up the stairs. She wrapped her arms around his shoulders and laid her head there. Wes shoved at the door with his booted foot. And then he was laying her down in his big soft, down-covered bed in his room. He was unbuttoning her shirt. If he'd asked her, she would have refused the refuge . . . but he hadn't asked. And it wouldn't hurt to love him one more time.

His fingers roused her. The gentle brush of his flesh on hers brought her further from sleep but into a dreamy state. She had no idea what time it was or what day it was or what month it was. She knew only that he was there with her. The man she loved with all her heart. Nothing mattered anymore. Not the screaming warnings that echoed off in the distance of her mind, telling her, reminding her that she was putting an end to this relationship.

Gently, he lifted her, pulling the blouse away from her. Laying her back, he shed her of all her clothes, tossing them across the room. Then he was under the light cotton blanket beside her. Gathering her in his arms, he pulled her across his chest. Wes kissed the top of her head, as he would a child's, and closed his eyes. He wanted her badly but he knew she needed to be undisturbed. She had been through so much. He would have to be content with just holding her, knowing she was here, with him and safe.

All during the night, she tossed and turned, groaned and fought, pleaded and cried softly. Drifting between sleep and wakefulness, Wes soothed her and calmed her. And gently held this woman he loved close to his heart.

The first streams of the faint light of morning drifted between the curtains. A breeze lifted them gently, bringing the aroma of wildflowers into the room. Victoria became aware of where she was and that her body lay cradled against his.

She felt the hard softness of him as she ran her fingers over his taut abdomen. Her fingers brushed against his jeans. Bless him. He was being cautious. She pulled at the snap. Soon enough they would be parted. Soon enough, she would no longer know the ecstasy of making love with him. There would be time for missing him later. Her mind and body needed him. Demanded him. Just this time. She wanted to be free and in love, one more time. And she wanted him to remember her. When he went to bed at night, he should remember the woman who loved him with all her heart, the woman he had tricked.

He awoke quickly and smiled at her. He kissed her chin lightly. She turned her mouth up for full contact. Sensing the welcome in her movements, in her eyes, he rained open-mouthed kisses down her face. Turning her so she lay flat on the bed, he bent over her and slowly but surely, gently and with reverence, devoured her.

His hands, his lips were everywhere at once. Running her hand through his hair, she brought his mouth up to hers. He held his face inches away from hers, looking at, soaking up that eager gaze in her eyes that even the shadows of morning couldn't conceal and he was happy. Happier than he had ever been. Life with her was going to be the best. He closed the space between them. This was only one in a million times when he would be inside her, filling her and being filled.

She traced his mouth with the tip of her tongue and then met his lips with her own, open and inviting. Their warm breaths mingled and merged, branding-iron hot and just as effective.

Under his hands, her breasts blossomed. Beneath his hands, her body arched, needing more and more contact. Licks of hunger drove the moans from her lips. Drew his whispers. All she knew, all her entire world consisted of was him. His hands, his mouth, his hair. His long, hard torso. His feet as they tangled with hers. His knees as they trapped hers.

Her lids shuttered closed and she was lost in a world of dark red sparks and flowing lava. He kissed her fingers one by one, and the soreness from the fire, the splintered wood disappeared as the feel of his mouth spiraled from her fingertips to the very center of her. Then his mouth was trailing over her breasts, slowly down the center of her body, and then along the inside of her thighs. Grabbing handfuls of sheet, she held on for the ride as he continued his journey to her ankles, behind her knees and back.

Despite the weakness caused by her ordeal, together they rolled across the bed, tangling sheets and spread. Pillows slipped silently to the floor.

He could never get enough of her. He wanted her now but he forced himself to keep a tight rein on what pushed for release. She was like velvet, soft and yielding. She was like long grass in the wind, undulating and flowing. Still he guided her, took her along the path of higher places. He felt her hand reach for the zipper on his jeans and he helped her.

Sizzling. The secret pleasure of her haste threatened to explode in him. Then when she pushed gently at his shoulder, he rolled over on his back and she bent over him. He was a locomotive coursing down the tracks at top speed. He was skydiving, floating and twirling through space and time. And all the while, her hands, her lips glided softly here and then there and back again.

Her mouth was like the soft, sweet petals of a rose as it poured over his flesh and seeped through his mind, killing any awareness of anything except her. Her gentle rovings drove him mad.

The only pain that racked her body now was that of need. Of want. The need to please him. To bring to him all the love she had for him. When he reached to draw her close, she pushed his hands away and continued her exploration. Their bodies were slick and hot. She tasted him, tested him, and made him wait. Sultry. Lazily and then with speed, her mouth brought him pleasure that threatened to send him over the edge.

Yet she made him wait. And want.

No more. A man could take no more without . . . rolling her under him, he looked into her shuttered eyes. His hand moved slowly, down . . . down. Weak now, she let him have his way.

Thunder echoed in the distance, trumpeting the imminent arrival of a storm. A cooling breeze ducked in the window, fluttering the curtains and carrying the scent of roses to linger there.

His touch, his gentle words of love sifted through the light veil of sensation. Driven to peak after peak, her body writhed with delight. A kaleidoscope of colors twirled in her brain. Each color bringing its own heat, its own speed. A whirling pattern of sensations spun on a hot axis, dizzying her. Like a pinwheel spinning in the wind. A roller coaster ride of speed and thrill.

And then he stopped. Reaching over to snap the little night-light on the stand, he looked down at her in the dim light. He ran his fingers over her lips. She nipped him. He pushed her unruly hair behind her ear. She kissed his chin. Rearing his head, he positioned himself over her. "I want to see you when we're together. I want to watch you become mine. Only mine."

He took her hands, twined his fingers with hers. She opened for him. He lifted, poised, for seconds only touching, only reveling in the heat of hot, wanting flesh against flesh. Pushing forward, ever so slightly, and so very slowly. Sliding, growing, filling, deeper . . .

She took all of him. United. Complete. Pressure point to pressure point. Core to core. Heart to heart. Polestar to apex.

Volcanic. Ebb tide. She arched toward him. He drove, meeting her only to retreat and charge again.

A carousel whirled, a rainbow arched, a flash of voltaic lightning zipped, ripping white into a rolling black sky.

Her eyes drifted closed as he kissed the smile that came to her lips. In that place reserved for lovers, saved and hidden until joined, until together and pleasing one another, they sailed.

She ran her hands down to his buttocks. In the age-old, rhythm of lovers throughout all time, they moved. Locked together, one in mind and body, spirit and heart, he pulled her even closer. As the tempo increased, became out of control and urgent, he reared back and whispered her name. As her eyes opened, focused on his beautiful face, they soared, exploding and fusing, sinking and disintegrating, melding and forging. Together they jettisoned over the edge into a scalding aura of force.

He rolled over, the cold light of day dragging him from the most peaceful sleep he'd ever had. Through the fog of a contented mind, he reached for her. Feeling nothing but empty bed, he opened one eye, half expecting to see her standing nearby. The room was empty. Sitting up, Wes looked around. It was as if she had never been there.

No sign of her was left in his room, except for the slight indentation on the pillow next to his and the light, sweet scent of her on his skin.

Pulling on his jeans, he padded barefoot out of the room and down to the kitchen. She'd be there. Playing with Katie. Fixing him something delicious to eat. Bacon, eggs, potatoes. He could smell the coffee. He smiled.

His mother was there setting the table. Katie was there, smiling up at him, hugging that nearly burned up rabbit. Victoria wasn't there. A quick jolt of panic rocked through him. "Is she outside?"

The sound of his own voice in the room brought his senses to full stand. And the reality of his words.

"Who, dear?" his mother asked absently from her place by the sink.

If she had to ask who, then Victoria wasn't there. Hurriedly placing a good morning kiss on Katie's cheek, he sprinted back to his room to dress. He was fighting the growing suspicion that she left him to get a point across. After last night she couldn't doubt that they had a life to live together. All that nonsense in the hospital about blaming herself for almost killing Katie and Joe was just that. Nonsense. And he had tried to talk to her about the hurtful words she had overheard before the fire. She had to listen to him. After last night, could she still doubt that most of this had been a misunderstanding? Anger feathered around the corners of his mind.

On his dash through the rain, he stopped to pick some of his mother's favorite roses. He tossed them in the truck and keyed the engine. As of this minute, no more time was to be wasted. None.

On the ride to Glory Town, Wes thought about Nick. They'd have to talk. A decision on his mental competency would have to be made. If he were a danger to anyone, including himself and especially Victoria, he would have to seek medical help. Now that everything had worked out the way it had, he could feel sorry for Nick. For his loneliness. For losing the one woman he loved.

He had slept late this morning. It was almost ten o'clock by the time he reached the old town. In the rain, it looked bleak. It even more resembled the sometime dreariness of the world so long ago. Sure it was filled with dash and romance most of the time, but he knew there had been plenty of lean times back then, too. He was a little surprised at his reaction to the pretend place. When had Glory Town become his home? When he'd fallen for Victoria. When his heart had opened up and embraced that lady and everything she loved.

Parking behind the still-smoking remnants of the barn, he hurried toward the hotel. If he'd had time, he'd have gone to the jewelry store. He wanted her to look at him and say yes first. And he wanted her to be with him. He wanted them to choose the engagement ring together. As they were going to do everything from now on.

She was on the steps when he burst in the hotel, roses wet and limp in his hand. She paused and looked up. He saw but didn't understand the pain in her eyes.

Some of this morning's panic made its way to his heart again. There was just something about the way she turned to look at him. Something in her eyes . . . a resignation?

Just the sight of him had her blood swimming, had her remembering the touch of his hands on her body, hers on his. "Morning, Wes. I was just on my way to my room. How is Katie this morning?" Her words were strong and that surprised her. It was the last on the list of the way she felt just now. It was hard to keep to her decision and even harder to accept the fact that she couldn't just run away. She had planned on facing Wes. A little later in the day, she was going to drive over on her way out of town. Her bags were packed and already stashed in the car.

Cold fear drilled down his back. "Didn't you see her

before you left? Why did you leave? How did you get back here?''

"I saddled one of your horses. He's in the barn on the back lot." She had ridden as though the devil himself was after her. Fast and furious. They had jumped fences and splashed through streams and slid down the hill. She had fooled herself into thinking distance between them would change things. It had only increased her longing and misery.

Wes dropped the roses, rushed up the stairs and trapped her in the circle of his arms. She drifted toward him unsteadily. Over his shoulder, Victoria could see Joe grinning up at them. Wes kissed her, full and deep. And she remembered so well, too well and too vividly, the way they were in his bed, in his room. Her resolve wavered and then she gave it a kick. What had to be done had to be done.

His lips on hers boosted his confidence. With the kind of conviction only a man can harbor, he began to feel relief when her body fit so well to his. Whatever it was that was still bothering her, they'd work it out. "We're going to town. Come on."

She stopped him. God, he was so handsome. His Western-cut clothes accented his build, enhanced his roughness. She remembered how it felt to run her mouth over his body. If only things had been different. How happy they could have been.

"I have other plans, Wes."

Her words cut through him with the swiftness and sureness of a saber. "Nick?" What else could it be? Resolve stiffened his backbone. "Are you still worried about Nick?"

Still he didn't understand. All that she had to say had to be said now. "Let's take a walk."

"It's raining."

"It's down to a drizzle." She took his hand and they left the hotel by the back way. As they walked past the

uined barn, he felt her tense. So that was it. He was
expecting her to rally after all this much too soon. That's
all it could be. He wouldn't let it be anything else. Up on
the hill they stopped, the rain now merely a mist that
swirled around them. She stood looking up at him, the
wayward breeze lifting and tossing her hair around her
shoulders. Wes waited.

"I saw Nick a little while this morning. Sally is with
him. Do you know he doesn't even remember yesterday?
It makes me feel so bad to see a man suffer so much.
Sally is taking him to the hospital this afternoon."

"It's best. He needs help. We aren't qualified to give
it to him."

"No. But we should be around to support him. At least
you should. He needs that." She drew her gaze away from
his beautiful face, afraid her resolve would waver after
all.

"I can do that." He tried to read her mind. He was
getting jumpy. This is stupid to walk all the way up here
to talk about Nick. What was she getting at? He felt ice
begin to trip through his veins. She turned to look at him
and the new sun narrowed her pond-green eyes.

She removed her hand from his and, to keep from
merely grabbing him and hanging on, tucked them behind
her back. "I'm going away, Wes." She waited, trying to
gauge his reaction. It didn't take long.

"The hell you say," he thundered. His voice was low
and unaccepting. "You're smarter than this. If the fire
hadn't broken out, I could have explained. The hospital
wasn't the place to talk and you needed time to think it
all out. You should be able to go over it. Make the right
decision about this. Hear me out. You know damn well
I'm in love with you no matter how it all started out.
You're the one who generated this frenzy."

Anger jumped to the forefront of her mind. "Me! How
dare you think I'm jumping to conclusions when I heard
it come from your own lips." And such wonderful lips.

"You heard part of a conversation. And yes, dammit, I hired on here to get rid of Buck's stubborn Eastern partner. Don't you see? It was Buck's plan all along that we get together. He knew I was at loose ends, beginning to doubt myself. He saw that a woman like you would be good for me. It's all been an act. For Pete's sake, Victoria, I thought you could see through that. Buck planned this and most of it went according to plan."

Taking both her hands in his, he forced her to look at him. "If I only hired on as a favor to Buck, what kept me here? Think about it. It was you. Watching you go from being that spoiled, pampered Virginia lady to a competent, capable Oklahoma woman. Every day I watched you grow and learn. Did I laugh out loud the day you fell off the fence? Did I snicker behind my hand that day in the barn when you watched the blisters forming on your pretty little hands? Did I make fun of you when you dressed the part of a gunslinger and killed off all the bad guys? Watching you, being around you, learning about you was teaching me that you, all this, was what was missing from my life. I could have walked away. Any time. But I was falling in love with you, bit by bit, day by day, and hour by hour."

Pale. She went absolutely white. Blood drained to her toes. The urge to laugh hysterically bubbled inside her. But then she saw her own reflection in his dark, sleepy eyes and was reminded of her stupid stunt that almost cost him his life . . . his little girl. This added information that might have fixed everything before now only made it worse.

"I don't believe you." She circled him. She had to move. Her nerves were surfacing and making her jumpy.

"We were both duped. And it was done because that old coot likes both of us. If he had asked me to drop over and take a look at the new lady in town, I would have laughed at him. So he put it to me as a challenge. He said his new partner was a stupid, pushy Easterner and he wanted him gone. Discourage him, make life miserable . . . get this person to throw up his hands and catch the next flight back home . . . where he belonged. He never even told me you were a woman. Until we met that morning in the hotel dining room, I assumed he was asking me to get rid of a man.''

He paced as he talked, there amidst the tall, waving grass, the sun that appeared from behind the black storm clouds, glinting off his belt buckle as he turned. ''He knew. That old codger knew, once I saw you, got to know you, I wouldn't leave without you.''

The stupidity of the entire situation washed over her, but the tarnish of knowing that she endangered Katie with her own childishness kept everything from shining.

''I was afraid you really didn't love me. I was scared I really didn't love you. And Buck never wanted me here. Then the fire. How can you ever forgive me for not keeping Katie with me?''

His eyes darkened and he took his time to think over his words clearly because he knew what he said next was very important, vital to the rest of his life. ''Buck didn't want you here at first but then he used that wily old head of his. He purposely kept you stirred up. He started liking you but he doesn't know how to tell a person he likes them. He figured you needed a man, being the chauvinist that he is. And so he picked me. Hand picked. In the old goat's mind we're the perfect match. And I know he's right. As far as Katie being in the barn with Joe, Victoria, I have often let Joe take her to the barn to ride. If it had happened then? Should I shoot myself?''

''No. Yes. I don't know. I don't know what I think. This is all so off the wall. I thought I had this all figured out. I'm not sure I want to believe any of this.''

He stalked over to stand an inch from her. He didn't touch her. Afraid his hold would be so tight he might hurt her, he kept his hands at his sides. The intensity in his eyes could be felt more than physical contact. "Do you believe in this morning?"

She felt the heat wash over her cheeks. Yes. Yes, she believed in the love they made together. And maybe she had to trust the last weeks. Their time together. The things they shared. The teaching times. The arguing times. The quiet times.

"Yes." And she meant it. She silently prayed she was making the right decision. Her brain booted her with a mental shrug. *It's worth a try. It's worth a damned good try.*

"Good. You'd better believe in it."

The booming sound of Buck's raspy voice had them both turning. He sat, the sun at his back, astride his horse. When had he approached them? Where had he come from?

"You guessed right that I duped you, Wes. But what you don't know is that I tricked both of you."

Victoria slipped her hand from Wes's. She didn't like the set to Buck's mouth, the frown on his face. "Almost backfired. The whole bloody thing almost blew up in my face. I did ask Wes here to move in on my Eastern partner and make life miserable. What better way to get action than to throw two cats in a bag and watch 'em go at it?" He dismounted and, holding the reins loosely in his hands, walked closer to the two of them. The two of them standing there looking at him as if he'd been found chewing on locoweed.

"A long time ago, Victoria, back in the East, I used to tag along with your dad when he snuck you down to the swimming hole. Your mother never let you go skinny-dipping and your father thought all kids ought to enjoy it. Your nanny, Martha, would come with us and bring a towel along. She'd always have you shined back up by the time we went back. You were all of two big, fat years old."

Victoria experienced a deluge of conflicting emotions.

What was he telling her? That he knew her father? What kind of a shenanigan was this?

"We used to hide you out at the stables until your mother went into town and then we'd all three head out on horseback, you sitting up there in front of your dad, clapping your hands together and yelling 'Faster, Daddy, faster,' and he would laugh and urge the horse into a gallop."

She found her voice. "You knew my father? Then you and Uncle Henry knew each other in Virginia?"

Buck looked from one of them to the other and took a deep breath. "I am your Uncle Henry."

Victoria's brain fogged. Words buzzed around in her head as she fought to comprehend what was being said.

"What's this Uncle Henry stuff?" Wes asked, half expecting this and more to be fabricated.

"I faked a will and notified Victoria that her uncle had died and left his half of this town to her. I told you I had let a silent partner buy in and then was surprised when he showed up to participate. I figured you two wouldn't bother discussing mundane matters like that."

Victoria swayed and Wes caught her from behind and let her lean back against him.

He was her Uncle Henry. Her father's brother. Stunned, nearly speechless, she murmured, "Did you and my father look much alike?"

Buck smiled, touched. "Yes. Quite a bit, being only one year between us."

"Then he would look like you now. God. Had he lived, this is what he would look like. Why? Why did you send for me?"

"A friend of mine back there kept me current on you. I couldn't do much about the life your mother forced you to live while you were young, but after your divorce, after I heard that she was trying to marry you off to some other rich dandy . . . well, I couldn't stand it anymore."

"Why," her voice faltered as she moved a few steps toward him, "didn't you let me know I had an uncle?"

Pain darkened Buck's face. He looked her squarely in the eye. "God only knows why, but your father loved that bitch. She was a cunning, conniving . . . I was never good enough. I was a rowdy. A drunkard. A devil-may-care idiot I think were her exact words. I was ashamed."

Victoria cocked her head and tried to comprehend what she was hearing.

"Sam and I used to sneak out once in a while, after you two were asleep. She never knew. She had her own room and only cut tracks to his when she felt like it. Anyway, we went to a bar and drank too much. I was drunk. I was driving. There was an accident. Sam died. I didn't."

The torrents of emotion pushed tears to the backs of her eyes. She blinked them away.

Buck continued, hurriedly. It was getting harder and harder for him to say the words that hurt this girl, the grown-up woman of the little girl he loved so much.

"She shrieked, she screamed, she pounded on my chest. Murderer. Killer. She said I was jealous of all Sam had so I took him out, got him drunk, and drove him into that tree." He hated that he felt the heat of tears at the corners of his eyes.

Shifting from one foot to the other, he continued. "I loved Sam. I never would have hurt him. You and me . . . and him. We spent a lot of time together. She said I could never come near you again. That I was bad for you. She convinced me. I left the state after a while. After I tried to see you and she would grab you up and run away. She made you cry. You see, you loved me, too."

Nothing. She remembered none of this but a feeling was rising to the surface, like a sunken ship blown full of air and floating, creaking and groaning to the top.

She nodded her head, and as if in a dream, she heard her own words. "Yes. Yes, I did."

Moving away from Wes, she walked closer. To look closer. To try to see her father there, in his eyes.

Buck let go of the horse's reins. "I called the whole town together. Told them I had a niece out East that didn't know about me. How I was getting you out here. How I was hoping you could be happy out here. I planned on not making it too easy and counted on the stubbornness you displayed as a little squirt. And Wes. I knew he would be good for you. I was hoping you two would get together. He deserved better than life handed him, too."

Victoria took another step and was only twelve inches from him. She reached out and touched his cheek, felt the tear roll from the corner of his eye, across her fingers. This man was her uncle. Her father's brother. Her family. She reached up with both arms and wrapped them around his neck. Tucking her face, she pressed against his chest. She felt it heave as the man fought his own release of emotion, felt the warm, wonderful protectiveness of his embrace. They cried.

Wes swallowed a lump in his throat. Why, that cagey, old codger. By God, he would enjoy having him for an almost father-in-law. And he would be grandfather to Katie and the rest of the kids. The tough, no-shit cowboy had a hard time keeping his own eyes dry.

Buck pulled back and looked at Victoria. "You forgive me then?"

"There's nothing to forgive, Uncle Henry. I only wish you had just called me and told me."

"So do I. But it just didn't seem the way and I was afraid you would tell me to keep riding west. This way, if it didn't work out, well, at least you'd never know."

She hugged him once more. Growing just a little embarrassed by now, Buck returned the hug and then swung back into the saddle. "You kids get all this straightened out between you. And don't take long. This town needs your attention."

With that, he whirled the horse and thundered away over and down the hill.

Wes walked up and turned Victoria to face him. She cast one more look in the direction Buck had disappeared and then turned back to Wes.

He leaned forward slowly and rested his mouth against hers. Her arms automatically moved to encircle his waist and pull him closer. She deepened the kiss. Now that the weight of the world had been lifted from her shoulders, she felt invincible.

When they parted, she laughed. Then at his perplexed look, she laughed even harder. "This is unbelievable. The entire thing."

He swept her up in his arms and twirled her around and around. Tripping, he ended up slamming them both to the wet ground.

As kids will do, they lay there, arms outstretched, watching the sky clear and holding hands. Victoria listened to the drumming of her heart. Her very happy heart.

Wes rolled the words over and over in his mind before he spoke them, all the while wondering why it's so hard for a man to say them sometimes. It must be because if it didn't turn out right . . . if she didn't give the right answer . . . Hell. "I want you to marry me, Victoria."

The thrill of his words jolted through her. Yes, her mind screamed. Yes. Suddenly she felt light. A breeze could carry her away. She felt like laughing and crying some more. Before she could answer, he pulled her to lie in the crook of his arm.

"Old towns like Glory Town always had one thing in common. Do you know what that is?"

She thought a minute, as much as her reeling mind would let her. "No. What?"

"Think. What one thing do you see as a constant in every Western movie you've seen?"

He answered for her, because it had been in his mind for so long. "A huge two-story blindingly white house with a big, long wraparound porch towering right at the edge of Main Street. Sort of higher up and out aways. Can you picture it?''

She could. ''Green shutters at every window and a gabled roof with lots of gingerbread trim everywhere. In the winter, when the streets are covered in snow and all of Glory Town is muffled, smoke would spiral, lazily and heavily scented with kitchen smells that it's pulling up the chimney. In the summer, you can hear the creak of the porch swing as the couple sits and watches the goings-on.''

It was his picture, too. ''It's our house, Victoria. Big and spacious and room for lots of kids. Katie needs brothers to pick on her and stand by her, dunk her in the mud, and watch over her when her boyfriend brings her home from her first date. And I need you to come home to. To sit with, to look at, to talk to. To love.''

Victoria drifted on the dream. ''The rich people. The owners of the bank or the thousands of acres of land lived there.''

''You love me. Being married and having Katie and lots of other kids qualifies us as rich, doesn't it?''

Her heart soared. ''Yes, it does.''

''I want to build that house for you, Victoria. I want us to be that family. Of course, now we have to add a rocker to the porch for Grandpa. I think I've loved you from the first moment I saw you.''

She sighed, all the broken chips of her life falling into place. ''You should have convinced me. We could have saved a lot of heartache.''

''I didn't know how. And I wanted to be sure that you loved me. You and I have both made some mistakes in the past. We needed the time it took so we were both sure.'' He slipped a long stem of lush green grass between his lips.

She rolled and propped herself on his chest. ''And now that we are, I feel I should warn you. I'm not an easy person to live with. I won't make your life all rose gardens and cherry pie. I won't stop being independent and active with this town. There'll be times when you come home that you'll have to fix dinner for yourself and the kids."

He rested his hand on her shoulder while he twirled the blade of grass with his tongue. He didn't want it any other way. "I can cook."

She punched him and snuggled against his shirt. "I should have known."

"Is that a 'Yes, I'll marry you'?" Tossing the grass aside, his mouth played with hers.

"Can you do laundry?" she asked, enjoying drawing this out as long as possible. Let him squirm a little.

"Sort darks from whites. Hot for towels and cold water for cottons. Bleach and fabric softener." He nipped her chin. "Never bleach colors and always put . . ." he kissed her soundly, "my jeans in for the long cycle."

"Sweep the floor?" she goaded.

"With a broom," he confirmed.

Harassing him, she went on. "Clean closets?"

"Salvation Army donations."

"Change the sheets on the bed?"

"In my sleep. In your sleep." He fitted his warm mouth to hers.

"You'll do," she mouthed against his lips.

"I sure will."

They stood beneath the morning sun in front of the small chapel at the end of the road in Glory Town. The sun glinted off the little steeple and bathed everyone in soft, warm sunlight.

Flowers, mountains of them, lined the sidewalk. Ribbons fluttered in the wind. Tables laden with food waited off to the side for the reception. A fiddle band waited to begin the festivities.

The construction workers erecting the big white house

on the edge of town set down their saws and hammers long enough to watch.

Wes's parents stood near the buckboard that was decorated with crepe paper, flowers, and ribbons. His father put his arms around his mother and pulled her to him for a kiss.

Wes, dressed in his black suit and go-to-hell hat, stood beside Victoria. She was the vision of any man's dreams. Her dress, yards of long, long white silk, white lace, and tiny pink rose buttons, flowed down her body and onto the dusty walk. The veil framed her face and invited an ethereal aura. She and Katie, who stood between the two of them, clutched bouquets of wildflowers. Buck stood next to Victoria, chest poked out and dressed in his Sunday-go-to-meeting clothes.

"Dearly beloved. We are all gathered here in the presence of man and God, and Buck," he grinned, "to join together . . ."

As the preacher, dressed in 1870s garb, began the ceremony, a horse nickered at the wind. A restless child pulled the trigger on his cap gun and broke off the sidewalk chasing his squealing sister. The sign on the general store creaked as the breeze brought a tumbleweed to bounce down Main Street. A door slammed. A car honked its horn from the distant road. Changed yet unchanged, Glory Town witnessed the joining of two of its permanent residents. It was only the wind, but it could have been a sigh.

Over the scratchy intercom came the sweet strains of "Finest Kind of Lady," the song Wes had written for Victoria. Katie had insisted. It was her contribution to the wedding ceremony. She twisted and squinted up at her daddy and waited as he bent to plant a kiss on her cheek.

Sally blew her nose into a floral handkerchief.

Victoria looked at Wes. It all seemed so picture perfect. Past him she could see the huge, looming frame of their new home. It stood right at the end of the road as Wes had promised. It would be a cheerful, warm house with the sounds of lots of kids and Katie. Katie could ride her tricycle down the hill . . .

"Well, do you?"

Wes's words brought her back from her daydreams.

"What?"

Laughter rose over the crowd and drifted on the wind.

"Marry my daddy?" Katie piped in, impatient to get to that big white cake that was waiting on the table.

"That I do, Katie, my girl. I do."

Other books by Joey Light:

SHARE THE FUN . . .
SHARE YOUR NEW-FOUND TREASURE!!

You don't want to let your new books out of your sight? That's okay. Your friends can get their own. Order below.

No. 47 STERLING'S REASONS by Joey Light
Joe is running from his conscience; Sterling helps him find peace.

No. 136 HIGH-RIDING HEROES by Joey Light
Victoria was going to stand her ground whether Wes liked it or not!

No. 25 LOVE WITH INTEREST by Darcy Rice
Stephanie & Elliot find $47,000,000 *plus* interest—true love!

No. 26 NEVER A BRIDE by Leanne Banks
The last thing Cassie wanted was a relationship. Joshua had other ideas.

No. 27 GOLDILOCKS by Judy Christenberry
David and Susan join forces and get tangled in their own web.

No. 28 SEASON OF THE HEART by Ann Hammond
Can Lane and Maggie's newfound feelings stand the test of time?

No. 29 FOSTER LOVE by Janis Reams Hudson
Morgan comes home to claim his children but Sarah claims his heart.

No. 30 REMEMBER THE NIGHT by Sally Falcon
Joanna throws caution to the wind. Is Nathan fantasy or reality?

No. 31 WINGS OF LOVE by Linda Windsor
Mac & Kelly soar to new heights of ecstasy. Are they ready?

No. 32 SWEET LAND OF LIBERTY by Ellen Kelly
Brock has a secret and Liberty's freedom could be in serious jeopardy!

No. 33 A TOUCH OF LOVE by Patricia Hagan
Kelly seeks peace and quiet and finds paradise in Mike's arms.

No. 34 NO EASY TASK by Chloe Summers
Hunter is wary when Doone delivers a package that will change his life.

No. 35 DIAMOND ON ICE by Lacey Dancer
Diana could melt even the coldest of hearts. Jason hasn't a chance.

No. 36 DADDY'S GIRL by Janice Kaiser
Slade wants more than Andrea is willing to give. Who wins?

No. 37 ROSES by Caitlin Randall
It's an inside job & K.C. helps Brett find more than the thief!

No. 38 HEARTS COLLIDE by Ann Patrick
Matthew finds big trouble and it's spelled P-a-u-l-a.

No. 39 QUINN'S INHERITANCE by Judi Lind
Gabe and Quinn share an inheritance and find an even greater fortune.

No. 40 CATCH A RISING STAR by Laura Phillips
Justin is seeking fame; Beth helps him find something more important.

No. 41 SPIDER'S WEB by Allie Jordan
Silvia's quiet life explodes when Fletcher shows up on her doorstep.

No. 42 TRUE COLORS by Dixie DuBois
Julian helps Nikki find herself again but will she have room for him?

No. 43 DUET by Patricia Collinge
Adam & Marina fit together like two perfect parts of a puzzle!

No. 44 DEADLY COINCIDENCE by Denise Richards
J.D.'s instincts tell him he's not wrong; Laurie's heart says trust him.

No. 45 PERSONAL BEST by Margaret Watson
Nick is a cynic; Tess, an optimist. Where does love fit in?

No. 46 ONE ON ONE by JoAnn Barbour
Vincent's no saint but Loie's attracted to the devil in him anyway.

Meteor Publishing Corporation
Dept. 393, P. O. Box 41820, Philadelphia, PA 19101-9828

Please send the books I've indicated below. Check or money order (U.S. Dollars only)—no cash, stamps or C.O.D.s (PA residents, add 6% sales tax). I am enclosing $2.95 plus 75¢ handling fee for *each* book ordered.

Total Amount Enclosed: $_____.

____ No. 47	____ No. 29	____ No. 35	____ No. 41
____ No. 136	____ No. 30	____ No. 36	____ No. 42
____ No. 25	____ No. 31	____ No. 37	____ No. 43
____ No. 26	____ No. 32	____ No. 38	____ No. 44
____ No. 27	____ No. 33	____ No. 39	____ No. 45
____ No. 28	____ No. 34	____ No. 40	____ No. 46

Please Print:

Name _____

Address _____ Apt. No. _____

City/State _____ Zip _____

Allow four to six weeks for delivery. Quantities limited.